IMPERFECT

A STORY ABOUT LOSS, COURAGE, AND PERSEVERANCE

A NOVEL

KATY MOTIEY

MANUSCRIPTS PRESS

COPYRIGHT © 2024 KATY MOTIEY
All rights reserved.

IMPERFECT

A Story about Loss, Courage, and Perseverance

ISBN	979-8-88926-054-7	*Paperback*
	979-8-88926-055-4	*Hardcover*
	979-8-88926-053-0	*Ebook*

IMPERFECT

Katy Motiey

This book is dedicated to my mom for her positivity, perseverance, and for instilling a strong sense of right and wrong in my brother Kaveh (Karl) and me.

Contents

———

*"All that I am, or hope to be,
I owe to my angel mother."*

— ABRAHAM LINCOLN

Author's Note

The "*sofreh aghd*" in a Persian wedding is a ritual where the bride and groom sit under a lace cloth, like a *chuppah* in the Jewish ceremony, while traditionally "successful and happily married women" hold each corner of the lace and rub sugar cones together to pass along their good fortune. The sugar cones cause a stream of granulated sugar crystals to drop onto the lace. The ritual is meant to symbolize the sweetness of the life the couple will create together. The setting is intimate, and only close family and friends are invited.

Many years ago, after the Iranian revolution and while I was in college, the son of one of my mother's close friends was getting married. My mother, brother, stepfather, and I were invited to the ceremony. During the revolution, my mother had helped the groom get a student visa to come to the US, and after that his parents had immigrated to the US. The parents were forever grateful for my mother's help.

Prior to this wedding, my mother had visited me in Washington, DC. At a dinner with some of my friends, she had shared the story of her legal challenges with my father's side of the family after my father died. It was the first time

I'd heard the story from start to finish, and it weighed on me. Perhaps it was cultural for her not to tell me the story directly, or she simply didn't know how to share the painful details.

Now at this wedding, we were hovering in the bride's parents' living room with thirty or so close family members when the bride and groom arrived. The couple sat on a bench, and the mother of the groom quietly tapped four women on the shoulder to drape the *chuppah* lace over the bride and groom's head. She tapped a fifth woman to start grinding the sugar cones. My mother was not one of the women called to action.

A few minutes into the ceremony, my mother and stepfather strolled outside and sat on the patio for the rest of the ceremony. I noticed them walk out, and I followed them to ask why my mother was not chosen to hold the ceremonial lace. My stepfather—a highly educated businessman who had lost his work, his company, and his assets under the Shah's regime and had strong negative feelings about the Iranian culture—announced it was because my mother was considered to carry a bad omen because she was a widow. At that moment, I felt like smoke might come out of my ears. Even today, thirty plus years later, when I think about that wedding, I cringe. Clearly, in the Persian tribal and superstitious culture, you are considered neither successful nor happy if you're a widow. And because of your unfortunate status, you are not welcome to play a meaningful part of a wedding ceremony.

The story of the imperfect life my mother lived during the 1970s weighed on me for years, and I couldn't get scenes like that wedding out of my head. Not only did she have the misfortune of losing my father when I was three years old, but she also ended up with legal challenges with family members. Now, years later, in the US, she was and is considered a "bad omen"? How is that right under any cultural norm?

In October of 2009, while I was winding down a company and had free time, I took pen to paper, or rather fingers to keyboard, and turned on the figurative faucet. My mother's story poured out of me. I wrote the entire first draft of this book in exactly twelve months.

I wrote the story from my mother's perspective and, for a variety of reasons, decided to fictionalize it. I changed all the names, and in many cases I simplified the story. For example, my mother has several siblings, aunts, uncle, and cousins, and all of them are omitted from the book. She also comes from a large extended family from each of her mother and father's sides with over eighty cousins. Many of these siblings and family members were available to support her emotionally and morally during her hard times in the 1970s, and none of them are mentioned in the book. So, while this book is fiction, it is very much based on a true story. In fact, in 2011, my mother read an earlier version of the manuscript, and her only question to me was why I had changed the names.

I have always had a strong sense of right and wrong, and my mother's story ultimately inspired me to go to law school. In 2018, over twenty-five years into my legal career, I won a Lifetime Achievement Award from the *Silicon Valley Business Journal* and the *San Francisco Business Times*. The title of the article was "A Strong Sense of Right and Wrong." The injustices my mother had to suffer no doubt instilled in me a black-and-white sense of right and wrong.

Women, especially single mothers, will enjoy this story. Those who grew up in the 1970s and remember the initial turmoil in Iran that led to the overthrow of the Shah and the Iranian revolution will recognize many of the scenes in this book. After reading it, my lawyer friends, colleagues, and employees will better appreciate the legal differences between the laws in Western countries like the US as compared to those in a country like Iran, even under the Shah's 1970s regime.

The little girl in the story is based on me, the main character is my mother, the boy is based on my brother, and so forth. Cyrus is the person my mother ended up marrying, "successfully and happily."

Readers of this book will understand why I have developed a hostile tone toward the Iranian culture and certainly Iranian laws. All of that said, both my parents and I were born in Iran, and over the last nearly fifteen years of working on this manuscript I have developed a small amount of appreciation for the culture I was born into.

More than anything, my admiration for my mother is endless. How she survived, grew in strength and character, and eventually thrived in 1970s Iran constantly amazes me. Her story is one of great resilience and flexibility. It became important to me that others read her story and admire her fortitude as well as her never-ending love for my brother and me.

May this fictional story based on true-life events bring you as much enjoyment and insight as I received while writing it.

PROLOGUE

January 1979, Tehran

———

Everything around Vida went dark. So much lost already, and now the power outage for the sixth time this week.

"Roya *joon*!" Vida called to her daughter. "Stay in your room until I light the candles."

Vida slid her hand across the cool surface of the wooden end table and searched for the box of matches she had left along with a lighter next to the candle the night before. She bit her lip. Was she already getting used to the changes being forced on her—on all Iranians?

The electricity, she had noticed, went off at 8:00 p.m., when the nightly news was scheduled to air. It came back on at sunrise, before morning prayers, when most people in Tehran were still sleeping. Electricity was being used like a soft drug.

Fiddling, she sent the lighter skidding off the table. It bumped its coating against the striped wallpaper and fell on the soft carpet with a thud. The flare of the first match briefly illuminated the whole room. Its sulfur smell lingered. It, too, was part of this new life.

At least we've already eaten, Vida thought as she rounded the room, lighting other candles. Roya had eaten her light supper favorite, a tuna fish sandwich with lots of mayonnaise on white toast, while Vida ate pieces of lavash bread spread with feta cheese, sprinkled with walnut bits, topped with a few basil leaves, and rolled into bite-size pieces. As always, she finished her meal with coffee whitened with the powdery non-dairy creamer she bought at the commissary, where she had access because of her American Embassy job.

"Mom, what are we going to do *tonight?*" ten-year old Roya asked. Standing in the dark doorway of the family room, she pushed her fingers against the opening, swaying gently side to side. She was a moving shadow, a stream of candlelight making her hazel eyes sparkle. *Eyes so much like Kamran's,* Vida thought with a sudden ache, missing her late husband both for herself and for their daughter.

Vida went to Roya and stroked her thick bundle of short black curls. "Maybe you can write in your new diary, *azeezam.* Can I help you find it?"

"Mommmm… I know where I put it," Roya complained.

At first the thirty-eight-year-old had worried her daughter might develop a fear of the dark, but Roya had adjusted to the blackouts and the routine that came with them. Now Vida wavered between relief and concern that her daughter took it all in stride and was adapting to a dangerous situation.

"You better put on the wool sweater Maman knit for you," Vida said. "It gets cold at night." The last thing she needed was Roya getting sick.

The little girl retrieved the striped sweater Vida's mother had knitted for her and stretched it over her head. She then settled on the love seat close to the candles, her legs folded to the side the way her mother sat. Vida smiled. Roya wrote with the paisley-fabric-covered diary on her lap, glancing up and pursing her lips now and then, as if concentrating hard on what to write. *A real thinker like her father,* Vida thought. Soon her determined daughter wrote and wrote with her head lowered.

On the couch opposite her, Vida held a book near the candlelight, trying to relax. She read the same few sentences over and over, her mind skittering between the airport shutdown the week before, the snowstorm expected to hit Tehran the next morning, the latest bomb scares at the office, and what would be essential to take if they had to leave the country with little notice. She stretched her legs in front of her, bending her toes back and forth and making a slight cracking sound. It was a minor release of pressure.

Out of the silence, a thunderous boom rattled the windows and brought Vida's hands to her ears. She leapt, grabbing Roya by the arm and pulling her toward the bathroom.

"Mommy! What's happening?" Roya cried, tugging at her mother's pants.

"I'm not sure, *azeezam*. Maybe some people in the streets." Vida's whole body was trembling. She clenched her jaw to keep her teeth from knocking against each other. She tried to keep her voice light so Roya would not get alarmed. Once her daughter broke out in hives at the sight of her frantically searching for car keys when she was late for an important meeting.

In a brief moment of quiet, thinking about all that had and could go wrong, Vida gazed at nothing in particular.

It was just the two of them, mother and daughter, alone in the middle of Tehran in the upstairs unit of their duplex. All the rooms had floor-to-ceiling windows facing the street. The only room without the windows was the bathroom where they huddled now, waiting for the booming to stop.

Vida could hear people outside, demonstrators. She gripped her daughter tightly until her knuckles went white.

The apartment was close to a community center where young people gathered to exchange ideas. Recently, students had begun meeting there openly to protest the Shah's regime.

Now Vida heard yelling, screams, and gunshots. Close. Escalating riots. *What if the bullets hit the windows, and the glass gets all over the floor?* She curled up on the floor of the bathroom with Roya next to her, shoulders shrugged with beads of sweat forming on her forehead.

"Stay right here, okay? I'm going to make a phone call," she told Roya, and squeezed her daughter's perfect little hand.

"But Mommy…"

"Stay here. Do you want me to get Mrs. Beasley?"

"Mommm... remember? We gave her away last year," Roya whined, declaring herself too old for dolls.

Vida caressed Roya's cheek.

She recalled Roya had given the doll away. A few times a year they gave away old clothes and toys to Ali, the janitor at the library where Vida worked. Vida figured one of Ali's many daughters would make use of Roya's hand-me-downs.

"Oh, that's right. Just stay here. Don't leave the bathroom."

Vida bent down and walked close to the ground, past the several rooms to her own bedroom. She took the orange phone from the dresser, crouched on the floor in the corner between the bed and the nightstand, and nervously inserted her index finger into the coil of the cord. Her heart was racing.

"Linda, Linda... it's me," she said in a soft voice. She took a deep breath and tried to sound calm. She didn't want Linda to worry. She could handle this.

"Oh, Vida." She sighed. "I'm glad you called. We heard about the demonstrations near your house. They're closing Pahlavi Avenue from both sides."

"I can hear the shooting. They're on our street."

The windows rattled.

"Oh gosh." Linda sounded worried.

"Moommmy... my stomach hurts," Roya yelled from the bathroom. Vida looked out the bedroom. The bathroom door was open, and Roya was spread out on the floor between the bathroom and the family room, her face ashen.

"Roya *joon*, I told you to stay in there," Vida raised her voice.

"I don't feel good, Mommy."

Why is Roya so pale? "Okay, I'm coming."

"Linda... I can't talk. I'll call you back in five minutes," Vida said.

"What's happening?" her American friend asked.

"I better go." Vida hung up. She grabbed a pillow, the flower-patterned bedspread, and the blanket folded at the foot of her bed—the one Maman, her mother, had knitted the year before. She shuffled to the bathroom, bent low to the ground, and shut each of the bedroom doors along the way.

She sat close, placing her arm around her daughter's shoulder and pulling her in. "Roya *joon*. It's okay. We're going to sleep in here tonight."

"Mom, I want to sleep in my own bed." Roya's voice sounded weak.

"I know... I know, *azeezam*." She rocked Roya back and forth.

The tiles on the bathroom floor were cold, and Vida pulled her daughter closer. They sat on the bathmat by the sink, the mother cross-legged, the little girl held in her arms as Vida stroked her locks. Roya lay limp.

"What's wrong? Are you nervous?" Vida kissed her daughter's forehead.

"No," Roya whimpered.

Vida could barely hear her voice, and she wasn't convinced.

"We're going to be fine. A few people are on the street, but they'll go home soon. Don't worry."

Vida remembered two weeks before when she drove to work the morning after midnight marches. She had witnessed pages ripped out of books flung all over the sidewalk next to the Abraham Lincoln Library where she worked. A half-burnt poster picture of the Shah with hand-drawn horns rising out of his ears and one of his eyes poked out hung from a building wall. A large white sign lay on the side of the street covered in blood-red handprints that read "*Marg Bar Amrika*"—Death to America. She shivered at the leftovers of a partially burnt US flag and a woman covered in a *chador* clenching the black cloth with her teeth. Only one eye was showing, the one eye that had stared Vida down as she snuck into the library that morning.

"Mommy, I don't feel good."

She touched her daughter's forehead. Warm. What would she do if Roya got sick? That cursed curfew prohibited moving around the city, even for medical emergencies. Even with no restrictions on being outside, Vida didn't have enough gasoline in the car to get her to Tehran Pars hospital. The oil refineries were on strike, and gasoline was rationed.

The week before, Vida and Roya had emptied the refrigerator, taken whatever food was in the apartment, and moved in with Linda and her family for four days. She didn't have enough fuel to get home. At nights, the two mothers would tuck the children in bed and, together with Linda's husband, would listen quietly to the battery-operated shortwave radio for any news from the BBC. One of the nights they went to the rooftop and heard demonstrators chanting "*Allah o'Akbar.*" They even heard a few gunshots. Once Vida was able to get gas, she had returned home with a few remaining groceries.

Now, she held Roya in her arms, hoping, praying it was nothing serious. She noticed Roya's eyes rolling to the side. Her skin even more pale.

"Roya, Roya," she yelled slapping the little girl's face and squeezing her cheeks.

"Mommy… maaaa… I'm going to…" and then the girl's body jolted forward.

"Sit up, sit up." Vida moved her close to the toilet and lifted the seat. Bracing Roya's head over the bowl, she held back the curls so they wouldn't get in the way.

"It's okay. If you need to throw up. Just do it."

"Uhhhhh..." Roya cried out. A lump-filled white mixture splattered into the toilet bowl. Roya jolted again, and more came up. Tears were streaming down her face, but she wasn't crying. She stayed bent over the porcelain bowl.

"Did it all come out?" Vida asked, hoping it was over. She looked away, fixing her eyes on the pale blue wall to keep herself from throwing up. She rubbed her daughter's leg, knowing that would calm her.

Roya jolted forward again, but nothing came out this time.

Vida grabbed a tissue and wiped her daughter's mouth. She ripped off a piece of toilet paper, held it up against her little nose, and told her to blow. More stuff poured from her nostrils. Vida's hands were shaking, and she tried to keep still.

Peering into the toilet bowl, Vida noticed a push against her own stomach. She held back and then flushed it. She touched Roya's forehead and then the side of her face. She rested Roya's cheeks in her sweaty palms and stared into her eyes. Her daughter was running a fever. *Is she going to throw up again, or is it over? How will I get her to the hospital?*

The sandwich! It was the tuna fish. The half-used jar of mayonnaise in the refrigerator, the power going on and off for weeks, ten or twelve hours at a time. It had gone bad. *Poor baby*, she thought. *What was I thinking, letting her eat tuna and mayonnaise?* Vida had bought feta earlier that day at the Jewish deli near the library where she worked for her own dinner, but she hadn't thought about the hidden risk of Roya's tuna fish request.

"Stay here. I'm going to get you a Seven Up."

"Okay, Mommy," Roya moaned.

Vida dashed through the family room and the entryway into the kitchen—windows all around her, shots outside, the building across the street up in flames. She didn't notice any of it. She swept her hand across her forehead to get rid of the sweat before opening the refrigerator. Her hand shook as she grabbed the bottle sitting in the door. She darted back to the bathroom, hearing a loud booming from beyond the living room window.

Smoke surrounded the building, and sirens blared through the night. Someone yelled into a bullhorn, and masses of people repeated after him—"*Allah-o-Akbar*"—God is great. Women screamed.

Vida quickly made it to the bathroom and shut the door. For that instant the sounds were gone, but she knew closing the door only gave them temporary relief. They would be safe, at least for a little while.

Vida sat on the ground and poured the drink into a glass, the bubbles making a fizzy sound. She took a deep breath.

"Here... *ghorboonet beram*... drink this. You'll feel better."

Roya rested on the tile floor and leaned against the wall, her head bent to the side. Her color was back.

"You're going to get cold. Sit on the mat," Vida insisted.

"It feels good here." The little girl's body was limp, but she carefully pushed herself up to take a sip.

Vida could tell she was feeling better. She let her daughter lie against the wall for a few minutes, drinking the soda. She thought frantically about food poisoning and hoped Roya's prompt rejection of the bad food would lead to a quick recovery.

A few minutes went by, and Roya seemed more relaxed. Vida padded the inside of the bathtub with her bedspread and put her pillow at the end, opposite the waterspout. Roya crawled in, and Vida covered her with Maman's blanket, tucking it around her so she was completely covered, as if in a sleeping bag. The sounds outside diminished, at least for a moment. Vida slid out of the bathroom and blew out the candles. When she came back Roya was dozing off. Vida ran her finger along her daughter's face, kissed her on the forehead, and knelt, leaning on the tub.

"Where are you going to sleep, Mommy?" Roya whispered, her eyes almost shut.

"Don't worry about me. I'm going to sit right here next to you. I'm not going anywhere."

Out of the silence came the shrill sound of the phone, startling Vida. She stood to get it.

"Who's that, Mommy?"

Maybe it's Kasra calling from Munich? The knot in her stomach grew. She didn't want her fourteen-year-old son to know about the demonstrations. He was only four years older than his little sister, but he had grown up so much during those four years. *Maybe it's Linda calling back?*

She got up to walk out of the bathroom, but then the phone stopped ringing.

"It's nothing. Go back to sleep."

Vida watched as Roya's eyes grew heavier and eventually shut. She looked cozy in the white tub, like when she was a baby in her basinet. *I must get her out of this country,* Vida thought.

PART I

PART I

CHAPTER 1
Summer 1971, Westchester County, New York

———

"I'm home," Kamran said in his deep masculine voice as he lightly shut the front door.

"Upstairs… taking a bath," Vida sang.

Kamran was doing so much better from his first brain cancer surgery. Three years before, during a trip to Iran where he fainted, he had been referred to a specialist in London. Vida was then three months pregnant. She and their three-year old son Kasra had traveled to London with him. After a fourteen-hour brain surgery and months of chemotherapy and radiation treatment, Kamran was finally released. The family had moved back to Iran where Roya was born ten days later, and after which they moved back to their home and life in the US. Now, it seemed he had never been sick.

When they returned to the US, at first Kamran joined the cardiology practice of an older doctor on a part-time basis, but when the partner died, Kamran took over the practice. He worked four days a week and taught one day a week at the Albert Einstein Medical Center, where he had completed his residency. In the summertime, he played tennis in the late afternoons. Vida helped in the office with accounting and insurance matters. The young couple had a steady flow of income and a routine schedule, a pace Vida enjoyed. Life in New York was the most stable it had been during their married life.

Vida had already piled the kids into the tub for their nightly bubble bath, her favorite time of the day.

Kamran made an entrance into the bathroom in his tennis shorts, the home movie camera in hand. He grabbed her stomach from behind, accidentally touching her breasts, and kissed her on the cheek. She had a wide grin, and her eyes sparkled. Her sleeveless button-down shirt was partially wet from the splashing of the water.

"Oops, sorry," he said, giggling and then lightly caressing her French twist.

"Not now," she complained. Her cheeks felt flush, and she turned to see if the kids had noticed. The children were too young and clearly didn't care, but still she felt uncomfortable displaying her affection in front of them. Expression of romantic feelings simply didn't happen in the Iranian culture. She felt conflicted about this. Love and affection were natural feelings for a young couple, but with this traditional civilization, you were not permitted to share them. You had to bottle them up, which was one of the many reasons she didn't like living in Iran, being Iranian.

She gazed at her husband with her large black eyes, exchanging smiles with him.

"Daddy," Roya screeched and stood up in the tub, her arms reaching out to him with a cloud of bubbles resting atop her curly black hair. A layer bubble foam covered her three-year old chubby stomach and round bottom.

"Roya *joon*. Sit down. I don't want you to slip in the tub." Vida tugged at her arm.

"Hi, Dad," said the seven-year-old Kasra, smiling up at his father as he pushed his plastic boat on top of the bubbles methodically, as if the boat was gliding across a glacier. The boy's thick straight hair was evenly parted to the side, and he had jumbo black eyes like his mother's. His eyelashes were so long that to an American they might have looked false.

Now in the bathroom, Kamran moved his hand back and forth. "Smile, everyone… wave." He held up the home movie camera with the other.

"Again? What are you going to do with all these movies?" Vida ran her hand over Roya's head to wipe off the foam, preparing her little girl for the shoot.

"You'll be begging for these films when they grow up. They are never going to be this age again."

"The birthday parties are one thing. But with Roya taking a bath… naked?"

"Who cares if she's naked. She's only three." He continued filming. Even though Kamran was raised in a religious family—his parents praying five times a day, fasting during the month of Ramadan, and his father having traveled to Mecca, the obligatory good Muslim journey—in many ways Kamran himself was more liberal than Vida. "Leave me alone. I want to make a movie. A real movie about the perfect mother."

Squinting with one eye pushed against the camera and the other looking at Vida, he poked at her taut stomach and then ran his slender finger along her hip. She moved closer, cupping her hand around his.

"Very funny... go take a shower," she said.

"Aye aye, captain." He searched for the power button on the camera.

After Vida put the kids to bed, she turned the stereo on in the living room at a low volume and went into the kitchen. She made two weak Bloody Marys, adding a touch of Tabasco and a few drops of fresh lemon juice. Rosemary, their neighbor, had given them the lemons the week before from the tree in her backyard, and Vida and Kamran had stayed up late one night squeezing lemons and storing the juice in empty bottles.

She carried chips and dip on a plastic tray and carefully placed it on the wooden coffee table. She lit white tea candles and sat on the loveseat in the living room. Leaning in, she stared into the bright lights and waited for Kamran to join her downstairs. The flames from the candle blew short and steady. As she stared at them, she took a deep breath and exhaled. One of the flames bent to the side as if it might go out, but then it stood up again, pointing upward. It reminded her of Kamran and his brain cancer, and how she had almost lost him. Like the flame, he had recovered. Now Vida felt things were indeed looking up.

When he finally got downstairs, he smelled clean and fresh from the Johnson's baby shampoo.

"Don't use up all their shampoo," Vida protested.

"But I love smelling like them." He leaned in and kissed her on the lips.

The few strands of hair that remained on the sides of Kamran's head were wet, and the bald spot, on top was shiny. Kamran's tendency toward baldness had accelerated after the chemotherapy. He sat next to her, his muscular leg warm against hers. After ten years of marriage, she felt closer to him now more than ever.

He sang out loud, imitating Perry Como's "It's Impossible." He got down on one knee holding out his hand as if he was going to propose marriage the American way. "Come on. Let's dance," he said and pulled her off the couch. She threw back her head, and he held her close, swaying to the music and dipping her. Vida laughed and felt giddy as if it were their first date.

They sat back down on the couch. He pulled her close, pushing his fingers into her back. The massage gave her an unexpected release of tension.

"Have I ever told you that you look like Sophia Loren?" he asked.

"Oh, that feels good." Vida smiled. She closed her eyes, and her voice softened. She felt a tad dizzy. "Rose came to watch Kasra's baseball practice. She is so wonderful to our family."

Rosemary and her husband Carlo lived next door. Vida spent most mornings at their house while the children were in school. Her friend dictated recipes for lasagna and spaghetti and meatballs as Vida took copious notes. In between, Vida sipped a cup of coffee, sharing her anxieties about living with a husband recovering from cancer.

"I know," he said. "We're lucky to have them as neighbors..."

She interrupted him. "Neighbors? They're good friends."

"I suppose they are. But we haven't known them *that* long, a couple of years. I mean... it's not like they're family."

"Well, I feel as close to Rosemary as I would with any of our relatives. She's always so kind, a good mother, a great wife. She has a model marriage with Carlo. I love that about her."

"How do you know?" asked Kamran. "We don't know that."

Vida paused for a moment, her eyebrows bunched, but she didn't want to argue with him. She reached for her drink. "You're right. We don't know about their marriage. I'm guessing, okay? I'm just saying. I get a good feeling when I'm with her."

Vida was thinking about so many relatives in Iran in unhappy marriages, pretending to be happy just for show. She loved how transparent Rosemary was in their friendship.

"That's all that matters," he said. He stroked her hair and reached for a chip.

"Hey, those are mine. Eat your own." She feigned anger and smacked his hand.

"Okay, okay, you don't need to get so bossy." He wrestled her onto the couch.

Lying on her back, pinned to the couch laughing, she announced, "You got a letter from Iran today." She had forgotten to tell him.

"Who's it from?"

"I didn't open it. It's in the kitchen. Do you want me to get it?" She lowered her gaze. *I should have remembered to tell him. Darn it.* It made Kamran so happy to get letters from home.

"No… you relax. I'll get it," he offered. Jogging into the kitchen, he raised up his hands in victory as if he had won a wrestling match.

She smiled and leaned her chin on her hand, gazing out.

"It's from Doktor," he yelled from the other room.

Vida had a rolling feeling in her stomach. Doktor, pronounced with an emphasis on the "k" as if it was a sophisticated fancy European name, was Kamran's older brother, a surgeon. Kamran and the rest of the family looked up to Doktor simply because he was older. Both brothers had been admitted to medical school, the highest scholastic achievement for Iranians. Kamran, however, had gone further. He had completed a US internship and residency program. Kamran was clearly the smarter one. *Why is Doktor so special?*

Once before, Doktor had sent Kamran a letter, and Kamran had not shared it with Vida. She secretly read it the next day. In the letter, Doktor asked Kamran to come back home to Iran. He had said if something happened to Kamran, Vida would not be able to handle their life. He indicated although Vida was bright, she couldn't handle their finances on her own. She was a young woman, and women should only have to worry about raising children and taking care of the home and their husbands.

When Vida had finished reading that letter, her pulse had elevated. She confronted Kamran when he came home. *Who was Doktor to pass judgment on her?* At that time, Kamran had listened to her and defended his brother for caring for their family.

Now Kamran dropped himself onto the couch, ready to read this letter.

Vida sat up, crossing her arms as if against a chill. When she had announced her first pregnancy to her in-laws in a letter, she got an immediate response from her mother-in-law, demanding names like "Ali" and "Mohamed" for her grandson, as though naming the child was an extended family decision. The thought of giving her child a religious name made Vida's head itch, thinking of the turban-covered head of the mullahs. When she was little, Maman had told her the clergy men wore their turbans because their heads were covered with lice.

"What does the letter say?" she asked as Kamran folded the letter.

"It's about a piece of property in the north Baba *joon* bought for us several years ago," he said referring to his father. "Doktor sold it."

In Iran it was customary for parents to buy property in the name of their children. The family assets were protected from any legal action, and it secured the children's future.

"How did he sell the property without you?" She wanted to ask him if Doktor had forged Kamran's signature, but she held her tongue.

"He has power of attorney from me," Kamran said, getting up.

"A power of attorney?" Vida asked. She set down her drink.

"I gave him a general power of attorney to handle all my financial affairs when we were in Iran three years ago. I'm sure I told you."

Vida sat silently, her heart pounding. She would never have approved of giving Doktor power of attorney.

"I can't believe you did that." Raising her eyebrows, Vida leaned forward. Her breath blew out one of the tea candles.

"What are you so upset about? I was sick. Remember? Anyway, how else is anything supposed to get done when we're all the way here in America? It's not a big deal. We agreed we would sell the property and invest the money." Kamran looked upset at having his decision questioned.

"I understand, but you and I… we're married. And everything we own is ours, and these kinds of decisions are ones we should make together… as a husband and wife," she said raising her voice. She was surprised at how forcefully she was saying this.

"I'm sorry. What do you want me to do now? Tell him to give the money back because I didn't want him to sell it?"

Vida pulled back with her arms crossed. She felt a tightness in her eyes and took long, deep, calculated breaths.

Kamran reached for her limp hand, holding it in his. He lowered his voice. "This is good for us. The money is ours." He kissed her on the forehead. "Now, do we want him to send it here or keep it in Iran?"

She didn't respond. She pressed her lips together. *Is this what it means to be married? Secrets and lies?*

"Come on. Don't be that way. I'm asking *you*," he said.

"Oh, so now you ask me for my opinion?" She had a dry throat from rushed breathing. But she didn't want to fight with him. *It's not good for his health to get angry.*

He stood up. "Yes… you are my wife, and I want to know what *you* want to do."

"Do whatever you want. It's your inheritance and your money." She purposely looked in the opposite direction. Doktor selling the property was one thing, but giving him power of attorney without consulting her felt like a betrayal.

"No, it's not my money. It's ours." He pushed a strand of loose hair behind her ear.

"Well, since you ask… I think he should send the money here so we can buy a house."

"Why would we want to buy a house in America?"

"Because we want to live here. We live here now. Remember?" she said, wondering why he was asking.

"I understand."

"No, I don't think you do. I don't want to ever live in Iran. I don't like the culture, and I don't want to raise my children there."

"I understand," he said, lacking any emotion.

"I don't think you get it. I want to stay here." Her hands felt clammy, and she felt a cold sweat.

He put his arm around her shoulder, kissing her cheek. He whispered in her ear, "Okay. I'll tell him to do that, to send the money to the US. Are you happy now?"

Vida looked at the table. The flames had gone out on all the candles. She looked at him and gave him a half-smile, almost forgiving him.

Rubbing his hands together, Kamran asked, "So… now… what's for dinner?"

* * * * *

On Monday of the following week, Kamran went in for his routine cancer checkup. Usually when he returned from one of these visits, he cheerfully announced he had passed his blood tests with high marks, as if he had taken a school exam.

This time, though, when he came home it was different. He seemed withdrawn. Vida could tell something was bothering him, but he didn't say anything out of the ordinary, and she was afraid to ask. She thought he might have gotten negative news about his recovery. She wondered if his cancer was back, but it terrified her to even think about that. She considered it a bad omen to talk about it.

That night, while she was brushing her teeth, he stood in the bathroom gazing at her reflection in the mirror. Finally, without any warning, he said, "I want to go home."

She was already wearing her light cotton nightgown. She spat out the toothpaste and eyeballed him in the mirror for a few seconds.

"We *are* home." She gave him a half smile. *Please, God, please don't say you want to go to Iran.*

"I mean Iran."

"When? Kasra's school starts in a week." She bent over the sink, still gazing at him in the mirror.

"I don't mean for vacation. I mean I want to move back."

She felt lightheaded. She couldn't believe what she was hearing. She rinsed her mouth, grabbing a hand towel, and turned around.

Kamran pushed himself back against the wall, his hands behind him, gazing down as if he had said something he shouldn't have. After a few seconds he looked up. The light bounced off his eyes. "Look. I don't want my life to pass me by," he said loudly. He seemed agitated. "I want to live. I mean *really* live."

"What?" She propped herself up against the bathroom counter on her hands. It made her angry to think he had made such an important decision without consulting with her.

"We will always have a tie to America," he said. "And I want the children to go to university here. But at this time in my life, I want to teach in Iran and give back to my country."

"What do you mean? You've been writing all those articles you sent to Tehran University. You *have been* contributing. Why the guilt?"

"It's not about guilt." He turned around, walked into the bedroom, and threw his jacket on the bed.

"Then what? You just started your practice here, and everything is finally falling into place. Only last week our green cards arrived. Remember? And... the house... we're going to buy a house. Did you forget about that conversation?" She followed him into the bedroom, standing behind him with her hands at her hips.

She noticed the photograph of Kamran and his siblings at the Caspian Sea when they were little children. It was placed in a silver antique frame Kamran's mother had given him when they left Tehran the last time.

Vida took a deep breath and put her hand on his shoulder. "Is it your family? Do you miss them?" she asked in a sweet soft voice.

He brushed her hand aside.

"Why don't you go for a visit?" Struggling to understand, the questions and suggestions rolled off her tongue.

He turned, pounded his fist against the wall, and then shook his hand as if he might have hurt himself. "It's not about the family." The room vibrated, and the picture frame fell face down on the dresser. He paused and took a deep breath before resting his hand on his head. She worried the children would hear them.

Her heart was about to explode. Something big was happening, something she had no control over. The only other time she had seen him this upset was when they found his mother feeding Kasra scalding tea when the baby was barely six months old.

Kamran placed his hands on Vida's shoulders, peering into her eyes. His voice soft and methodical, he said, "Vida *joon*, it's not about my family. I want to go back. Just for a little while. We need to. It will be better for us and the kids. They will get to better know their grandparents, aunts, uncles…"

She gently pushed him away and moved to her side of the bed. Pulling back the bedspread, she propped up the pillows and sat up in the bed. "I don't understand. Please don't do this."

"It's best for all of us," he insisted, leaning his head back against the wall.

Their eyes fixed on each other as if they were dueling. She knew she couldn't convince him to change his mind. She remembered him in the hospital after his surgery the first time when she visited him, lying there, helpless, not knowing if he was going to see his unborn daughter. Was his cancer back now and he wasn't telling her? She wanted to ask him. But how? And maybe she didn't want to know.

Finally, she pulled the covers over her head and pretended to go to sleep. Her back turned to him, she buried her head in her pillow, sobbing quietly so he couldn't hear her and knowing he surely must. But he didn't try to comfort her.

* * * * *

The next morning, she drove Kasra to school and Roya to preschool. When she walked back into the house, Kamran was sitting at the kitchen table dressed for work and reading the paper. He didn't look at her. She grabbed a dishrag and started to dry breakfast dishes.

When he remained silent, she sat tentatively on the edge of her seat across the table from him. "Can we talk about our conversation last night?"

"I'm not changing my mind," he said without looking up.

"Is it the cancer? Is it back?" she whispered softly.

He gazed straight into her eyes. He looked like he was going to share his secret, he was going to blurt out what she already guessed, but he didn't. "Why is it always about the cancer? Everything is about the cancer. Can we once just forget it ever happened? Can you please pretend?" He slammed his hand on the table, grabbed his briefcase, and marched out.

She sat for a moment with an unfocused gaze. She took the dishrag and threw it on the floor, tears streaming down her face. Feeling desperate and alone, she called Rosemary.

"Vida, is that you?"

The tears gushed out, and Vida couldn't utter a word.

"Honey, are you okay? Say something… please."

But Vida sobbed uncontrollably. She wanted to speak but couldn't say anything coherently. Rosemary hung up the phone, and within a few minutes she appeared in the kitchen with Carlo behind her.

"What happened?" her neighbor asked, out of breath.

"Where's Kamran?" Carlo asked in a loud voice.

"Everyone's okay," Vida said.

Standing against the kitchen table, Rosemary put her hand on Vida's shoulder. "Oh. Thank goodness." She sighed. "What happened, sweetie pie? Do you want to talk about it?"

Vida reported what had happened. She reached for a tissue. "Please talk to him." She felt a tightness in her throat.

"Did something happen yesterday?" Rosemary asked.

"He had the checkup. I'm worried it's about the cancer."

Rosemary eyed Carlo. "Oh… don't be silly. He would tell you if there was a problem. He probably just wants to go back home for a while."

"You think so?" Vida's eyes widened. She could barely see but felt a sudden sense of hope.

"Sure. Why wouldn't he tell you what's going on?"

"Maybe you're right," said Vida looking down. "Do you think I'm overreacting?"

Rosemary pulled her chair closer to Vida and put her arm around her shoulder. "Look. He's been through such a rough time—physically and emotionally. It's been a hard three years. If he wants to move back to Iran for a while, just go. You can always come back. We will all be here." She grinned.

"Please ask him to stay. You ask him." Vida turned to Carlo.

"You know I can't do that," Carlo said.

"You can. You're older, and he respects you," Vida insisted.

"No. He won't. It's for the best that you go."

"I'm sure you'll be back. It's not like you'll be stuck in Iran forever," Rosemary said.

"I don't want to go." Vida brushed away the tears with the back of her hand.

"Look. Clearly this is what he needs right now. Leave your furniture in our basement," Carlo said, as if that would console Vida. "And book your return flight for six-months from now."

Vida bowed her head and sobbed. She felt like the kitchen walls were caving in on her.

Within two weeks the entire home was packed, the dishes, glasses, and ashtrays cushioned in bubble wrap. Carlo helped move the antique desk and matching bookcase, the ones Kamran inherited from the older doctor's medical office, to the basement of his house. The rest of the medical equipment they left in the locked office space. Kamran and the landlord agreed he would pay the office rent for six months until he figured out a more permanent plan. Vida sent all the patients a typed form letter notifying them that they were leaving the country due to a family emergency. She didn't know what else to say. She didn't know then that she would not be back.

Rosemary drove them to the airport the day they left. When she said goodbye to Vida, she cried and whispered in her ear, "I know you don't want to go. Do it. Do it for him."

* * * * *

Kamran, the children, and Vida flew to Frankfurt to break up the ten-hour flight from New York to Tehran. The kids and Vida stayed overnight and then took another flight to Tehran the next day. Kamran took three days to visit with a former classmate, who lived in a suburb. He bought a Mercedes, packed it with home appliances, a toaster, blender, and vacuum cleaner, and drove to Tehran by himself. The move would change the family forever.

CHAPTER 2

December 1971, Tehran

———

On the day of the lecture, Kamran was jumpy. He rubbed the back of his neck while he paced the living room. Throughout the day, he misplaced his reading glasses several times. The head of the cardiology department at Tehran University had invited him to speak to a group of medical students. Kamran was grateful to Hassan for introducing him to the department head. Hassan was Kamran's closest medical school friend, one of the few classmates who did not lose his humanity in the process of becoming a doctor.

Kamran kissed Vida on the cheek and squeezed her fingers before he left the house in the afternoon. His hand shook a bit when he released her fingers. *This could be the beginning of his teaching career, the reason he brought us back to Iran,* Vida thought. She had a floating sensation, thinking their lives might finally settle down.

It was the middle of December, and the German neighbors downstairs had decorated their Christmas tree with live candles. Vida loved Christmas and thought the lights were so beautiful in a soothing way.

"I'll be done by five thirty and home no later than six," Kamran announced.

"Are you sure?"

"The professor has another class at five thirty. Trust me, we'll be done by then. He's prompt."

Vida rolled her eyes. She and Kamran regularly joked about Iranians not honoring the clock and had struggled with that since returning to Iran. They had shown up at 8:00 p.m. for parties only to find dinner served at 11:30 p.m. They attended a concert once where they took their seats at the announced time and waited nearly two hours while the audience continued to pour into the concert hall, chatting and greeting each other.

The young couple had met at her cousin's engagement party in Tehran ten years before. The next day he flew to New York to start his medical residency. They wrote letters back and forth, lots of them, until he proposed in one of the letters. On their wedding day, he called in, long distance, for the ceremony, but only for a few minutes. His father had signed the wedding contract on Kamran's behalf. The next day the new bride flew to New York to join her husband. Right from the start, their marriage was not conventional, living as nontraditional Iranians.

"He'll stick to the schedule," Kamran said with a determined face. "I'll be home on time. I promise." He lifted three-year-old

Roya and threw her up in the air, her skirt flying up, pudgy legs exposed. The little girl's eyes fixed on her daddy, her mouth wide open, thrilled to be tossed into the air.

Vida smiled and had a feeling of weightlessness.

Roya rubbed the top of his still-bald head and giggled. "Do it again, again, again," she screeched as he gently set her on the carpet.

"Be good. Don't give your mommy a hard time," he said, squatting to her size and looping his finger into one of the short curls.

"Maybe we can go have *bathtanee* when you get back," she said lisping, as she attempted a word in Farsi with an American accent.

"It's *bas-ta-nee*," Vida enunciated carefully. Even though she wasn't happy about living in Iran, it was important the children speak the language.

"*Ah-fareen*, your Farsi has gotten so much better," Kamran said, kissing Roya on the forehead. "I'm so proud of you. Sure, I'll take you and Kasra out for ice cream when I get back. Vanilla… chocolate… or strawberry?"

"*Daddy*, vanilla is my favorite," she scolded, as if she had been reminding him for a lifetime.

By 6:00 p.m., Vida had picked up seven-year-old Kasra from his despised piano lesson and was home preparing dinner. It hadn't started to snow in Tehran, but it was cold and gray, and a storm was expected.

She looked at the clock in the kitchen and noted the time. She dipped strips of boneless chicken breast, first in a pile of flour, then softly in an egg batter, and finally in a bowl of breadcrumbs, laying each piece on a plate, ready to be thrown into the frying pan.

Kamran was late, which wasn't like him.

Maybe the students asked a lot of questions? she wondered. *Maybe the professor was running on Iranian time? He would have called if that happened. Maybe Kamran decided to sit in on the next class as a visitor?*

A piece of chicken fell off the fork into the egg batter, splattering the yellow mixture onto the white tile counter. *Shoot.* She wet the sponge, squeezed the water onto the counter, and scrubbed it down hard, her brows wrinkled.

She waited until 7:30 p.m. and then started frying the pieces of chicken cutlet, wondering if she should call family members or the police. *It's taking way too long. Did he have a car accident?* She busied herself making sure the oil didn't spatter the counter or walls. *Who am I going to call? I don't want to alarm anyone.*

Finally, she heard the front door open and then slam loudly. Her shoulders dropped, and she gently closed her eyes. She let out a sigh of relief. Vida poked her head out the kitchen door. Kamran marched right past Kasra who had lined up the Matchbox cars in the living room. He bumped into Roya who jumped up and down on the couch, yelling, "You stink, you stink, you stink." Then he brushed his daughter aside as he walked into the kitchen.

"Kamran *joon*, I'm glad you're home." Vida approached him calmly even though he looked preoccupied. She reached to help him take off his suit-jacket. "How did it go?" she asked, not wanting to mention his lateness in case the lecture had not gone well.

He paused for a minute with a look of doubt. He burst out, "I lost my car. I lost it."

She was taken aback.

He didn't look angry, only puzzled. He was surprisingly calm about losing the new Mercedes.

"What do you mean, you lost the car?"

"After I got out of the lecture, I walked around the parking lot for an hour."

"Huh?" she asked. *Something was wrong.* She had not seen him this way.

Roya was still running around in the family room, chanting, "You stink, you stink." The night before Kasra had embarrassingly said this to one of their doctor dinner guests who happened to have terrible body odor. Fortunately, the man did not speak a word of English, but Kamran and Vida had gotten a bellyaching laugh about it after the guests were gone.

"I just couldn't find it," he said. He had dark circles under his eyes. "I looked and looked and walked all over the parking lot. Then I forgot what I was looking for."

Vida's heart started to race. Kamran took off his suit-jacket and hung it on the back of one of the kitchen chairs. As the two of them were talking, Roya launched in between them, jumping up and down. "You stink, you stink."

"Roya, stop it, I said. Now!" Vida snapped.

Her daughter darted out of the kitchen.

Trying to appear calm, she turned to Kamran, "What do you mean?"

"Can you get me a glass of water?" he asked. "I have a throbbing headache."

He took a sip and held the glass with both hands. "It's okay. After a while I found it. I was standing right in front of it," he said, his voice flat. He turned and stumbled out of the kitchen. "I'm going to take a short nap. Wake me up when dinner is ready. Okay?" He shut the bedroom door behind him.

Taking a short nap? At this hour? Vida stared at the closed door, her heart beating with an unnamed fear. Her hands were sweaty, and she wiped them on her apron. *This is not like him.*

She was reaching for drinking glasses in the kitchen cupboard when she heard a loud thump in the bedroom and the sound of breaking glass. Her heart stopped mid-beat, and then she ran to the bedroom and threw open the door.

Kamran lay on his back on the floor, fully dressed except his shoes, shaking in every direction, jerking up and down. He was foaming at the mouth, his eyes rolled back.

"Kamran… Kamran… oh my god… oh my god." Her jaw dropped and her hand flew to her chest. She tried to still his shaking body by pushing his shoulders toward the floor. It felt as if she were trying to shut a door against a hurricane, but the shaking continued, and its force pushed her away.

"No." She gasped, trying again to hold him down. The force of his body was too strong, and this time it threw her to the ground. She picked the phone up off the floor and tried to dial, her fingers shaking. *I have to dial faster.*

"… yes… yes… *kheylee mamnoon…* please tell him it's an emergency," she said in as calm a tone as she could manage. Then when she heard Hassan's voice on the line, she stuttered, "Hassan… Hassan… he's dying… he's dying." She was out of breath and sure her heart would stop beating.

"What's wrong?" Hassan asked in his typical measured voice.

"He's foaming... his mouth... shaking... up and down," she said. "And his eyes... his eyes..." She started to choke on her own words.

"Do you have ammonia in the house?" he asked.

"What are you talking about?"

"Forget it. Take a bottle of perfume or cologne and put it under his nose," he said. "Do it. Now."

Dropping the phone, she grabbed the bottle of L'Air du Temps. Her hands were shaking as she popped up the lid. She dropped to her knees and tried to hold him down with her arm as she waved the bottle from left to right, back and forth, under his nostrils.

For an instant she thought she was in one of Kamran's home movie's, projected in slow motion. The jolting slowed down until it came to a sudden stop. Kamran lay flat on his back. His hands and feet lay limp. His head dropped to one side. The pillows settled on the ground. The sheets were tangled up. He rested perfectly still, his eyes shut. With a dazed look, she lifted his right arm and let it drop to the bed. She leaned over and put her right cheek next to his mouth. She could feel his breath.

She let out a sigh, whispering, "Thank god." There was silence for what seemed like an hour, but only a few minutes had passed, maybe less. Now she could hear a beeping sound coming from the phone off the hook. The kids were standing in the door of the bedroom, facing her, holding hands. Both sets of big eyes were fixed on Vida. *They must have seen everything.*

Reaching for the phone, she put her finger on the button to make sure it had hung up. But then the phone rang before she began dialing.

"*Allo, allo*," she answered with unexpected composure.

It was Hassan.

"He's breathing... but he's unconscious," she reported.

"I'm sending an ambulance. I'll be right there."

What if he's dying? Who am I going to call? What will happen to the kids? Then she started picking up the shards of broken glass. The kids were still standing in the doorway with their little fingers interlaced. Tears were rolling down Roya's face, and she was shaking, but she didn't make a sound. Kasra looked ahead, stunned and quiet.

"Kasra, come here," she said, reaching for him and combing through the limp hair covering his eyes. "*Azeezam...* Go downstairs to the neighbors and take Roya with you. I want you to stay there until I come get you. Okay?"

"Okay, Mommy."

They started to walk out, but Kasra turned around. He cupped his fingers around his mouth and whispered, "Did

Daddy die this time?" His tone was matter-of-fact, as if he was asking for another piece of chicken cutlet.

"No, no. Everything's going to be okay. He's just not feeling well," she said. She felt guilty not explaining what was going on, but she didn't know how to explain it if the unthinkable was happening. "Go. Go on downstairs. Take care of your sister." Vida had a knot in her stomach. Her heart broke to lie, sending the kids away, but she didn't want them to see their father this way.

Kneeling, she cradled Kamran's hand in both of hers. She kept rubbing it, hoping he would wake up, but he looked as though he was in a profound and peaceful sleep. Every few seconds she reached over and put her hand on his chest. *He's still breathing. He's still breathing.*

She heard the siren approach and rushed to the window. Two men in white outfits pulled out a gurney. Another car drove up right behind the ambulance. Hassan climbed out, holding his black leather case, brushed one of the paramedics out of his way, and rushed into the building.

Within a few seconds Hassan was in the entry, gasping for air.

"Where is he?"

"In the bedroom."

She let out a huge breath.

"Tell me exactly what happened," he said, putting his ear against Kamran's chest.

She repeated what she had seen, wiping away her tears with the back of her hand and trying to stay focused. Her fingers brushed against her tangled hair that had become undone while she was struggling to quiet Kamran.

"It was a seizure," he said. "You're lucky he didn't swallow his tongue. He could have choked."

"Is it related to the cancer?"

"I don't know."

Does Hassan know something he isn't telling me?

"Maybe he didn't eat enough food today, or he took a fall. Or he's having a reaction to something that happened," he said as he walked her outside.

A reaction to what? Her mind drifted to the children. She had sent them downstairs. Were the German neighbors even home?

"He ate fine today, and I don't know about any falls. All I know is he was nervous about the lecture. He was distracted when he left this afternoon. Do you think it's that?" she asked with hope.

"Could be the stress of the lecture. Go downstairs and get the paramedics. We'll take him in for an X-ray and a brain scan."

Stupid lecture. Why did Hassan even introduce Kamran to the university professor if it was going to stress him out? She started to run downstairs but remembered she forgot to tell Hassan about Kamran losing the Mercedes. She marched back up. When she walked into the bedroom, she saw Hassan sitting on the floor, cradling Kamran's hands. His head was lowered. Hassan tugged a handkerchief from his pocket, wiped the tears, and patted his nose.

CHAPTER 3

December 1971, London

———

After Kamran recovered from the seizure and a long six-hour flight from Tehran, he and Vida arrived in London. They headed straight from the airport to the hospital in a cab.

The National Hospital for Neurology and Neurosurgery in Queen's Square was familiar to Vida—Victorian in design, multiple stories, red brick with white painted window sashes. It looked like it might have been home to many people, an apartment building perhaps. For several months, it had been home for them three years earlier. Physicians in Tehran had told her then they were not equipped to handle brain surgery the way he needed it. Hassan had told her to go overseas.

The hospital floors were white and shiny, and she could smell ammonia from the fluid used to wash them. A large Christmas tree covered with white lights, bobbles and tinsels, and an angel placed on top stood in the front entrance. Except for the Christmas tree, the hospital displayed no other signs of the holiday. *Such a contrast between the British and American celebration of the event.*

"My husband's name is Dr. Kamran Shamsa. We just arrived from…"

"Oh, yes, ma'am," said the older lady at the front desk.

Vida smiled when she heard the cockney accent.

"Dr. Mitchell said you would be traveling today. He should be here soon. Would you like a cup a tea? The trolley will be around shortly."

When Vida had called Dr. Mitchell the day before from Tehran, the doctor suggested they meet at the hospital where he had a small office. He had said this was preferable to meeting at his Harley Street office. It would be easier because they would probably need to run tests.

The woman at the front took them to his office where they sat waiting. Vida remembered all the times they had sat in the Harley Street office, waiting for the doctor. The last time they had felt hopeful, ready to start a new chapter in their lives. The surgery had been a success, the six months of chemotherapy followed by radiation treatment had worked, the cancer was gone, and Kamran was officially in remission. She was more than eight months pregnant that last time, stretched to her limits physically and emotionally. She had thought then it would be their last medical visit to London.

Vida noticed the awards on the wall—an Order of the British Empire and a Commander of the British Empire—like the ones in the Harley Street Office. A picture of Dr.

Mitchell shaking hands with the queen at a garden party at Buckingham Palace took up most of the wall.

The picture comforted her, and she felt relieved to be sitting, waiting for a doctor, as if the responsibility was no longer hers. She knew one of the best neurosurgeons in London was caring for her husband; he was in good hands. The best surgeon in Tehran would not be helpful at a time like this.

Dr. Mitchell hurried in with his briefcase, large umbrella, and a beige raincoat folded over his arm.

He dropped his keys as he organized his belongings. He shuffled over and shook Vida's hand when she stood up from her chair. He looked at Kamran, who said nothing. He didn't even look at Dr. Mitchell. Instead, he looked like he was inspecting the dark red Persian carpet, as if tracing the paisley designs in his mind.

Vida wondered if it reminded him of the carpets back home. His father's house on Avenue Pasteur was covered in them. *Does he even remember Dr. Mitchell?*

"Tell me what's been going on," asked the doctor.

"He lost his short-term memory and doesn't recognize anyone. On the flight over, he asked the stewardess to dance with him. He thought he was at a dinner party. He then told the stewardess I had been following him for days. On the plane he walked down the aisle, asking strangers what they thought about his lecture and flirting

with women, even with the religious ones wearing a *roosari*."
She was rambling and running out of breath but needed
to share this information so she alone was not carrying
this burden.

"Wearing what?" the doctor asked.

"The customary head dress," she said.

"Ahhh," he said deep in thought, observing Kamran.

Kamran looked like he was in a trance. It wasn't clear to Vida
what he was looking at, perhaps everything or nothing. She
could tell he was in a different world.

"Do you have the results of the tests?" Dr. Mitchell asked.

She pushed her camel coat sleeve up and flipped through
the stack of papers in her bag as if she was looking through
a filing cabinet, past the American Express traveler's checks
her father had given her and the maroon passports. Finally,
she pulled out the results of the X-ray and scan, along with
the notes Hassan had written for Dr. Mitchell. She hadn't
read any of it, not even the notes. She'd had no time.

"As I said on the phone, his doctor in Iran said it was a seizure.
He…" she said, glancing over at Kamran. "When he saw his
children, he thought they were his younger siblings. Since
we have landed, he's been quiet. I'm not sure he hears me."

"Maybe just tired," Dr. Mitchell said apprehensively. He put
on his spectacles and started to review the paperwork.

Vida watched him for any clues.

Finally removing his glasses, he looked up at her.

"Seizures happen if the patient has a brain injury, is epileptic, or has a brain tumor. It happens when there's a miscommunication of electrical signals to the brain. There could be another mass in his brain, and maybe it has spread. We won't be able to tell until we do surgery. Given the loss of his short-term memory, I would suggest we do it soon, tomorrow morning. It doesn't make sense to do any more tests."

"He's going to be okay. Right?" she asked, lacing her fingers and pressing her hands together as if it was her world, as if letting go would mean it would fall apart.

Rapid thoughts went through her head, mostly bad ones, but she wanted to stay positive. Dr. Mitchell had cured Kamran before, and she had no reason to think he wouldn't do it this time.

"We do not schedule surgery the few days before Christmas unless it's an emergency. In this case, I think its best we go in right away. I'll do my best, love."

She could tell it was serious, but again she didn't want to go there with the bad thoughts.

"How long will the surgery last?"

"Can't say until I know what we're facing."

He stood from behind his desk and walked around, placing his hand on her shoulder, and smiling. "We're going to do the best we can."

The doctor pushed the button on his intercom. "Send Nurse Brighton in, please."

A few moments passed before the matron nurse entered. She exhibited no emotion. She might have been in her forties, with graying hair she had pulled back in a bun under a white cap. Dr. Mitchell introduced her to Vida, and the nurse escorted the young couple to the hospital room carrying their luggage.

It was a private room with a single metal hospital bed in the middle. Vida couldn't see anything through the window above the bed because of the steam from the heating system. To the right of the bed was a small green leather couch with wooden arms. Vida didn't know it then, but the room would be home for the next few days.

That night the head nurse directed her to sleep in the nurses' station on a small cot. "I will not have you sleeping in his room. He needs his rest for the surgery," she had barked.

At first Vida hesitated to go because she didn't want to leave her sick husband alone, but she had no choice. The exhaustion of the last few days and the flight had set in.

Early the next morning, she walked over to Kamran's room. The luggage was stored beneath his bed. She pulled it out to retrieve her toiletries, changed her undergarments and clothes, and freshened up in the bathroom.

Kamran was still sleeping on his back, his head to the side. His body was covered with a white blanket. It was still dark outside when the matron nurse arrived with two others. The two looked like younger versions of the head nurse but slimmer, dressed the same, with pale skin, blue eyes, and white caps over their hair buns. They were both in their mid-twenties, probably a few years younger than Vida. One of them smiled, and Vida gave her a half-smile back.

The matron nudged Kamran's elbow. "Sir, sir... time to wake up."

Vida was annoyed at the lack of consideration or emotion. But it was clear she was the boss and they had to follow her rules.

Once Kamran awakened, all three nurses helped move him from his bed onto a surgical bed with wheels. The two young nurses quickly changed the sheets to his bed and carefully tucked the corners underneath the mattress so the bed would be ready for his return. Before they wheeled him out of the room, Vida held Kamran's hand, leaning over him. "Good morning, *azeezam*. Did you sleep well?" Her voice shook.

He was about to get wheeled in for brain surgery, probably not knowing he was in a foreign country and not knowing who she was or that they had two beautiful young children. In a way, it was best he didn't know.

"I'm sorry they won't let you eat. You're about to go into surgery, but everything will be okay. I'll be waiting for you when you get out. Don't worry."

She started choking but held back and tried to keep her smile, leaning over the bed and gazing reassuringly into his eyes.

He stared back at her, and for a passing moment, she thought, *Can he even hear me?* She continued smiling, as did he. He squeezed her fingers and said, "You are so beautiful. You remind me of that actress... Sophia... Sophia?"

"Sophia Loren," she finished his sentence. Maybe he did remember her.

"Ms. Loren, are you going to be upset if these pretty girls walk me to my lecture?" He grabbed the hands of the two nurses while gazing into Vida eyes.

Vida couldn't hold back the tears. She didn't say anything. She turned her back, put her hand on her forehead, and sat on the couch as they wheeled him out. After he was gone, she dropped her head in her hands, tears gushing out of control. She had held in her emotions during the last day, but she couldn't hold them any longer. She wanted to be silent so nobody could hear her, not wanting to draw attention to herself. But it wasn't possible. She cried so hard she thought she might gag.

About fifteen minutes later, one of the young nurses, holding a tray with tea, toast, jam, and an egg, came back and stood at the door. "Mrs. Shamsa... something to eat?" She seemed afraid to approach Vida, as if she had never seen a grown woman cry so intensely.

"Thank you. You're so kind."

The nurse set the tray on the table in front of the couch and walked backward to stand at the door. She bowed her head, her fingers interlaced in front of her.

"We've been married for ten years," Vida mumbled. She grabbed a tissue from the box on the table and wiped her nose before looking up and smiling at the nurse. It was not appropriate to talk to the nurse, but she needed to say something.

She remembered the earlier years when they lived in New York when he was doing his residency. She thought of the long evenings she waited for him when he had the all-night shift, and she would run off to the movies with her best friend. She reflected on the time he was late getting home from the hospital. She had called her best friend, and the two women had driven around Manhattan and looked for him in the streets, expecting to find him mugged and left for dead. Instead, they found him lazily leaning against the counter in the emergency room and chatting with a young candy-striper.

She thought about the days she and Kamran had driven to Coney Island in their red Volkswagen bug. They had piled their friends in the car and told Persian jokes all the way down there. They ate hot dogs on the boardwalk, rubbed oil on their legs, and sunbathed. Wearing oversized fashionable sunglasses, she and the other wife watched the husbands swim in the ocean. Vida had been filled with hope then— hope of building a life in America.

At the time her stepmother, Homa, had told her not to share too much about all the "good things" in her life, like marrying a doctor and moving to America.

"Nazarat meezanan," Homa had said. It was custom to hide good things because of the fear of getting struck with the fury of jealous thoughts, the stroke of the evil eye. Her stepmother had burned *esphand* the day Vida left Iran for America to join Kamran and chanted words as she moved the burned incense over the young bride's head to keep the evil eye away.

When Kamran eventually became ill, Vida couldn't help thinking she may have been pounded by the wrath of some unknown, or maybe known, person's *nazar*—jealous thoughts. She stopped herself. *Really? Am I going to fall for this Iranian nonsense? Nothing bad will happen.*

"It's funny… when I was in school…" she blurted out to the nurse, "an older lady looked after the boarders. Her name was Queenie. She read my tea leaves once. She told me I'd live out of a suitcase most of my life."

The nurse leaned against the door smiling, her eyes focused on Vida.

"Queenie told me there would be a terrible tragedy in my life." She started to choke on her words but held it back. She swallowed hard. "She also told me I would buy a pair of mismatched shoes. And two weeks later the orange pumps I bought in London turned out to be two different colors. One of them discolored from the window display."

The nurse started to giggle, and Vida realized she had been thinking out loud.

Her mind shifted to the surgery. "Could you please check on his progress?" she asked, pulling her legs to her chest and leaning over.

For five long hours she waited in his room. She distracted herself by figuring out the time difference between Tehran and London and wondering what the children might be doing. She had left the children with Agha Joon and her stepmother. When she called her own mother, Maman had said she would stay at Agha Joon's house to help Homa watch the kids. It was so unusual that her mother had such a close relationship with Vida's stepmother.

Vida wondered if Homa had made *aash*, with the lentils and wide noodles, the way Roya liked it. She hoped Roya had not added too much vinegar in the soup because it made her cough. Maybe Maman made kababs in the oven with white rice, Kasra's favorite. Had her children asked for her when they got up that morning? Did Maman sit them down and tell them a long story to distract them?

She walked down the hall and looked out the window. It reminded her of all the times she skipped classes when she was in boarding school and ran off with her Venezuelan roommate, shopping and smoking cigarettes in the city. Then she remembered riding around London, killing time when Kamran was in the hospital for chemotherapy and later radiation treatment. She wondered how long she would have to stay this time before she could go home.

She saw a black cab standing by the side of the building. It reminded her of the taxi ride to the hospital the day before. She had not paid the cab driver. He would not take her money once he learned Kamran was ill. She felt badly about not paying and under normal circumstances would have insisted. If they were in Tehran, it would have been customary for the cab driver to *tarof*, as a gesture of politeness, for her to offer to pay and for him to refuse, for them to go back and forth for several minutes, she holding out the cash bunched up between her fingers, thrusting her arm forward with force, he pushing her hand away, she insisting to pay, he swearing on the lives of his children and in the name of *Allah* he wouldn't take a penny, and when all that was done for the driver to overcharge her. *What a ridiculous custom they have in Iran.*

Finally, Dr. Mitchell entered. His surgical mask was pulled down below his chin, and the white cap on his forehead soiled, discolored in spots and sweaty. He sat beside her and put his hands in between his legs.

She inhaled and held the air as long as she could.

"I am so sorry. The cancer had metastasized throughout his brain. We tried to get it all, but it had grown. We removed some of it, but it didn't make sense to do more. We didn't think he was going to make it, but he did."

She took another deep breath, hoping the rest would be good news but knowing it was not.

"He's in a coma, and you will be lucky if he dies quickly. If he comes out of the coma, he will be nonfunctional."

The tears welled up in her eyes, and it felt as though her heart would stop beating.

"We will bring him back to the room in a few minutes, but don't expect him to wake up," he said. Then he walked out of the room as if he had said too much.

She gasped for air. She was afraid, for her but mostly for her children.

Within a few minutes, Kamran was wheeled in. The orderlies were wearing white pants and jackets.

Her husband was lying on his back, his eyes closed, his head bandaged with layers of white gauze wrapped tightly. Tubes stuck out from his nose, mouth, and arms, each leading to a separate apparatus. The bed the nurse had so tenderly fixed for him was pushed aside, and the surgical bed, with Kamran lying in it, was wheeled in its place.

One tube coming out of his mouth and attached to a transparent pump collapsed and rose with the rhythm of his breath, as if he was blowing up a balloon. After the men in the white jackets left, Vida was alone with Kamran.

She stood next to the bed holding his hand and crying silently. She didn't want to believe what she had just heard. His hand was limp. He looked to be in a bottomless sleep, and it didn't feel as though he was with her in the room.

After a while, she sat down in the chair next to his bed. For the rest of the day and into the night, and then the entire next day and into the following night, she was there. Occasionally, she looked through the steamy window; sometimes it was light out, at other times completely dark.

The nurses brought her food on a tray for her meals, but she wouldn't eat. They would come in and prop up his pillow, fiddle around with the tubes, as if it might make a difference, as if he was going to wake up if they did their jobs. For the most part, though, they didn't do anything.

She sat hour after hour hoping for a miracle. She would doze off to the whistling sound of his breath from the respirator. Each time, when she woke up, she would jump out of the chair, go to the bed and listen again, anticipating the hissing sound. That was how she knew he was still with her.

Early morning on Christmas Day, she woke up. The whistling sound was getting faint, and then suddenly it stopped.

She looked at him, afraid to touch him. She ran out of the room yelling, "Nurse, help, help. He's not breathing. Please do something."

The matron rushed back to the room with her and took his pulse. There was nothing. The nurse glanced at Vida, and then she looked toward the ground, pulling the white sheet over Kamran's head.

"Sorry, love… but he's no longer with us," she said without any expression on her face. She turned around, straightened her white jacket, held her head up, and marched out of the room.

Vida stared at her husband's covered body, and then her world went dark.

CHAPTER 4

December, 1971, London to Tehran

———

Vida woke up in a hospital bed, her right arm feeling numb, sore, and uncomfortable. She wondered if it was broken. She could barely open her eyes. She noticed her arm was hooked up to an IV. She was on a hospital bed. Two men in black pants, black jackets, and black ties sat in the room. They had dark hair and looked Iranian. She remembered what had happened to Kamran, and she wailed.

"I'm so sorry," one of the men said, standing up. "When your husband passed away, you collapsed. The hospital contacted the Iranian embassy. They didn't know who to call." He paused. "It will take a few days to finalize the arrangements. Tomorrow is Boxing Day here in England. It's a national ho…"

"I know what Boxing Day is," she said with an angry tone.

"Do you have family here in London? You are welcome to stay in our home," said one of the men.

She sat up and reached for a tissue on the table next to the hospital bed.

She looked at her moist tissue. "No."

She was uncomfortable lying in the bed with strange men staring at her.

"Can you hand me my purse? Where is the telephone?" she asked, sniffling and reaching toward the floor.

Her husband had an English friend in London. The man and his wife had lived in Iran, and Vida met them the last time she was there. The friends picked her up at the hospital and were kind to her for the few days that followed. They helped book her flight and get official copies of the death certificate, arranging for the body to be sent back with her on the plane. They sat with her when she made the dreaded phone calls back home, first to her own father and then to Kamran's. She couldn't bear the emotional outburst if she talked to his mother or either of her own.

Finally, she arrived at Mehrabad Airport in Tehran on the last day of the calendar year, 1971.

Hassan had arranged for the ambulance to come up to the plane to receive her and the coffin. About thirty relatives were waiting in the airport—hers, his, young, old, all in black, sobbing and clutching each other.

* * * * *

They drove up to the house from the airport at 9:30 p.m.

"Where are the kids?" Vida whispered to Homa. She could barely see, and her eyes were swollen.

Her stepmother pointed to the second floor.

As they walked in, Vida took her shoes off and tiptoed.

She suddenly heard a squeaking sound and footsteps running up the staircase.

Vida eyed Homa.

Kasra must have woken up from the noise of our arrival back into the house. Vida's eye bulged, and she couldn't blink. Her muscles tensed. She was not prepared to break the news to her children. She stumbled, her legs feeling weak, toward the staircase. *No child should have to hear about their father's death.* She had no formal speech prepared.

When she got to the upstairs family room, Kasra was playing with his toy cars. She sat next to him on the floor and folded her legs to the side. Her palm was sweaty, and she rubbed it along the carpet.

He didn't approach her.

She reached to hug him, but he wouldn't look up.

Vida cleared her throat. "I need to tell you something important."

Kasra was spinning the wheels on one of the Hot Wheels.

She wasn't ready to tell him, but she had no choice now. *He's old enough to understand,* she convinced herself. She knew he knew something awful had happened.

"This last week I flew to London with Daddy," she threw out, caressing his hand. What else was there to say? She looked down, gasping for air.

"And…" she ran her fingers through his hair.

He pushed her hand away. "I know, Mom… you don't have to tell me. Daddy died in London. Right?" He stared up at her with his black eyes wide open, his long lashes curled back. His thick hair was parted at the side, and he looked like a little man about to grow up much faster than any seven-year-old should.

"Yes, he did," she said, fingering the navy-blue paisley shape on the red carpet. She couldn't look at him.

He stood up, made a fist, and raised his voice. "I hate London. I know *Babajee* would have said goodbye to me before he left. He always says goodbye." The little boy dropped his head and began to wail.

Without making any body contact, she said, "*Azeezam…* don't cry. I want you to be a big boy. I don't ever want you to cry. Okay?" It was too hard for her to see her little boy cry.

He stood on the rug with his arms to his sides, zeroing in on the racetracks and taking quick shallow breaths. After a few seconds, he wiped his tears, his eyes fixed on his mother.

She wanted to hug him but was afraid she might lose control. Instead, she sat on the carpet on her knees, her hand holding her up, feeling the teardrops fall onto her own flesh. She avoided making eye contact, not knowing what else to do or say, feeling like Kamran's unbearable death was her fault.

He sat back, and their eyes met. Then he reached for his mother.

She held him tightly, rocking back and forth. How could she not? He buried his head against her shoulder, and while he sobbed, he repeated, "Mommy, I'm not going to cry."

She held him and soaked in his scent, comforting him. The loss was no longer hers alone. She rubbed his head until the whimpering stopped.

After a long minute, he sucked in the moisture streaming down his nose, rubbing the back of his hands against his eyes. He separated himself from his mother, and without looking back at her, he continued lining up the Hot Wheels, one in front of the other. Then he took one and moved it back and forth, so its wheels started to spin before releasing it onto the railing and watching the car turn at a high speed, going through loops and eventually launching into the air and landing on the carpet.

She interlaced her fingers, pushing them against her forehead so he wouldn't see her crying. But he must have seen her.

"Everything will be okay for us. I promise," she whispered. Vida finally unfolded her legs and slowly walked out of the room, her heart pounding inside her chest faster than the toy car that had raced off the track.

* * * * *

The next day the driver arrived at Agha Joon's home at 7:30 in the morning. Vida, her father, and Homa drove to Qom, the holy city, that morning for the burial. Kasra and Roya stayed behind with the hired help. Vida didn't want to subject the children to the sadness, knowing the children would get frightened by the wailing relatives. She was grateful they had been asleep when everyone left for the funeral. Having told Kasra didn't make it easier for her to face her daughter. *Was the child even old enough to understand?* She didn't know if her little girl could make sense of it. She was in a daze herself, weakened from the weeklong trip to London and back, and in disbelief that her husband was now gone.

It was a three-hour car ride. During the first hour, they drove through the southern part of Tehran, swarming with women covered with black *chadors*, holding bunched-up fabric beneath their chins with one hand and dragging small children with torn shoes and winter jackets hanging off them with the other. Vida wondered how many of those women were widows. With little money, would she end up like one of these women, dragging her children with torn shoes in the Tehran winter?

Older girls ran through the streets like children, too, but looked like grown women with their flower-patterned *roosaris* wrapped tightly around their heads and faces. Would Kamran's family impose Roya wear a *roosari*? Men carried fresh-baked *sangak* bread, wearing dress shoes with the heels pushed down as if the shoes were in fact slippers. All the drivers, including truck drivers with dark bushy mustaches, honked furiously and drove without order, with no respect for lines on the road or traffic lights, as if they were racing in a Grand Prix motor race. How could she ever drive in this city with children in the vehicle?

In the car, Vida's head rested against the window. She had lost the love of her life, and her heart ached at losing the one she loved more than any other person, other than her children. At times, she moved her head to wipe the steam that would build up from her breath and tears, with the sleeve of her coat. She was stuck in the memory of the events in London.

After they drove through Tehran, there wasn't much to see, except dirt on both sides of the two-lane road and an occasional unattached thorny bush blowing in the wind aimlessly as if, like Vida, it was finding a place to belong. How could she ever raise her kids without her husband? About an hour into the ride, they passed the gates of *Beheshte-Zahra*, the graveyard where her grandmother, and most Tehranis, were buried.

"I don't understand why they had to bury him in Qom," complained Vida's father. He turned around to look at Vida and his wife in the backseat, his wire-rimmed reading glasses halfway down the bridge of his nose. "It makes the ride so much longer."

After getting the news of Kamran's death, Doktor had gone off and purchased a mausoleum in the holy city to host ten of his family members upon their deaths. It was costly and extravagant to buy a mausoleum, and she didn't understand why he had gone through with the expense. They could have simply bought one plot of land for Kamran. Doktor had also made arrangements to have the entire extended family and friends make the three-hour trip to the burial on a luxury bus. Vida didn't know about any of these decisions. She was just told where to show up for the burial.

Vida's father had insisted they drive separately because they wanted to get back to the children. Vida told him she didn't want to waste time stopping to have *chelokabab* and raw onions for lunch after the burial, which was customary and the plan. Normally she loved *chelokabab*, especially when the gardener and his son would grill the skewered meat on top of the charcoal barbecue in the backyard for family gatherings. But she didn't have an appetite for it as part of the post-burial program for her own husband.

Her mind wandered to the days after Kamran's death, strolling in and out of stores on Oxford Street without an umbrella, in shock, her hair soaked, shopping for black clothes, the black clothes one had to wear for a full year after the death of a close relative. *How much closer do you get than your own husband?*

Homa sat in the backseat of the car with Vida. She was tall, thin, and fair, raised in the northern part of Iran, near the Russian border. A quiet and soft-spoken lady, she was only ten years older than Vida and a privately religious woman herself. A black scarf tightly wrapped around her short blonde hair and tied underneath her chin, Homa cradled a flask of tea, sweetened with cubes of sugar, and looked at Vida with her gentle blue eyes. A couple of times during the ride she poured the tea, the scent of cardamom floating in the air. Her stepmother held her hand in front of Vida. Every time Vida politely shrugged and nodded, refusing the offer.

*   *   *   *   *

By the time they arrived at the gravesite in Qom, the bus full of Kamran's family had already unloaded. A shiny navy-blue Mercedes was parked next to the bus like the one Kamran had driven to Tehran from Frankfurt a few months earlier.

Women were walking slowly so their heels wouldn't get stuck on the patchy grassy spots in between the gravestones embedded in cement. The French glass doors of the mausoleum, a four-hundred-square-foot room, were open. A few people Vida didn't know were mounting an oversized framed picture of Kamran on the front wall above the hole in the front center of the ground. Next to the opening was a white marble tombstone with engravings from the Koran.

She had seen many of these people the night before at Mehrabad Airport in Tehran.

Now in the mausoleum, Vida's mother-in-law, draped in a black *chador,* kneeled at the side of the hole in the ground. She sobbed and chanted, "My child, my darling, why did you go before me… Where have you gone… Why did you go so soon… What am I going to do without you… How am I going to live?"

Kamran's sisters knelt beside their mother, unsuccessfully trying to lift the sixty-year-old woman up, away from the gravesite. Ten years before, Kamran's older sister, Nasreen, who had been married to one of the wealthier landowners in Tehran, had lost her husband to a sudden heart attack when she had six small children. Kamran, who was then in medical school, had moved in with Nasreen and the kids so they wouldn't have to be alone. Now Vida looked at Nasreen wondering who was going to help her with her children for the coming months?

The widow was wearing a black tailored pantsuit with low-heeled pumps and a long black winter coat. After she walked up the stairs and into the mausoleum, she placed a sheer black scarf on her head and tied it loosely under her chin. She stood with her head down, her father and stepmother on either side of her, Maman next to Homa.

Doktor stood behind them with his head bowed down. His hand was covering the bridge of his nose, and his glasses were folded in his other hand resting by his side. He was not crying but appeared rooted in thought. Vida couldn't help but think he was hatching a plan. She didn't see who else was there, but many were, it seemed. Numb to her surroundings, she stood.

Occasionally, she would lift her head as her mother-in-law's shrill sobbing reached a higher pitch. She was tired, her energy sucked dry from not eating, although she had not noticed her hunger.

The men of Kamran's family, his brothers, and male relatives paused a few moments after opening the coffin. Doktor did not join them, as if he was Don Corleone and the others holding the coffin were his Mafioso cronies. In line with custom, the body had been washed in a mosque that morning while an imam read a certain prayer. Then it was wrapped in a white linen sheet, the *kafan*, and taken to the mausoleum to be buried in the linen alone.

From where she was standing behind Vida, Maman whispered loudly so most people on her side of the grave could hear, "Is *Aghay Doktor* afraid to get his hands dirty? Why is *he* not helping?"

Vida leaned over and glared at her mother. "Mamaaaan," she softly screeched in anger. Her mother was so bold and outspoken, a non-Iranian quality for a woman in that country, a quality Vida did not appreciate at a time like this.

Even though divorce was rare in Iran, Maman had divorced Vida's father when Vida was a few months old, and Vida never forgave her for that. She had felt isolated as a little girl, living with her stepmother, father, and stepsiblings until she was shipped off to boarding school. She had heard stories about her mother and her mother's cousin dressing up and going to nightclubs. She had missed having a mother to talk with, a mother who would dress her up, fix her hair, and tuck her in bed at night. Vida couldn't understand why a woman would voluntarily leave her husband, especially now when she had been forced into being a single mother.

Maman looked back at Vida and said, "*Azeez*, am I not right?"

Vida didn't have it in her to argue with her mother and turned her head back.

Vida's body jolted forward when she heard the base monotone voice of the imam start to read prayers from the Koran. What had been a dream-like state was now a reality. She didn't look up when they lifted the *kafan*-wrapped body out of the coffin. She suddenly felt violently nauseated and started to retch. Her two mothers held her up. She needed fresh air.

Maman and Homa led her outside, each holding one side close to her armpits. They stood beside Vida as she dry-heaved, looking as if they expected this to happen. The two mothers cleared the snow from the steps of the mausoleum before helping her sit down. Homa sat next to Vida, her arm over the thirty-one-year-old widow's shoulder. Maman stood on the steps, glancing inside the mausoleum and adjusting her scarf.

"I have to go inside. Please help me get up," Vida whispered from lack of energy, her body limp.

"No. You don't *have* to do anything. You're going to kill yourself from exhaustion. Just sit for a minute. Nothing will happen. Let them be offended," said Maman, referring to Kamran's relatives who would have looked down on Vida for not joining the ceremony.

Homa got up and stood on her toes looking over Vida's shoulder, trying to eye what was going on back in the mausoleum. She adjusted her *roosari* as if she was going to back inside.

Eventually, Vida's father came outside, demanding they drive back to Tehran. The imam was still chanting inside the mausoleum when they veered off. Doktor and the other family members were bowing their heads as if they weren't judging the obvious sudden departure.

During the ride, her father cracked smoked *tokhmeh*, watermelon seeds, in the front seat.

"Your ulcer is going to flare up. I should never have brought these," complained Vida's stepmother from the back.

"I can't believe they had an imam at the service. *Khanoom*, promise me when I die nobody is going to read from the Koran," he said. "And I don't want any *akhoonds* there either." Her father referred furiously to the clergyman.

Exhausted from lack of sleep, food, and stress, Vida fell asleep with her face against the cold window.

CHAPTER 5
January 1, 1972, Tehran

———

Now this doorbell. As Vida pulled and tugged at her locks, noticing the dark circles under her eyes, she put her turtleneck back on. She felt a tightening in her chest like she did at the gravesite. *Who is coming to the house so late in the evening after a burial?*

By 8:00 p.m., the night Kamran was buried, Vida, her father, stepmother, and mother had finished dinner. Maman had her winter coat folded over her arm ready to head back to her apartment.

After the burial Vida had told Roya about her dad, and the little girl had cried and cried, until she fell asleep in a puddle of tears. Now, the children were tucked in bed upstairs, fast asleep.

By the time Vida got downstairs to the living room, Agha Joon was gesturing for Vida's father-in-law Mahmoud and Doktor to sit down.

Maman was holding a silver tray laden with cups of tea, sugar cubes, and dates.

Homa, who covered her short blonde hair with the same black scarf she wore at the burial, had brought one of the plates of *halvah* sprinkled with pistachios from the kitchen. The day before she had prepared several plates to take to Vida's in-laws the next day for the mourners. Vida felt uncomfortable with her family entertaining as if it was a party, but hospitality was Iranian custom. *What are Doktor and Mahmoud khan doing here so late?* she wondered.

Both men were still wearing their black suits, their ties in place, as they had been at the burial earlier in the day.

They haven't gone home yet. She crossed her arms.

Doktor reached into his interior jacket pocket and methodically withdrew an envelope like a gangster pulling out a revolver. He took a long uninterrupted breath and removed his jacket, still holding the envelope and making sure he didn't bend it.

Kamran's father was a jovial, short, stocky man, shorter than his sons. With a mix of light brown hazel eyes and perfectly straight white teeth, he barely had any hair on his head, only a light strip around the sides and back.

Doktor was taller and leaner, with lighter eyes and a full head of hair. He might have looked handsome to some, but not to Vida. "It's too bad you missed the lunch at the *chelokababi* after the ceremony," he remarked.

She wondered why he, a doctor, didn't understand how drained she must feel after this last week. She could tell he wanted something, and her stomach churned.

Finally, Doktor sat down and leaned back on the couch, crossing his legs and stretching his arm along the back, looking entirely too comfortable. "It's been a long day, but this will only take a few minutes," he said.

Mahmoud sat inspecting his own shoes, his legs crossed at the ankles and his eyebrows crunched like he was unsure of what was about to happen. He crossed and uncrossed his arms until he pulled out an ornate *tasbeeh* from his pocket and moved the beads methodically. He shook his head. He seemed restless, not physically but emotionally.

Doktor slipped a piece of paper from the envelope and handed it to Agha Joon. Without taking his eyes from the two men, Vida's father reached for his glasses on the coffee table and lowered his head to study the piece of paper. He kept his head bent for a few minutes. Vida shifted in her chair.

Maman sat on the side sofa next to Vida, opposite Doktor and Mahmoud, narrowing her eyes as she studied their expressions. Maman had never approved of Vida and Kamran's marriage.

Homa pushed the *roosari,* her headscarf, back and forth, pulling at the ends to make sure it was tight. "*Befarmaeed, chaee*," she said, pointing toward the cups of tea, making a peace offering.

Vida's insides were quivering, and she rested her hand on her belly to hold it in, as if it might all tumble out. Finally, she moved to sit next to her father, who shifted the piece of paper her way.

Vida glanced at the paper but couldn't focus on the words. It was a legal document with technical words. A seal had been imprinted at the top of the page with the royal emblem, a lion with a sword, like the one on her maroon Iranian passport. Along the top it read: "Order from the Family Protection Court," and next to the word *deadline* it said "For Immediate Execution."

She scanned the page and made out her children's names, except it referred to them as the *sagheer*, orphaned children, of Dr. Kamran Shamsa. She struggled to focus on the rest of the document. Her heart pounded so fast, she thought it was skipping beats, like her eyes, which were skimming over the words.

The court order stated the custody of the children was granted to Vida's father-in-law, in accordance with the law, and the family had the right to act upon the order right away.

Taking a deep breath, Vida wanted to say something, but it seemed she lost her voice. She felt a tightness in her chest. She wanted to scream, but something held her back. She had her head bowed down, her eyes blinking fast, still making out the document's words, when her father got up and walked toward the front door. His legs were planted wide, and his nostrils flared. The cold winter air rushed in.

"*Aghayoon* (Gentlemen)… *befarmaeed*," he snapped, pointing with his finger outside the house, demanding they leave. "You should be ashamed of yourselves."

Vida eyed Homa with a disoriented look.

The in-laws stood up. Doktor loosened his collar, his face red. "We don't want to make this difficult. This is our right under the law," he said, his voice shaking as he scanned the room.

"The law?" Agha Joon yelled, the vein in his neck engorged. "The law? You can shove the law where… It's time for you to leave. Now," he barked, holding his arm out toward the door.

Doktor stood straight up with his hands bunched together in fists. "I will come back to take the children to my father's house in a couple of days. I will take them kicking and screaming if I must." His eyes were protruding. "She," he said pointing to Vida, "can do what she likes. But the children… They are ours."

"My daughter and my grandchildren will live right here where they belong," Agha Joon yelled as the two men stumbled outside into the snow. Then he slammed the door.

The family stood facing the door with arms crossed. A heavy silence hovered over the room. Vida collapsed on the couch, her mouth open, holding her stomach as if someone had punched her. Her knees shaking, she looked around the room, unable to focus on any one thing. Homa rushed over and lightly rested her hand on Vida's shoulder.

Rolling up his sleeves and swearing, Agha Joon said, "Those *pedarsookhtes, madar...* I can't believe it."

Vida looked at her father in a daze. Her eyes felt like they might pop out of their sockets. She felt like she was drowning and couldn't come up for air. *What if I pack the children's bags and take them back to America? We could leave for the airport tonight.* A family friend owned a travel agency. *I can book the tickets and be out of here by the morning. Nobody will ever know.* Her mind was racing, and she wanted to race with it out of the country. But she couldn't. She couldn't take her two children and live on her own in the US. How would she live with no money? Where would she live? That would never happen.

"I spit on these backward Islamic legacy laws," her father said. "If there's one thing the Shah and his parliament need to do, it is to reform this goddamned legal system. There is no reason custody of the children should revert to the father's family."

Vida stood up, spreading her fingers out in a fan against her chest bone. Her breath uneven. She didn't realize she was screaming until Maman grabbed her.

"Keep your voice down... Keep your voice down," Maman whispered loudly. "What do you think you're doing? The children are sleeping." Her arms were in the air as she stood close to Vida.

Holding Vida's shoulders, Homa gently pushed Vida down on the couch.

Vida sat back down, digging her teeth into her lower chapped lip until it started to bleed, a silent screech leaking out of her while she cried uncontrollably.

"*Madar joon*, don't do this to yourself. Breathe. You're going to faint," said Homa.

Vida's father paced the room. "Backward laws."

"Of course they are backward. That so-called prophet Mohamed was a self-absorbed politician, creating rules for his own self-interests," Maman chimed in. She was a strong-willed, quick-witted lady who came from a highly educated prominent Qajar dynasty family that shunned Islam for not keeping up with Iran's modernity.

"There must be a mistake?" said Homa.

"No... there's no mistake. It's the law," said Agha Joon.

"*Agha*, she's just asking," Maman defended Homa.

"*Ehh...*" He swatted at Maman for her interference. He put on his reading glasses and looked down at the document again. "I just didn't think they'd go about it like this."

Vida ran her hands through her hair. "This can't be happening. This just can't be happening."

"Yes, it's the law... but these days families discuss these sorts of things. We are a modern country. Families don't march into court and get a court order."

They must have done this while I was still in London,
Vida thought.

Her father sat back on the couch, lost in thought. He
interwove his fingers and twirled his thumbs.

"As angry as I am about this, we must resolve this within
the family," he whispered loudly enough for everyone
to hear him.

"Good luck with that," Maman said sarcastically. She turned
to Vida. "Go to court and challenge them," she said. "You
will beat this system. I know you can do it." Maman jabbed
her finger and tried to make strong eye contact with Vida,
who avoided her gaze.

"*Khanoom*, what are you talking about?" Agha Joon said in
an angry tone. "The families must resolve this. Look at her
face. She's lost so much weight she looks like a skeleton." He
pointed at Vida. "You expect her to fight these people in
court? In this country?"

"She can do it. She's strong," added Maman. "I know she
can do it."

Homa sat next to Maman with her hands together between
her legs. Her *roosari* had fallen off her head and lay limply
around her neck. "Maybe it's a formality," she offered. "They
don't mean it. They are so kind, a religious family. Can't we
speak with them openly?"

"How do they expect to communicate with Roya and Kasra who don't even speak Farsi?" Maman interjected. "They're doing it for the money," she added matter-of-factly. "It's obvious."

"There is no money," Vida reminded her, standing up, her hands in the air. She raised her voice like she was convincing them of the obvious facts. "He was only a few years into the medical practice, and he's been sick."

"You're going to need to be with his family until we get through the *hafteh*," said Homa.

"Yes, the *hafteh* is very important," said Maman trying to minimize the importance.

The traditional *hafteh*, seven days of mourning with the long-established seventh day of gathering, was meant to keep those who were grieving occupied, surrounded by loved ones and together, so they would not feel so deeply the loss and loneliness resulting from death.

"*Agha* wants you to move into the upstairs apartment," Homa blurted out looking over at Vida's father.

"Of course she's moving upstairs. Where else is she going to go?" Agha Joon emphasized.

Vida rocked back and forth. *This is not what I had planned for my life. Moving into an upstairs flat in my father's house?* Normally she wouldn't appreciate her father making decisions for her, but at this moment, she didn't want to decide anything. She needed others to decide for her.

They had a brief discussion about Vida's belongings left in America. Maman suggested they have it all shipped back to Tehran. Vida disagreed and said she wanted to move back to America.

"You're not moving back to the US by yourself," Maman commanded. At the time of her marriage, Maman had preached a rose would never grow out of a bunch of weeds, referring to Kamran's family. Maman's father was a general in the army, her brothers university professors. Back then, educated people didn't trust the religious ones.

"Why does it matter to *you*?" Vida blurted out.

Stretching out his arms as if splitting up a fight, Agha Joon interjected, "Let's not get into it right now. Everything will get shipped back."

Vida's mind drifted to Rosemary and Carlo's basement, where she had stored boxes of her belongings. "How much will it cost?"

"How much will what cost?" Agha Joon stood up, holding Vida's head in his hands and kissing her forehead.

"To ship everything back to Iran? The furniture, the books? I don't have any money," Vida said, burying her face in the tissue, sobbing.

"Stop worrying. Your father is here to help," Homa said. "And I'm sure Mahmoud *khan* and Doktor will too. That's what family is for."

Vida sat up. She stopped crying for an instant. *I'm going to get a job. Yes, that's what I'll do. I'll show them what it means to be a good mother. But who's going to hire me?* When she lived in New York, she had gotten a degree in library science.

She could feel another surge of emotion, and the tears were building up again. "And who's going to watch the kids?" she said out loud.

"I will… and Maman will help too. Right?" said Homa elbowing Maman.

"Of course I will," said Maman seemingly afraid to add to the discussion.

Homa put Vida's head on her shoulder. "We are here for you," she said.

* * * * *

It was now 9:30 p.m. Vida's heart was racing. She had to do something and rushed to the phone to call Hassan.

"They came for the kids!" she burst out. She could feel the adrenaline rushing through her body. "I need a lawyer right away."

"What do you mean? Please, please slow down."

Her speech was rushed. She could feel her heart pounding as she explained what had happened.

"Hold on a minute. What did you say?"

"Yes. They want me to hand over my children, like they're a pair of shoes."

"Under the law I suppose they can. But I'm shocked," he said, his voice softening. "I've met Doktor. He's a good man." Hassan had a calm tone.

"I need a good lawyer. Can you help?"

"Yes... but... I mean... do you really want to get an attorney involved?"

What is wrong with Hassan? Why is he taking Doktor's side?

She cut him off mid-sentence. "What else do you want me to do? It's not going to happen. I'm not going to..." Her voice was rising, and she felt a swelling in her throat.

"Breathe. Breathe. Take it easy," he said. "I'm sure whatever is going on can be resolved within the family."

Is Hassan in on this? Kamran planned all of this before he died. He told Hassan not to help me and to let Doktor raise the children.

"I don't think so. They're serious," she said. Her throat was closing now. "And I am too."

"Okay. Let me make a couple of phone calls. I'll call you back," he said.

When she hung up the phone, she had beads of sweat at her hairline. She took one long, deep, drawn-out breath. *Kamran wouldn't do this to me. He would have told me if he wanted Doktor to take custody of the children. He was open with me. Breathe. Breathe.*

At night Vida paced back and forth in the living room, alone, while the rest of the family slept. She would go into the kids' room and put her hand on their backs to make sure they were alive. Afterward she resumed pacing. *What if they take the children?* She imagined Roya wrapped in a blanket crying out to Vida as Doktor carried her to the car; Kasra dragging his legs, head down after him. And what about her life? It would be empty and meaningless without the children. She imagined herself on her knees, tugging at Doktor's pants and begging him to leave the children with him shooing her away like layered dust on the mantel.

Vida thought she heard sounds outside. When she looked out the window past the curtain nobody was there.

* * * * *

Dr. Vakeelee arrived at the house the next afternoon. The forty-year-old scholar looked Oxford-educated, as Hassan had described him. He carried a dark briefcase and wore a black suit, a white shirt, and a black bowtie. He carried a beige trench coat folded over his arm. A thin mustache outlined his upper lip.

Hassan had described the attorney as a prominent human rights and family lawyer.

Vida was impressed by his educational and family background.

Vida and her father sat across from him at the dining room table. Vida leaned in while her father sat back at a distance, twirling his thumbs and evaluating the lawyer's manner and appearance like he did when he was playing *takht-e nard*, backgammon.

The attorney removed his spectacles. "I'm so sorry to hear about your husband," he said, followed by a deep sigh and a thoughtful expression. He paused. "I understand from Hassan your mother is from the Maleki family?"

She sat up in her seat with a faint smile. "Yes, she is." *Does he know Maman?* Her eyes widened.

"Doctor Maleki?" he asked.

She leaned in, gently biting her lip. Dr. Maleki was Maman's brother, a professor. "Yes, he's my *da-ee*."

"*Azam Joon* is my *kha-leh*," he announced with a smile.

The lawyer's aunt was married to Vida's uncle. How had she not known this? They were from the same stock. She sighed and slowly smiled. Any family connection would bring an outsider one step closer to her. She knew then she could trust this man.

She skipped the details about Kamran's long illness and death, recounting the visit from her father-in-law and brother-in-law. She asked questions, and the lawyer answered in his scholarly tone while playing with his spectacles, folding and unfolding the handles, and twirling them at times.

"The Family Protection Laws created significant advancement for women's rights in Iran, but the legal system is ancient. It's based on Islamic laws, and they are not friendly toward women, as you know."

She listened patiently, struggling to stay polite. "Can they really take my children?" Vida asked, hoping the lawyer would know of an exception.

He put his fingertips together, forming a steeple. "The family courts distinguish between *hezanat*, custody, and *velayat*, legal guardianship. By law, the paternal grandfather is the *qayem* and has legal guardianship. In terms of custody, whether the children can live with you?" He paused twirling his glasses. "Well, the courts have the ultimate discretion in a case like this."

Her father sat back nodding in agreement, a small teacup resting in front of him.

Vida rubbed the back of her neck and put her head down. Softly she asked, "What are the chances the court will grant me custody?"

"Most progressive judges will grant custody to the mother," he said without hesitation.

She paused and closed her eyes for a moment.

"Are you okay?" her father asked in a low voice.

"I'm fine," she said, not making eye contact with him. Her head felt heavy and unstable.

"What does it mean for me not to have guardianship?" she asked.

"You cannot manage the children's money, you cannot take them out of the country without your father-in-law's permission, and if you get remarried... you will automatically lose all of your rights."

Vida unfolded her arms and legs and then crossed them all again. She wanted to run out of the house and go somewhere, anywhere, but she held back her emotions. It wasn't appropriate to lose her temper.

Making a fist, her father's nostrils flared. "Well, she's not getting remarried! *Mashalla*, we shouldn't talk about that... not at a time like this." He looked away.

The lawyer seemed embarrassed he had mentioned remarriage and started to defend his position. He tried to make eye contact with Vida.

She used a careful and controlled tone, not wanting to show her anger at the system. Although this man was a relative of sorts, he wasn't family. "Kamran has a sister. She is a widow with under-aged children. How are her children living with her?" She turned to her father. "Nasreen?"

"I know who you're talking about," he said. Agha Joon's eyebrows were bunched together.

"If the deceased husband has no male relatives, the courts will automatically grant custody to the mother. Still, the mother cannot be the legal guardian. In that situation the court will appoint a guardian, and that person manages the children's finances," he said.

Vida started to push back her cuticles with her nail digging into her thumb. She remembered Nasreen telling her about a man who would come to the house the first Wednesday of the month with a suitcase full of cash and a notebook where he would record how the funds would be spent.

Her father took a breath and sat back in his chair, his fingers interlaced, twirling his thumbs first in one direction and then another.

The lawyer nervously opened his briefcase, as if searching for something. After several seconds, nodding, he shut the bag and folded over its leather flap, as if he had forgotten what he was looking for. He straightened his bowtie.

"Vida *khanoom*, don't you think it makes sense to resolve this issue within the family?" the lawyer spoke forcefully.

"*Afareen bareekala*… Bravo." Her father slammed both hands flat on the table. "I told her the same thing."

Vida stood up, her fist on the table. "How could you suggest a compromise? They already have court papers. If they wanted to resolve this in a friendly way, they would have come to me first," she said.

Vida's father rolled his eyes and pushed back from the table.

"Can we try? I can talk to them," the lawyer said, his eyes moving nervously back and forth between father and daughter.

"They said they were going to take the kids in a few days," she said, sitting back down. "We haven't even had the *hafteh*." Now her voice was cracking.

"Let me call your father-in-law and set up a meeting. I'll arrange it for after the *hafteh*, and I'll tell them to hold off doing anything for now."

Vida hesitated, glancing at her father for guidance.

Her father nodded as if to say, *It's the reasonable thing to do.*

* * * * *

The lawyer made a phone call and arranged a family meeting for the day after the *hafteh*.

CHAPTER 6

January 1972, Tehran

———

When Vida arrived at Nasreen's house for the seventh day of mourning, she removed her snow boots and left them at the front door with the other boots, some with caked-on mud from the blizzard the day before. She slipped on short black pumps she had brought in the London shopping bag to wear inside the house. She took off her black sheer scarf and assumed her place in the living room, sitting between Kamran's sisters near her mother-in-law.

During the last seven days Vida felt more and more isolated, soaking in the ambiguity of her legal issues and the possibility of losing her children. Her jaw was sore from clenching her teeth at night, and Band-Aids covered her scabbed cuticles.

Kamran's parents, siblings, in-laws, aunts, uncles, cousins, cousins of cousins, and all those related to those people, as well as Vida's relatives, poured into the house. The eight-bedroom mansion live-in servants—including the maid and her children, the cook, and the driver—had organized the large gathering. Chairs were lined up against the walls of the living room so the guests, many of whom Vida did not know, could see each other. It was considered rude to turn your back to someone in any setting. So at all social gatherings, even those related to a death, chairs were arranged in a circular pattern. An oversized framed picture of Kamran rested on the white mantel with lit candles on each side. The frame was a duplicate of the one mounted above the grave in the mausoleum.

The ladies' attire, including nylons, was black from head to toe. The older ones wore headscarves. Since the men sat elsewhere in the house, none of the religious women were required by custom to wear a *chador* or to cover their hair. However, some did because that was their habit, and they were more comfortable with the headdress.

In front of every third chair stood a small ornate table of the Louis XIV genre. Each table held a small box of tissues, tiny crystal bowls, each separately filled with dates, raisins, or sugar cubes for the tea that would be served, and a small white plate spread with *halva*, the ones Homa had made the day before.

Vida hated *halva*. She didn't mind the taste of the sugar, oil, and flour paste so much, but the smell of rosewater made her stomach turn. As a child, she remembered walking through the Tajrish bazaar, a shopping center in the northernmost part of Tehran, on the weekends when Maman would pay her a visit. In the middle of Tajrish was an *Imamzadeh*, a shrine, and to get from one end of Tajrish to the other they had no choice but to walk through the structure. They usually strolled past at least one imam, usually three or four. Vida would hold her tiny nose because of the imam's strong body odor infused with the smell of rosewater. Maman had explained these religious men rarely showered and used rosewater to cover-up their stench. So Vida could not help relating rosewater to the smelly, sweaty bodies of the clergymen.

Besides the occasional whisper when one woman would turn to another sitting next to her to say a few words, perhaps to comment on the brand of another lady's purse, scarf, or blouse, to speculate as to where that other woman may have purchased the item, or to share words of pity for Vida and her children, the room was quiet. The women sat in silence, their heads bowed. Vida detested the Iranian women's gossip and preferred the silence.

Some cried, but it wasn't as dramatic as it had been at the burial. Vida cried, too, but she dabbed a tissue at the corners of her eyes and held back her tears.

Nasreen made her way toward Vida and sat in the empty chair next to her. Clenching her teeth while carefully eyeing the room, she whispered in Vida's ear, "You're not crying loudly enough. Everyone is looking at you." She patted Vida on the back, lightly rested Vida's head on her shoulder with a sad look, and surveyed the room before walking away.

Vida glanced at her without any expression, ashamed of being a part of this family, ashamed of being Iranian. This culture was all a show. She had no energy left to respond to her sister-in-law. She looked down again, the sound of Nasreen's voice echoing in the empty shell of her head, and her tears dried up like the bottom of a hollow well.

A couple of minutes later, Vida's aunt took a seat in the same empty chair. She placed her fancy handbag—a black scarf tied to the handle in a bow—on the floor. She dragged her chair closer to Vida. Holding a cup of tea, the aunt leaned over and whispered, "I heard about your meeting with Dr. Vakeelee. Such a good man and well-connected. I'm telling you he will fight your custody battle to the end, and he will win. I'm sure of it."

Vida gave her a half-smile. "It's the law. How would he ever be able to change the law?" Her hands fell limply in her lap, palms facing up and her chin lowered to her chest. *Really? Would the lawyer be able to save her children?*

The older lady then stroked Vida's face. "Look at you... so beautiful and young, and those eyes... they are something else. Don't let this custody issue get to you. Everything will work out. I just hope you continue to live your life." Then she sat back and scanned the room while sipping her tea, half-smiling, and nodding at the ladies with whom she made eye contact.

Vida knew then news about her custody issue had spread within the family. How could it not? This had not happened in her family before. She didn't like being the subject of gossip. Still, she breathed more easily knowing her own family was on her side and prepared for the battle that needed to be fought.

In the family room Vida imagined the men had a similar set-up. The doors that divided the living room where the women sat and the family room were shut so the two groups, although mostly family members, would not interact. It was custom within religious families.

This arrangement was a good thing for Vida, especially because she didn't want to face Doktor or witness his nasty smirks. The thought of him and what he was putting her through made her clench her teeth. The last thing she wanted to see was his grimace or his false tears. She couldn't imagine a brother who cared so little about his own niece and nephew as to go to court to forcefully rip them apart from their mother. Ever since Doktor had delivered the court papers, the tiny hair on her arms stood up when she thought of losing Kasra and Roya. A few times a day she imagined the kids curled up on an old mattress crying in a locked room in the basement at Doktor's house.

At lunchtime, various rice dishes were served buffet style in the dining room. The women served themselves first before the men were called in, as if it were a formal dinner party. Vida stood by the dining room table to let the guests go first. She had no appetite but thought it would be noticeable if she didn't take a plate. She was under a microscope, watched by the entire family. She scooped white rice and yogurt and placed a few pieces of chicken kebab on the side of the dish. Normally she would have sprinkled the maroon-colored sumac, *somagh*, on her rice, but she couldn't be bothered to walk over to the side buffet where the condiments were neatly arranged.

When Vida walked out of the dining room, she glanced up and saw Doktor at the entry. Her heart beat fast, like a metronome out of control. He was wearing a black suit and a black tie, his eyes red and puffy.

"Vida *khanoom*..." he said, as if he was going to strike up a conversation with her.

Vida wanted to dump the dish of rice and yogurt on top of his head and then throw the plate to the ground, the china shattering into tiny pieces. She didn't do that. She stopped and looked the other way, only for a second, to take hold of herself and her emotions. Finally, she turned around. Her body tense, she searched his hazel eyes and noted his hair. Even though Doktor was older, he had much more hair than Kamran. She wished Doktor had gone through chemotherapy for brain cancer, losing all his hair and then his life. The steam from the rice on her plate generated heat that burned her fingertips, so she moved it to her other hand and kept on walking.

In the living room she carefully set the plate on her chair. She picked up her purse, walked past the crowds in the hallway, and slipped outside.

She stood on the front porch, her arms crossed, trying to keep warm. She pulled out a Winston and lit it with the red plastic lighter she had bought at Heathrow on her way back to Tehran. She inhaled the smoke, at first taking short puffs and then long, drawn-out ones. She looked around, not wanting anyone to see her. The white smoke drifted up into the air, and her thoughts began to float with it.

Outside in the cold, she followed the vapor into the air, wondering what the meeting would be like the next day in this same house and whether Doktor would come to his senses and let her keep her children. It would be a miracle. She thought about what she could give up in exchange for her children, as if she were bargaining for a gold bangle bracelet at one of the jewelry shops in the Tajrish bazaar.

The complex breaths from the smoke had a soothing effect. She scanned over the porch and noticed all the cars piled in and around the large front yard. She gazed up and scanned the high trees, noting the missing leaves, and then she looked down and her eyes fell on a navy-blue Mercedes. It reminded her of Kamran's car, and she became curious. She walked around the vehicle over to the driver's side and rubbed her hand along the door, noticing the scratch from the day Kamran dropped off the movie camera at Doktor's house.

Doktor had asked to borrow the camera, the one Kamran treasured so much. On the day her husband dropped it off at his house, when Doktor said he would keep the camera *amn*, safe, Kamran had accidentally scratched the door with his key. This was, in fact, her husband's car. *How did the car get here? Did Doktor have keys? Why would he take it without asking her?* She took one last puff from the cigarette, tossed the butt to the ground, and stepped on it hard to make sure it went out.

When she got back inside the house, she returned to her chair. Still confused about the car, she could hear the clanking sounds of the other women's forks against their plates, scraping the last grains of rice. *How could these women eat?*

Glancing across the room, she saw Maman talking to a pregnant woman.

"I had a dream last night. Imam Reza came down from heaven and spoke to me," said the woman, referring to one of the Islamic prophets.

In a sarcastic tone, Maman put her hand to her mouth and said, "Really, the imam himself?"

Naively, not realizing Maman was mocking her, the woman said, "Yes, the imam came to me in my sleep."

"*Ajab*, interesting," said Maman, placing a fist to her mouth. Vida knew she was mocking the lady.

Does she need to ridicule people? Why can't she just let it go? Vida thought.

"The prophet told me to name my son Reza," she said, pointing to her belly.

"Hmmm, *ajab*," repeated Maman.

The lady didn't know Maman's sarcastic humor and disbelief for Islamic rituals, but Vida did and was embarrassed to witness the conversation. She hoped nobody else was listening. She made eye contact with her mother, her eyes shrinking in anger. She remembered how embarrassed she got as a little girl when Maman mocked the religion to strangers at the store.

* * * * *

The day after the *hafteh*, Vida, her father, the lawyer, Doktor, and Mahmoud met at Nasreen's house in the same dining room where lunch had been served the day before. The white china was cleaned and stacked on the buffet next to rows of crystal drinking glasses, and the dining room table was spotless.

On one side of the table Vida sat with her father and lawyer, the men leaning forward on their elbows. Her father twirled his thumbs back and forth. Her father-in-law sat across from them, methodically moving the beads of a carnelian *tasbeeh*. He seemed to be saying something underneath his breath, maybe a prayer. Doktor's chair was set back from the table, his legs crossed the way pompous men do at times. He sat back, observing the group as they took their seats across the dining room table, as if he was Imam Reza and the group was paying homage to him. Vida shifted in her seat, folding and unfolding her legs, anxious for the meeting to start.

Nasreen shuffled back and forth between the dining room and the living room with a variety of food. The group sat watching her move in and out of the room. Vida felt restless and wanted to help, but she worried if she left the room she might miss something important. She felt badly that Nasreen was troubling on her account. Vida knew why the servants were not helping. The subject to be discussed was too sensitive. Nasreen wouldn't want the servants to gossip about the family issues, but they probably still did.

"I thought you were going to sit in the living room I set everything up earlier," she complained, circling the room and offering tea.

Vida felt a cloud of tension in the room, like nobody wanted to start the discussion.

"*Zahmat nakesheed…* please don't bother, we're only here for a few minutes," the lawyer said, telling Nasreen not to go out of her way.

Vida thought it was his way of suggesting she leave.

Nasreen slipped out of the room through the swinging door to the kitchen.

"*Khob… Agahaye* Doktor… why don't you start?" the lawyer offered, using overly polite words, calling him "Mr. Doctor."

"Start with what?" Doktor asked arrogantly, still leaning back in his chair and making eye contact only with the attorney.

"What is the issue here with the children?"

"We need to know when the children will be delivered to my father's house."

"Delivered?" Vida leaped out of her chair outraged. Her arm struck the small cup of tea in front of her, splashing the warm liquid onto the dining room table. She started to wipe the table with napkins.

Vida's father and the lawyer rose to help. Even her father-in-law got up from his side of the table, reaching over to offer his napkin. Doktor ignored the mess and continued to sit back, observing others cleaning the spill.

"Yes, we want to know when the children will be handed over to my father. Don't worry. We will feed them," Doktor said, smirking sarcastically.

Vida wanted to throw all the wet napkins into Doktor's face, but she held back. She began to speak as she wiped the table, but her lawyer grabbed her arm and pulled her down, letting her know it was not her turn to talk.

The lawyer focused on Doktor. "Now... don't you think it's in the best interest of the children to live with their mother?" he asked, nodding back and forth.

"No. I don't think so," Doktor said with a dismissive glance.

Vida's father-in-law continued moving the *aghigh*, dark brown beads, even faster now. His gaze fell to the table, as if he didn't agree with Doktor but also as if he had no choice.

"What is your *daleel*?" her lawyer calmly asked for Doktor's reasoning.

"She's too young, and we don't agree with her upbringing... you know, having lived abroad by herself, boarding school, and all that. And look at her. She is so... well... I don't even want to put into words what can happen."

When Vida was in boarding school, she had attended some parties with a Lebanese boy. In the 1950s, in a typical Iranian family, it was wrong for a single woman to spend time with a man other than a close male relative. It was even wrong to pass time with a male cousin unless marriage was planned. But Vida wasn't raised in a traditional family. It's true she hadn't advertised to anyone she had a spring fling with the Lebanese boy. It would have been public humiliation for her family. She had told a few of her close girlfriends about her mini boyfriend, though. Had they blabbed her secret? But to whom?

"What are you suggesting? Too young for what?" Vida erupted, standing at the table. Her heart raced, and she was out of breath. "Was I too young three years ago, when I was pregnant and flew to London with your three-year-old nephew, to take care of your brother for cancer treatment? And was I too young to take care of him and Roya and Kasra by myself in America after that? And what gives you the right to judge my upbringing?" she yelled, pounding her hand on the table and shaking, heat flushing through her body.

Nasreen walked back into the room.

"*Khanoom*, go. Everything is fine." Doktor shooed Nasreen out of the room.

She dropped her head and marched out.

"Mrs. Shamsa… please… sit down," whispered the lawyer, pursing his lips, clearly disappointed with her behavior.

She sat, crossing her arms and facing the sidewall.

"She is too young, and we do not want my brother's children to be raised by strangers," Doktor said.

"Strangers?" Vida said clearing her throat.

"What strangers?" Vida's father, interjected.

"When she remarries," added Doktor.

"Who said anything about remarriage? My daughter just lost her husband. Why would you even think that? What is the obsession with marriage?" said Agha Joon, his nostrils flared.

"She's young… and, well, we know this is what she's planning…"

Vida couldn't imagine marrying another man, and she tasted something sour in her throat like she was going to throw up as she heard this conversation around her.

"And so, what if she does?" her father interrupted Doktor mid-sentence. "It's none of your goddamned business."

Doktor stood up and pulled his chair closer to the table. "What are you talking about? That man… that man she will marry…" He leaned in with his elbows, pushing down on the table. "That man will beat those children. We are not going to put up with it. Legally we have a responsibility to ensure their well-being."

"*Aghaye* Doktor, your reasoning does not make sense," Vakeelee said, removing his spectacles. "Your sister-in-law just lost her husband." He spoke slowly and methodically. "It's been a little over a week. She is still in mourning. Why would you say such a thing? It's not appropriate." He got up, gesturing for Doktor to sit back down in his seat.

Doktor held out his arm. "Because... Well, she cannot possibly look after these children properly on her own. If she raises them alone... well, her son will turn out to be a drunk, and that little girl... well, she'll grow up to be a... a... a whore." He smashed his fist on the table, staring at Vida.

She felt a pounding in her ears like she might explode. She was about to rise above the dining room table like a dragon when her father grabbed her hand.

Doktor had crossed the line, and Vida knew it. Everybody in the room knew it.

"Since we cannot have a civilized discussion, we will not resolve anything here today," said Vakeelee, placing his glasses back on his face.

"There is nothing to resolve," Doktor replied, sitting back in his chair, looking down sheepishly as if he knew he had gone too far. "We have a court order. The children are ours. She can move into my father's house," he mumbled, his tone scornful.

"Let's go. This meeting is over," Vakeelee said, standing up and pushing his chair in close to the table. "I can see this has been a waste of time."

Agha Joon, Vakeelee, and Vida marched out of the room toward the front entrance of the house.

Nasreen ran after them as they got into the car while she pulled on the ends of her *roosari*, tightening them so the scarf wouldn't slip off the back of her head. "Where are you going? Vida *joon*, please don't go. We are family. We can work this out," she pleaded, still adjusting her headdress. "Please don't be upset. We should talk about this."

Vida wanted to say, "*What family?*" but she didn't. She looked at her sister-in-law with eyes that appeared cold and then shut the car door. She rested her chin on her hand, looking out the window, past Nasreen. As they drove off, she saw the navy-blue Mercedes parked on the gravel. She wanted to say something, but the words wouldn't come out of her mouth.

"I'll go to the family court tomorrow with a request for temporary custody," her lawyer said, driving the car.

Her father was sitting in the front seat. "How are you going to do that?"

Vida was only half-listening from the back. In a daze, she softly said, "Doktor stole Kamran's car." She didn't say it loudly enough, and they didn't hear her in the front. Leaning her head into the backseat, she didn't see the point of saying anything at all.

"... the children do not speak Farsi and will not be able to communicate with these people. I will argue it will be disruptive and shocking. The children are not familiar with the culture. We may not be in England, France, or Germany, but this *is* Iran after all... I can promise you... I can assure you Iranian judges are forward-thinking," said Vakeelee, smacking the palm of his hand against the steering wheel.

Vida could tell her lawyer was angry, but she felt hopeless.

* * * * *

The next morning at 10:00 a.m., the phone rang. Vida's muscles twitched as she reached for the black receiver.

"I just returned from the court," the lawyer announced out of breath. It was customary for an attorney to attend hearings without their client.

"And?" Vida asked.

"You got temporary custody... I told you. Progressive judges."

Her eyes widened. She fell back in her chair with a wide grin. "For how long?" she asked.

"One year."

"That's it?" Vida asked, feeling let down again.

"Give me time. I'm going to make this work for you," Vakeelee said.

The line went silent. Vida ran her finger through a layer of dust on the table, and her shoulders drooped. She had not expected anything otherwise, given the ancient laws. She slouched in the chair, lowering her head. Her heart felt like it was shrinking.

"Look. I'm going to work on this for you, but you must be patient. It's going to take time. This is a marathon. Do you understand? A marathon," he said.

"I understand," she said with a heavy sigh. She twirled her finger in a ball of dust.

"You won't be able to leave the country," he said.

"Okay," she whispered. *Where would I go?* she wondered.

It was the end of January, and the next hearing was set for December, a lifetime away.

* * * * *

For the *cheleh*, the fortieth day after the burial, begrudgingly she went to the burial site with the family, a gathering like the *hafteh*. She didn't want to go but had to keep up appearances. So, once again, after visiting the mausoleum, the family congregated at Nasreen's house.

This time, fewer people came, and more conversations occurred. Vida surveyed the family members, and she could tell time was healing their wounds, but hers were still raw. She even saw her mother-in-law, whose sadness had consumed her up to now, smile a few times when speaking to relatives. Vida's own sadness floated like a fallen leaf making its way down a stream, drifting, and lost somewhere.

CHAPTER 7

April 1972, Tehran

─────

To support herself and her children, Vida started looking for a job. By April, the formalities surrounding Kamran's death were over, and she wanted to organize her life, generate income, and reclaim the independence she had lost. Normally, the Iranian New Year, *Norouz*, the first day of spring, would be a time of celebration. But with a recent death in the family, it was passed over. By practice, nothing was to be celebrated for an entire year.

She began by inquiring with a former acquaintance about possible job openings. "We met at an AFME party here in Tehran five years ago," said Vida when she introduced herself to Mrs. White.

Silence.

"The American Friends of the Middle East?" Vida reminded her.

Still, an awkward silence lingered.

And then with a soft tone Mrs. White said, "Yes. Yes, of course."

Mrs. White was the head librarian at the American Embassy Abraham Lincoln Library, prominent among foreign libraries. The library was visited by American and European students living in Iran as well as locals who were planning on traveling abroad to pursue academic degrees. Vida met her several years back when she was in Tehran on vacation with Kamran.

They set up the interview for 9:30 a.m. the next day.

The widow was still in mourning, and custom dictated she would be for a year. For the interview she wore black pants, a black turtleneck, and a beige raincoat, to break-up the darkness. The week before, her hairdresser cut her hair short like Audrey Hepburn's. The strands lay mostly flat on her head, but for the interview she spoofed them up a bit with rollers to give her hair the life that had drained out of every aspect of her life when her husband passed away.

She wore light makeup for the first time since she had left for London for the last surgery. She had become used to wearing a neutral-colored lipstick since Kamran's death, more as a moisturizer to keep her lips from chapping in the cold biting Tehran winter. For the interview, she used her light mauve one, which was enough to put color on her face but not enough to make it look as though she had stopped mourning.

At the beginning of their discussion, during small talk, they discovered Mrs. White's twins had graduated from the Tehran American School where Kasra was enrolled. Vida was not shy to express her limitations in doing the job, the need, for example, to leave at a certain time to pick up the kids from school.

Mrs. White explained the American Embassy's preference was to hire an Iranian for the job. Finally, Vida pulled out her résumé, which she had quickly typed and retyped the night before to avoid typos, unsure it was in a modern format. When she told Mrs. White why she returned to Iran and about the death of her husband, the head librarian shared she had lost her husband in a car accident when her twins were two years old.

The conversation led to an awkward silence between the two women. Vida noted a small American flag resting on the corner of the desk. She ran her finger along the stripes. A momentary distraction. The discussion was going in the wrong direction. She didn't want to talk about her late husband. Not now. *You don't even know this woman. Don't get emotional. Stay on the topic about the job.*

Finally, the librarian cleared her throat. "You would manage the operations of the library, help me hire, and manage a staff."

Vida felt relieved the conversation was turning back to the position. The library had four thousand members, mostly students, and with all the Americans and other foreign students coming to study in Iran, the embassy expected the membership to grow. Mrs. White talked about plans to open branches in Mashhad, Isfahan, and Shiraz, and they would consider moving the Tehran location. Already this office was too far south on South Saba Street near the American

Embassy, about a half-hour drive from where Vida's parents lived in the northern part of Tehran.

Mrs. White asked, "Does any of this sound interesting to you?"

Vida didn't want to look uninterested, but she was deep in thought, wondering whether she could handle the job, managing people, traveling, and the possibility of the library being moved further away from where she lived.

Mrs. White clarified, "The position does not require travel. Occasionally, *I* travel for seminars or conferences, but you don't need to." She got up, walked over to Vida's side of the desk, and placed her hand on her shoulder. "Any other questions?"

Has the librarian already made up her mind? "No," Vida replied.

"Okay. Let me review your résumé. I'll give you a call tomorrow morning. Does ten o'clock work?" Mrs. White walked toward the door.

"Yes, sure." Vida reached for the briefcase.

Mrs. White put out her hand and gave Vida a firm handshake, the way only a working American woman would, smiling as she made eye contact. "I'm so glad you called," she said.

At the library entrance, Vida fumbled to put on her raincoat. She had been back in Iran for only a few months and already back to thinking like an Iranian. *Maybe Mrs. White was taroffing? Maybe she didn't have a job opening?* During the drive home, Vida mentally canvassed her network of family and friends, wondering who else she might call to inquire about jobs. It wouldn't do to get her hopes up with this one. By the time she got home, she had convinced herself she was not getting the job.

* * * * *

Late that night she sat with Homa in the upstairs flat.

"I don't know if I got the job."

"You have to hope," Homa said.

Vida whispered. "I lost all of it the day Kamran died."

Quiet hovered over the room, like a thick cloud.

Homa was sitting on the floor. She got up and started to head downstairs. "Stay right here," she said. She came back holding a small cardboard box. The lid was decorated with flowers, and inside was a gold chain with a pendant. "Take it. It's for you," said her stepmother.

Vida lifted the chain from the box and held it up. It was a long, gold necklace that, when worn, would hang to the middle of her chest. At the end of the chain was a light brown, oval-shaped, flat stone. The *aghigh*, or carnelian stone, had gold trim around it. One side of the stone was smooth, and the other bore words engraved in Arabic.

Vida was familiar with this gemstone but didn't like its color. It wasn't cheerful. She associated the stone with Islam because she had seen religious people wearing it as a ring. Still, she adored the necklace because it was a gift from Homa.

"It has a prayer engraved on it. I bought the stone at the Tajrish bazaar a few days ago, and I had them make you the necklace." Homa ran her finger along the chain and the gold encasing on the outside of the stone. "It's all eighteen-karat gold. It will bring good luck," she said.

"It's beautiful," Vida said, rubbing her finger against the flat side of the stone, smooth and cold. "What does it say?"

Homa pronounced a few Arabic words Vida did not understand.

"But I'm not religious," Vida protested, replacing the necklace in the box.

Again, her stepmother lifted the necklace from the box.

"It's not about religion. It's about God. It doesn't matter what it says. Just wear it. God will be with you all the time, looking after you." While placing it around Vida's neck, she said, "*Aghigh* always brings good luck."

Vida held the chain. All the gold jewelry in Iran was either eighteen-karat or twenty-two-karat gold. Maman had told her, "If it's not at least eighteen-karat, it's not gold." She thought it was generous of her stepmother.

She held Homa. "Thank you. I'll wear it," she said.

"Every day?" added Homa with a big smile.

"Every day."

* * * * *

The next morning at ten o'clock, on the dot, Mrs. White called. It was so American of her to call on time.

"You know the library is affiliated with the American Embassy?" asked Mrs. White. "So, you'll be paid by the United States government. You will need to fill out paperwork. Security clearance. Once we hear back from the embassy that you have been cleared, you'll be able to start."

Vida swallowed hard, her fingers fanned against her chest. "You mean I got the job?"

"Yes. I'm looking forward to working with you."

"Unbelievable. Really great," said Vida. She put her hand to her mouth. "I can't believe it." She leaned back in her chair and sighed. It was the first time in a long time she felt exhilarated. She looked toward the kitchen, noting the bright sunshine glaring through the window above the sink.

"Homa *joon*, Homa," she called out as she ran down the stairs. "It worked. The *aghigh* worked…"

Two weeks later she started the new job.

* * * * *

The first week was busy, and she kept a tight schedule, dropping off Kasra at the TAS, Tehran American School, in the morning and then Roya at nursery school. A relative had opened the preschool, and it was a good place for Roya. Vida would pick up both children in the afternoon. The days Kasra had baseball practice, she had to pick him up later, and that threw off the schedule. It was hectic. It helped that Vida was living upstairs from her father and stepmother.

TAS had buses, but it was a big school, and Vida worried about putting her son on a bus unchaperoned. She had nightmares about Doktor taking the children and locking them up at her father-in-law's house in the *zeer zameen*, the basement. So she took Kasra to and from school herself.

During the first week on the job, she brought her lunch in a brown bag and ate at her desk. She took a late lunch, one day, to go to the *Bank-e Markazi*, the Central Bank, to open her own bank account. Her new boss had asked that she open an account there so the embassy could automatically deposit her salary. Vida was thrilled to be getting her own paycheck.

The second week, right before noon one day, Mrs. White walked over to Vida's desk.

"Lunch at the Jewish deli next door?"

Vida had already brought her own sandwich to work and preferred to eat at her desk so she could leave on time, but she wanted to be polite and accepted the offer.

"How are you liking your new job?" Mrs. White asked, biting into a mortadella sandwich.

"I like it," Vida said. She looked at her sandwich and squeezed the baguette. The crust was soft, like the bread she bought at a small bakery near her house in Westchester. *Why are we here?* she thought.

Mrs. White stared at Vida, and it made her self-conscious. She could tell her boss wanted to say something. *She better say it soon. I have so much to do, and I don't want to be late leaving the office.*

Then without any warning, the librarian uttered, "If you don't mind, I want to ask you a personal question."

Vida swallowed hard and looked up. "Sure." She heard herself crunching into a small bumpy cornichon.

"The salary you receive can't possibly be enough for a family of three. How do you support yourself?"

The question surprised Vida. She took her time chewing and then swallowing the pickle. How was she going to answer that? She was raised not to talk about money issues, another Iranian quality, and she didn't want to get into her personal situation. The question felt more than a little intrusive, and she didn't know how to answer it at first.

"I'm living at my father's house," she said. Vida took a sip of her drink, staring at the ice cubes in the glass. *Why is she asking me this? Maybe a raise... already? That would be nice.*

"Did you know you can collect social security benefits from the United States for yourself and your children?" Mrs. White asked.

This was news, and Vida wondered why Mrs. White would mention this. "No," Vida said, looking up.

"If your husband worked in America, by law you are entitled to collect social security benefits."

"He didn't work very long, just a few years."

"It doesn't matter. You *are* entitled to benefits," she insisted.

Vida stared at Mrs. White, her eyes wide, barely blinking. She was interested in what her boss had to say, but she didn't believe it could be possible. She was living in Iran and not entitled to any benefits in her own country. *How could I possibly get any US government benefits?* she thought.

Even if she and the children were entitled to get funds, she wasn't allowed to control any of the children's money because she wasn't their legal guardian. Her father-in-law was the legal guardian. Her lawyer had made that clear. Vakeelee had secured temporary custody, which meant Vida and the kids could live together, but she was not allowed to control their finances. If she or her children received any inheritance, or any funds whatsoever, Mahmoud, and therefore Doktor, would dictate how the money would be spent. It was the law.

She didn't want to get into the details of her legal situation with her new boss.

"Did your late husband have a life insurance policy?" the boss continued with her line of questioning.

Vida felt the sandwich stick in her throat, and she coughed. *What is she trying to do?* Vida looked around, hoping nobody could hear this conversation.

When she had first married Kamran and they were living in New York, he purchased a life insurance policy, but Vida didn't know about the details. When Kamran died, she assumed the children would have been the beneficiaries. However, she had decided not to inquire about the policy until the guardianship issue was resolved. She hadn't told anybody about the insurance policy, not even her own father, Maman, or Homa.

"Yes, he did…" Vida replied finally. "But the Islamic laws in Iran have created so many complications. I would need to speak to my husband's family if my children were to receive any money. It's different here than in America." Vida half-smiled. She would have to consult with her lawyer, but she didn't want to tell Mrs. White that attorneys were involved. It was too much personal information for her boss.

"Oh, that's interesting," said Mrs. White deep in thought.

"And I'm assuming the policy would be for the kids?" Vida said in an uncertain tone.

Mrs. White shuffled in her chair again and pulled it in even closer. "I don't think so. That's not how it works in America. It is standard for the spouse to be the beneficiary."

Silence again. Until then Vida hadn't contemplated the insurance proceeds would benefit her. In Iran, assets in a marriage were either in the name of the husband or the children. The wife was entitled to nothing except what she received from her own father as dowry. This type of insurance policy was not common.

Vida was deep in thought. She touched her neck and leaned her head to the side, touching the new carnelian necklace Homa had given her. She had mistakenly worn the gift on the outside of her sweater that day. Until today, she had been wearing it on the inside of her clothing as a reminder of her family support and because she was embarrassed to wear anything associated with religion.

Mrs. White reached over the table. "Can I touch it?"

Vida looked down at the necklace. "Sure."

"It's beautiful. *Ageeg,*" she said with a thick American accent about the carnelian stone.

Vida looked surprised Mrs. White knew anything about the stone.

"It's a common stone in Iran. It brings good luck. Right?" she said.

Vida looked down at the pendant. "Yes, that's what I was told." *This woman has lived in Iran for a long time.*

Mrs. White sat back in her chair with a half-smile. "By the way, I hope you know I'm just trying to help you. I'm not trying to be nosy."

"This information is helpful." A part of Vida thought Mrs. White was being intrusive, asking about her financial situation, but she appreciated the concern.

"I felt paralyzed when my husband passed away," said Mrs. White. "Thankfully, a relative was a social worker and educated me about the system. It would be a shame for you not to get these funds, especially the insurance policy. I would guess, based on your husband's age when he died, it would pay you a lot more than the social security benefits. But you must work on it now. Once the statute of limitations passes, you won't be able to get any of these funds. You might want to start thinking about all this right away."

"A statue of what?" Vida asked. She imagined the Statue of Liberty.

"Legally if you don't ask about the money within a certain amount of time, you won't be able to get the funds from the policy… Normally you have to inquire within a year."

"I have the written policy at home, but… I haven't looked at it." Vida wiped her mouth with the tissue in her lap. She was excited about her newfound knowledge.

"Why don't you bring it to the office tomorrow, and we can look through it together? And then you can decide if you want to call your lawyer. Although, if he's Iranian, he probably won't know anything about US insurance policies and how they work." Mrs. White wiped her mouth and tossed her napkin on the table.

Vida had tried hard to avoid mentioning the attorney, but clearly her boss had outsmarted her. It was as if she knew what Vida was thinking all along.

* * * * *

Rosemary had shipped back to Tehran most of the furniture and the seventeen boxes Vida and Kamran had stored in her basement before they left New York. At night, Vida plowed through the boxes. She found the insurance policy quickly. She had a passing thought her boss had ill intentions, but then she reminded herself to stop thinking like a suspicious Iranian.

"What are you looking for?" Homa asked, standing in the entrance to the empty guest room, watching Vida rummage through paper.

"Nothing important… just an old photo." Vida felt guilty she hadn't told the truth, but she didn't want to get into the details of the policy. Not now. No point in saying anything until she knew what she was entitled to.

* * * * *

The next day Vida brought the paperwork to the office. Mrs. White pulled up a chair next to her, and the two women reviewed the document together, Mrs. White pointing at the fine print on the last page of the policy. "See. You *are* the beneficiary," she said lightly brushing Vida's back.

Vida was in disbelief. Then she had a passing thought about moving into a brand-new home. She felt powerful. She would fight the custody issue and live in her own house with the children. She'd show her in-laws she could raise her children on her own. She didn't need anybody. But then she had an empty feeling in the pit of her stomach, a sense of shame. Her husband had died. She didn't want any money. She simply wanted him back.

Vida gathered all the necessary documentation and prepared letters. She felt a twitching in her muscles and decided not to tell her parents or her lawyer, least of all her in-laws. *Anyway*, she thought, *there's no way I'm going to get these funds. I'm in Iran. The insurance company is in America. Kamran died in England. What are the chances it could all come together?*

Still, any unexpected funds would make an enormous difference in her life. *How wonderful it would be to buy a home for the kids to have their own rooms,* she thought. She would place Kamran's antique desk and bookshelf in Kasra's room. She would throw birthday parties for the two of them.

At the end of that day before leaving the library, Vida walked by Mrs. White's office to thank her.

"One step at a time. Let's wait and see what happens." Mrs. White twirled her pearl necklace around her fingers. "Come in here for a minute." She motioned for Vida to take a seat across from her desk.

Vida's sense of doubt was probably apparent to her boss. The librarian took Vida's hand and held it. "When my husband died, I felt badly about calling the insurance company. I didn't want to benefit financially from his death. I avoided it for weeks and was ready to walk away from all of it. But after I thought about it, I realized he wouldn't have wanted that. He wanted me to be taken care of if he died. That's why he bought the policy. Does that make sense?"

Vida remembered her fight with Kamran when he demanded their family move back to Iran after his last checkup. She realized he had been protecting her. He brought the family back to Iran because he knew he was sick. He knew he might die. Somewhere in the back of her consciousness she must have known that too. He had wanted them to be safe with family in a familiar environment.

When Vida walked out of the library, she was conflicted about keeping all this information a secret, hidden from her father and Homa. *But why?* she thought. *It's my money. I don't have to tell anybody.*

* * * * *

Two weeks later, she received a letter from the Social Security Administration. Vida's heart pounded when she ripped open the envelope. It contained three checks, each about $100, providing for benefits going back four months to the date of death.

"Look what came in today," Vida said, showing Mrs. White the letters.

Her boss had a big grin on her face. She leaned her head to the side and put her hand on her hip, as she often did, as if to say, "I told you so."

It was a small amount and would continue to be going forward, but it was something. *Every little bit helps*, Vida thought. Two of the checks were in the children's names. She thought about calling her lawyer but instead decided to call her father-in-law directly. It would build goodwill with him.

She wouldn't mention the insurance policy when she called. She didn't need to. It was her money.

"Good to hear from you, Vida *jan*. Everything okay with the children?"

Her heart was racing. "Yes." A heavy silence settled on the phone.

"What can I do for you?" he asked.

She told him about the social security checks.

The silence between them was noticeable, like the tombstone on Kamran's grave. Then he said, "*Ey-baba*. Vida *jan*, don't worry about it. I'm not even going to mention it to Doktor. It's such a small amount. You don't have to tell me about these kinds of things."

Vida sank in her chair, only now realizing the strength it took to make the call.

"Thank you. Thank you so much," she said.

From her desk, she could see into Mrs. White's office, the door open. A beautiful arrangement of daffodils sat on the desk. Grinning, she hung up the phone. Her father-in-law would be more reasonable with her than Doktor. *Perhaps Homa was right. Maybe they are good people after all.*

* * * * *

In mid-May when she received an envelope at the office from the insurance company, it contained no letter this time, only a check for $50,000.

CHAPTER 8

June 1972, Tehran

——

The statement above the perforation read, "Life Insurance Policy of Dr. Kamran Shamsa." At the bottom of the page was the check.

Has there been a mistake? Did they send the check by accident? She noticed a red mark on her arm where she might have scratched herself. A welt. *That's what happens to Roya when she gets nervous. She breaks out in hives.* Vida's eyes skipped back to the check.

She folded the document, tucked it back in the envelope, and put it in her desk drawer. Then she opened the drawer to look at the check again. The week before while flipping through a magazine at the hair salon, she admired pictures of newly built homes in the northern part of Tehran. In April 1972, her $50,000 was enough to buy a Tehran house outright. She would even have money left over. It was not wise to let her mind wander too far, though, and she stopped herself before she got carried away. She placed the check back into the envelope and then into the drawer.

She wanted to tell Mrs. White, but her boss was out of the country at the USIS conference.

The safest place for the check—until she got herself to the bank the next day—was at the office. What if she got mugged on the way home? Or what if thieves robbed the house? These things could happen. The top drawer of the metal desk had a lock from which two keys hung. She locked and unlocked the drawer more than ten times until finally she stopped herself. When it was time to go home, she put the envelope in the top drawer, locked it one last time, and dropped the keys in a small-zippered pocket in her purse. *I must tell Agha Joon and Homa now.* This was important news for her.

When she got home, she smelled the sweet saffron from the steaming rice. She took in a deep breath. "Yum," she said, rubbing her stomach.

A towel was wrapped around the pot with the rice. She lifted the lid from the pot next to it to peek. She soaked in the delicious aroma when the steam from the stew rose up into her face. The tomato-based *khorest* had chunks of meat, the deflated *ghoorehs*, unripened grapes, floating, the strips of eggplant limp on top. Small bubbles surfaced slowly.

As usual, her stepmother had already set the table for the five of them. When she brought the rice to the table it was in the shape of a small white mountain, covered with strips of yellow from the saffron.

"Any *tahdeeg*?" Vida asked, referring to the crispy rice at the bottom of the pan.

"Yeah... *tahdeeg, tahdeeg, tahdeeg,*" yelled Roya, who was holding her fork in one hand and spoon in the other, banging on the table. Kasra joined her. The kids loved *tahdeeg* more than the rice itself.

"Roya, stop it. We're not in a playground," Vida said firmly to her daughter. Already anxious about telling her parents about the insurance money, the shrill sound of her daughter's voice made Vida more agitated.

Homa had her sleeves rolled up and was hovering over the rice pot, chipping away at the bottom of the pan with a knife.

"Don't worry about it," Vida called out. She glanced over at her children who had put down their forks and knives and sat staring at her like scolded puppies.

"Normally it comes right off," her stepmother said, banging away while shaking her head. "I must have burned it. I think I forgot to add the oil."

"It's okay," Vida insisted.

"Let me make another pot of rice. For the kids. It won't take too much time."

Vida raised her voice. "Can you please come sit down?" *Oh my god. I can't believe I just yelled at her.*

"Okay, I'll sit down." Homa put the pot to the side of the sink and washed her hands. "*Aaa-gha,* come on... Dinner is ready," she called out to Vida's father.

The children finished their dinner quickly and ran off to play in the family room. The three adults sat finishing theirs.

"I have good news." Vida noticed her knee was bouncing. She didn't make eye contact with her parents. She reached over to pour more eggplant stew over the small mound of rice on her dish.

"Oh?" said her stepmother, looking up.

"Remember when Kamran and I were first married, and he was working in New York?" Vida kept her head down, buried in her dish.

"Yes, of course." Homa put her fork down and rested her elbows on the table. "And?" She leaned in as if Vida was going to break unwanted news.

"It's nothing bad... It's just... uhh... apparently, he had bought a life insurance policy."

Her father didn't look up. He kept eating and coughing sporadically. Probably it was the *torshi,* the mixture of homemade pickled vegetables her stepmother often served with dinner. *Maybe too much vinegar in this batch?*

"A couple of months ago I wrote the insurance company a letter, and I sent them the death certificate."

"And?" asked her stepmother, focused on Vida, barely blinking.

Her father kept eating. "*Khanoom*, there's not enough salt in this *khoresht*," he said as he shook some over the stew.

Does Agha Joon know something? Is he mad at me? Vida's armpits felt sweaty. "Well, they sent me a check today," Vida said, eyeing her father. She had a fluttery feeling in her stomach. *Is he going to acknowledge what I'm talking about?*

He continued coughing.

"*Agha*, have a glass of water or a spoonful of yogurt." Agitated, Homa lifted the bowl with the plain yogurt, holding it in the air while looking at Vida and waiting for more information.

He ignored Homa and kept his eyes on his plate.

Frustrated, her stepmother put down the bowl. "What did you say?"

Vida knew she had heard, but clearly Homa wanted Vida to repeat it. Maybe she wanted Vida to say it again so Agha Joon would acknowledge what Vida was saying.

"The insurance company sent me a check today." Vida took a deep breath.

Agha Joon reached for the yogurt and scooped it from the bowl. He added salt and pepper and mixed it around with his spoon.

"Why? You don't need the money," he said, still looking down at his plate, again mixing the yogurt.

"I can't live here forever. You know I want to buy a house." Vida put her fork down, her elbows on the table.

Finally, her father looked up. He swallowed what was in his mouth. "I told you I'm giving you the piece of land in Niavaran."

Vida's father, who was retired from his Department of Treasury position, owned several properties in Tehran. Only the week before they had talked about dividing his assets between each of the children as part of an early distribution of his property.

"Thank you, but I can't live on a piece of land. I want to keep that and build on it someday," she said. "It's a great piece for an apartment complex if I ever save enough money for it. Right now, I need to buy a house."

"*Agha* means we don't want you living alone with the kids," her stepmother explained.

"*Khanoom*, I know what I mean." His face red, he stared down his wife. "You don't need to translate for me." Then he looked at Vida. "I don't want you living alone with the kids. I want you to live right here with us."

Homa rolled her eyes.

"I understand, and I need your help, but I want to have my own place. The kids are going to get older and..."

"And what is this about an insurance policy?" he interrupted, raising an eyebrow.

Vida was taken aback.

"And don't you need to tell Mahmoud *khan* about this money? He may not want you to buy a house with the children's money," he said, referring to Vida's father-in-law.

"No, the money is mine. Kamran chose me as the beneficiary, and the insurance company made the check to me." Then she proceeded to give them details of how she had gotten the money.

He listened carefully, nodding, the palms of his hands pressing against each other but not showing any reaction.

Vida pressed her lips together, rubbing the back of her neck. It seemed they weren't taking her seriously.

When the water in the kettle started to boil, Vida stood up. "I'll make the tea. You might not be interested to hear this, but this is enough money for me to buy a house without borrowing any of it. Plus, I have a plan."

The doorbell rang, and Vida was startled.

"It's your mother," Agha Joon grunted. "She had dinner next door and said she would drop by."

Ever since Vida had moved in with her father, her mother visited often. Too often. Maman had a good relationship with Homa, so she was welcome to drop by. Still, Vida believed her mother inserted herself into family business more than was appropriate.

Homa wiped her hands on a towel and hurried to the door.

Maman walked into the kitchen, her shoulder-length hair held up by clips. She leaned over and kissed Vida on the cheek as Vida poured hot water into the teapot. "Be careful. It's hot," Vida said, barely acknowledging her.

"How are you, *joonam*?" Maman said.

Vida did not respond to her mother as she poured tea for everyone, including Maman, who was now sitting at the kitchen table.

"Shireen says hello to all of you," said Maman, referring to her sister who lived next door.

Agha Joon glanced at Vida but didn't say anything.

Not wanting to make eye contact with Maman, Vida announced, "I was telling them I am going to buy a house."

"So what's this grand plan?" Agha Joon asked.

Raising her eyebrows, Maman eyed Homa. "Big news?" she asked. "What house, and what plan?" Maman glanced over at Agha Joon.

Vida repeated the details of the insurance policy. "I was saying I want to open bank accounts in the name of the children and then buy a house in their names."

"Why wouldn't you keep your own name on the title of the house?" asked Maman.

"It's Kamran's money, and I don't feel right about keeping it in my name. Agha Joon did that with his property," she said, referring to her father buying land in the name of his children. "Tomorrow I'm going to tell Mahmoud *khan*, and I know he'll see my intentions are to take care of the kids. I think this will persuade him to transfer guardianship to me."

Without hesitation Maman gawked at Vida, pointing at her, and said, "I wouldn't do it." Then she looked down at her tea as if embarrassed about the force of her comment.

"Why not?"

"If you have the money in your own name, you'll always have control over it. If you put it in the name of the children, you'll lose control."

It was so typical of Maman to think of herself before her children, and now Vida thought Maman was convincing her to do the same.

"If the house is in your name, you don't have to answer to anyone."

"But if I'm going to give the money to the kids later, why not put it in the account now, buy a house under their name, and maybe get the guardianship too?"

At that point Vida's father, who had been silent during the back and forth, interjected. "It's a good idea. Your in-laws will like it, and this is a step in the right direction to resolve all these issues. After all, we have *a-be-roo*, our family reputation, to look out for. We don't need any more problems, and you must end this legal battle right away."

Maman shook her head in disagreement.

Vida's father tapped Vida on the shoulder as he walked out of the room. "I think your plan is a good one."

Maman, raising an eyebrow, shrugged. "I'm just telling you what I would do. It's your money."

Homa, who had finished washing the dishes, sat back down at the table.

"What do you think?" Vida asked her.

"I agree with you and Agha. I would do whatever you have to do to get the guardianship," she said, glancing at Maman in disappointment for having to disagree with her.

Maman smirked, shaking her head back and forth with an apparent confidence. She kept the fear to herself that perhaps Vida was making a mistake, the fear no one was willing to express.

"*Ey-baba,*" her stepmother said. "Once they see that she's trying to put her own money into the children's name, they'll back off. They mean well. This *jarian* will end soon. I'm sure of it."

I hope so. I want this to be over, thought Vida.

That night they parted in disagreement, but what mattered most to Vida was her father had agreed with her.

* * * * *

Vida arrived at work a little earlier than usual the next day to make up for the extra time she would spend at the bank depositing her check during the lunch hour. In the kitchen in the back, Ali, the janitor, was sitting at the table, a large glass of tea before him. He added a tablespoon of sugar to the *chaee* and stirred, the *click clack* back and forth annoying Vida.

Ali, an uneducated timid man originally from the village of Malayer in the west of Iran, had come to Tehran with his wife hoping for a better life. One of the library staff members had hired him as a gardener. After complaining of a bad back, Ali was forced to find other work. He had taken odd jobs in Tehran, and the staff member supported Ali financially. So when the employee told Vida about Ali's situation, Vida made the case for Mrs. White to hire him as a janitor.

"*Sob bekheyer,* Ali *Agha.* You're here early," Vida said good morning as she reached for her coffee mug from the cupboard. She addressed him in a formal way, calling him "*Agha*" out of respect.

"Good morning, *Khanoom* Shamsa," Ali said, jumping up as if he was a soldier ready to salute. He also addressed her in a proper way, referring to her as Mrs. Shamsa.

"Please… Sit down. Go ahead and drink your tea," Vida said.

Ali's jittery nature gave her a strange feeling in her stomach. She didn't know him well and had a passing thought he might have gotten into her desk. Her thoughts were not logical, but she couldn't help it. She didn't like thinking this way. She quickly poured her coffee and went to her desk, worried the check would be gone. Her hand was shaking as she opened the drawer.

If she was thinking rationally, she would have remembered Ali didn't have a key to the desk and, because the check was written in English and he was illiterate, he wouldn't know what it was. But in her state of anxiety, she had lost her common sense. When she found the check in her desk, she sighed, lowering her head, embarrassed. She looked around the large room to make sure nobody was watching and then locked the drawer again.

During her lunch break she went to the *Bank-e Markazi*, the Central Bank, and opened the bank accounts in the children's names. She asked the banker to split the money evenly between the two accounts.

* * * * *

About a week later, one sunny June afternoon, Vida and her father met with a real estate agent and looked at two houses in Saltanatabad, a new neighborhood in the northern part of Tehran, close to her father's house and close to one of the schools where she was considering enrolling the kids. One of the houses, a one story newly built home, was in a gated neighborhood in Niavaran. *It's perfect for us*, she thought. Agha Joon liked it, too, because it was close to his home and was secure. During one of the car rides, Vida and her father decided it was the right time for her to tell her father-in-law about the plan to buy a house with her insurance proceeds.

*   *   *   *   *

The next day Nasreen held a family dinner at her home. Thankfully, Doktor was out of the country. Vida's father-in-law and mother-in-law were there with other relatives.

Vida's mother-in-law, who had seven children, often said Kamran was her favorite. Vida was not quite sure why she thought that. Was it because her late husband had left Iran to study, and she had missed him? Or maybe because Kamran had helped Nasreen when she was widowed with small children of her own? Maybe he was the favorite because he had died. Vida noticed in Iran, death was more respected than life.

After a long dinner, where the women sat at one end of the table chatting about cooking matters and the men at the other debating recent actions by the mayor of Tehran, Vida settled next to her father-in-law in the family room for the ritual after-dinner tea. He held a jade *tasbeeh* in his hands, lightly pushing the prayer beads back with his thumb.

"How are you managing?"

"Every day I am reminded I must get up and keep going… for the kids. They are the most important part of my life."

"I understand. You're a good mother, Vida *jan*."

"Thank you," she said. She was touched by his comment and felt moisture in her eyes, but she held back her emotions.

He placed his hand on her back and patted it.

Vida picked one of the cups of tea off the tray and placed it in front of her. Turning to her father-in-law, in a hushed voice, she said, "I have good news."

"Yes, tell me. Good news is always welcome." He crossed his legs, sitting back on the couch.

"Well…" She sighed, not sure how to prepare him for the information she was about to deliver.

"I am listening. *Khanoom,* where is my tea?" he called for his wife.

"It's on the tray. Right in front of you," she complained from the kitchen.

"Yes, of course," he said.

Her heart was beating faster than normal, but she had to say this. It was the right time.

"Kamran had a life insurance policy. In my name. The money arrived a month ago, and I opened two bank accounts, one for each of the children. I am going to buy a house in their name." She was running out of air; had she said too much? The glass teacup felt hot and was burning her fingers, so she put it down on the coffee table.

Her father-in-law dropped two sugar cubes into his cup and stirred, back and forth. The sound of the tiny silver spoon tapping against the glass rang in Vida's ear. He lifted his cup and peered into the tea as if he hadn't heard her. She wanted to grab the spoon away from him and throw it against the wall. *Is he not listening?*

"*Khanoom,* what is this? Why is the color so light?" he asked his wife, who had come back into the family room, probably to listen in on the conversation.

Vida's mother-in-law rushed over, tugging at the ends of her *roosari* to make it tighter. She took the cup and held it up toward the window, studying the color of the liquid. "You don't have to get all upset. It's just tea. It looks fine to me, but I'll get you another one. One of these days you're going to have a heart attack over nothing," she mumbled as she walked away.

The old man then turned to Vida, still holding the beads, and pushing them back one at time while moving his head up and down. "That is a good thing to do. I approve. You did the right thing."

Vida closed her eyes for a moment and let out a huge breath. "Then I'm kindly going to ask that you give me the guardianship of the children."

He paused and crammed the beads into one hand, bunching his eyebrows together as if he was going to say something. Then he reached over to the coffee table in front of them. "Are you going to drink your tea? Yours is the right color."

"*Befarmaeed*, please, I haven't touched it," said Vida. Her face felt flush. She could tell he was stalling. Her heart was racing, and she rubbed her hand against her skirt. Had she said the wrong thing? Was she naive to think she could resolve this issue right here and now?

He put a sugar cube in the corner of his mouth and poured the tea into the saucer and back into the cup so it would cool down, and then slurped while he drank it.

"Well, we know all of his money would eventually go to the kids, if he had lived," he said, referring to his own son as if he was talking about an unknown person.

"Yes, but you don't understand. The insurance proceeds are *my* money, and *I* chose to put it into two bank accounts in the children's names. I have split the money equally. I want to buy a house in their name…"

She started to raise her voice but then stopped mid-sentence. She grabbed at her purse like she was looking for something but didn't know what.

Vida's mother-in-law returned with the fresh cup of tea on a tray.

"Where did this one come from?" she complained putting her hand on her hip and referring to the cup Vida's father-in-law had taken from Vida. She was seemingly disappointed someone else had served her husband.

"It's okay. He took mine. I don't want one, thank you," Vida said.

He set down the cup Vida had given him and praised the one his wife had brought, steam rising from its top. *"Bah bah."*

Then he stood up to study the plate full of dates on the table, as if playing a game of backgammon. Finally, he selected one and popped it in his mouth.

"You've made a mistake," he said, his mouth half-full, examining the rest of the dates.

Vida felt a churning in her stomach. "What mistake?"

"Surely you know under Islamic law, boys inherit twice as much as girls, and so… Kasra *jan* should get twice as much as Roya *jan* because he is a boy. You should know these things."

She was annoyed he was citing Islamic law again, but if this was his only issue, she felt relieved.

"You are right," she said, straightening in her chair. "I've made a mistake. And I am sorry. But in the end, it doesn't matter."

"Why?"

"When I buy the house, it will be in both their names. Whenever we sell it, many years from now, we can split the money three ways, two parts to Kasra and one part to Roya." She spoke fast as if it might close off the discussion in her favor. "Roya, Kasra, get your things, we're going home," she called out.

He put his hand on her arm as she reached for her purse on the floor. "I meant to tell you Doktor sold the Mercedes.

I'll keep the money *amn*, safe, for the children for when they are of a proper age. And, about the guardianship… we can discuss it another time. This is not the right place," he whispered, taking another sip of tea. "What color!" he declared loudly, referring to the tea, probably so his wife could hear him.

Vida pinched her lips together and threw her hands up as if to say, "I give up." *Islamic law? And he sold the car without asking me?* She left the room in a huff.

*   *   *   *   *

At the end of the month, Vida waited for the bank statements to arrive at her work address where she received most of her mail. When they did not arrive, she thought there might be a problem. Every day, she waited for Ali to deliver the stack of mail wrapped with a rubber band. She ripped off the elastic and flipped through the envelopes, but the statements never arrived. Finally, one day, during her lunch break, she drove to the *Bank-e Markazi*.

"I want to talk to the *ra-ees*," she said, asking for the bank manager.

"He's out to lunch. Can I help you with something?" the bank teller asked. He was a bald plump young man wearing a dark three-piece suit with the jacket buttoned.

Vida explained what had happened. She handed him a piece of paper with the account numbers. The teller left as she stood waiting, consulting her watch. *What could be taking him so long?* She noted the long line of people forming behind her. In her hand she held the *aghigh* necklace, rubbing the smooth side, a comforting habit.

"Ma'am, there is no money in these accounts," the teller reported.

Her body was shaking, and she raised her voice. "How can that be? I opened the bank accounts myself, right here in this branch."

"I understand," he said with a calm voice. His face turned red, and it seemed his jacket might pop open.

"What? What did you say?" she was yelling. "Where is your *ra-ees*? I am not leaving until I speak to your boss. I am an employee of the American Embassy. I opened two accounts for my children with my money, less than two months ago, and now you're telling me the money is gone?" she yelled, leaning forward on the counter.

"The money is not gone, Mrs. Shamsa. The money is safe in another account."

A man came running out from the back, pulling on his jacket.

"*Khanoom... khanoom... khahesh meekonam, tamana meekoonam*, this is a bank. I beg you to lower your voice. Please... please, come sit down at my desk." He escorted her to his office and pulled the chair out for her at his desk.

Vida looked down on the ground, noticing the square gray and black tiles. She felt lightheaded.

"Can I get you a glass of water? Maybe some tea?" asked the man.

"I'm fine. I just need to speak to the *ra-ees* now," she said. She pushed a chunk of hair behind her ear and then moved the gold chain around her neck like a man adjusting his necktie.

"I *am* the bank manager. What happened?" He used his index finger to remove something from between his two front teeth. Then he sat back, crossed his legs, and put his fist next to his mouth.

In as quiet a voice as she could manage, Vida explained what happened. "And now I'm being told the money has been transferred to someone else's account?"

"That can't be true. We would never do such a thing without your permission."

"That's what *he* told me." She pointed at the teller, now standing in the corner, his jacket button open, *petch-petching*, whispering loudly, to other bank employees.

All of them were staring in Vida's direction, but she didn't care.

"Let me find out what happened. I'll be right back," he said. "*Aghaye* Mohammadi... Mr. Mohammadi... please come to the back with me." He grabbed the bank teller who had helped her by his jacket collar.

The two men moved behind the counter, and she could see them pointing down at a piece of paper. Vida hadn't eaten lunch, and her anxiety level was rocketing. She couldn't believe there could be a problem with the bank accounts. A couple of minutes later, the manager returned.

Waving his arms in the air, he said, "Mrs. Shamsa, I have good news. The funds are safe. There's been a misunderstanding."

"*Khob...* that's great. Thank you very much," she said sitting on the edge of her seat.

"The money is in *Dr.* Shamsa's bank account."

Her eyes felt they might pop out. She knew then what she had suspected when the bank teller told her the money had been transferred. "Dr. Shamsa" was Doktor, who had intrusively taken money from her children's bank accounts. She clenched her teeth and forcefully hung her purse over her shoulder, pulling at the strap. She banged her hand on the branch manager's desk and marched briskly out of the bank.

"Mrs. Shamsa... Mrs. Shams..." the bank manager called after her.

She didn't turn back.

* * * * *

When Vida and her lawyer got together, they speculated her father-in-law, the legal guardian entitled to control the bank accounts, had given Doktor power of attorney to access the funds. Immediately, Vida's lawyer filed a civil lawsuit against Doktor for taking her money.

At first, the lawyer reprimanded Vida for not consulting with him before opening the bank accounts, and she felt stupid for having gone forward with her decision without letting him in on her plan. But after a few days he called and said they could win the case if he found a "hook," and she felt somewhat relieved about the situation. He did warn her the matter could take several years before there would be any resolution. It was out of her hands.

She had to move forward with life.

CHAPTER 9

September 1972, Tehran

———

"Do you have what you need?" whispered Vida into eight-year-old Kasra's ear as she walked with him into his new classroom.

He nodded, his head close to her shoulder, glancing down.

She kissed him on the forehead and brushed the invisible lint from his blue blazer uniform. "You will make good friends here."

She felt a knot in her stomach while leaving him in the new British school. What if Doktor kidnapped him? She tried to erase these irrational thoughts. Her father had told her the night before to think positive thoughts. "Doktor will never take the children away. I promise you," he had said. *But Doktor seemed capable of anything.*

Up until now the children were in different schools, Kasra at the all-American, Tehran American School, and Roya still at a relative's preschool. Vida wanted them to be together. Logistically it was easier for her, but more importantly, she felt safer having them in the same location. Her biggest challenge was finding a bilingual environment so they could learn Farsi while keeping up with their English. After all, she was hopeful they would all return to the United States someday, soon.

A childhood friend who had also returned to Iran after having lived in the US suggested Vida enroll them in one of the leading British-run schools. Without having visited the recommended school, Vida called the principal who agreed by phone to enroll Kasra in the second grade that week. If things worked out with her son, later she would move Roya to the same school.

When she walked out of the classroom, she wiped her tears away, careful not to smudge her makeup. She sat in her car in the parking lot, staring out the window. Her little boy was growing up. *Is this the right school for him? I should have spent more time getting to know the principal and some of the parents before enrolling him.* After a few minutes, she convinced herself everything would be fine, and she drove to work.

It was early afternoon when she received a call from the principal.

"We need you to come to school. It's urgent," he said.

Her face turned white, and her hands felt clammy.

"Not to worry. Your son is right here in my office safe," he added.

Vida reached for her keys to unlock the bottom drawer of her metal desk where she kept her purse. She inserted the key into the hole, but it wouldn't budge. She banged on the drawer, and again nothing. Stuck.

Finally, Ali stood towering over her.

"I can do it. Let me try," he said with his calm village accent. With one turn he unlocked the drawer. "Here you go," he handed her the keys. He stood innocently gazing at her holding the keys.

"Thank you," she said, biting the inside of her cheek. She felt uncertain about him. Reaching for her purse, she darted out of the library.

Weaving in and out of Tehran traffic, where drivers had no respect for lines on the road, she kept her hand on the horn. Running a red light, she parked unevenly over two spaces in the parking lot. She rushed to the principal's office.

"I'm here for my son."

"Name?" said the overweight American redhead sitting in the front. She was on the phone, and it looked like she couldn't be bothered.

Vida was out of breath, and her hair had come undone. "Kasra. His name is Kasra," she said.

"Take a seat." She motioned with her hand. "I'll be right with you."

Vida sat for a few seconds, fidgeting with her fingernails, and tapping her foot on the ground. She looked at the secretary, who had now swiveled her chair, her back to Vida, giggling on the phone like she might be telling a friend about a new lover. Finally, when the assistant hung up the phone and strutted away from her desk heading into the hallway, Vida marched right into the main office without knocking.

The principal sat at his desk, focused on a piece of paper. Kasra sat on a bench with his head down, teeth clenched, his back straight, staring down at the floor. Vida didn't see anyone else in the room. The little boy didn't look up at his mother when she put her hand on his shoulder. He didn't say a word and had no tears. His face blank, his fingers crunched together resting on his thighs, he looked as if he was ready to throw a punch. His eyebrows bunched together were connected as one, a sure sign of rage.

"Kasra *joon*, what happened?" She placed her hand on his chin, forcing him to look up at her.

Nothing. He said absolutely nothing. He just looked at her blankly with his big black eyes and a look of fury.

She squeezed his shoulder to say, "I'm here for you." Still, his mouth was constricted, and he refused to speak.

The principal had gotten up from behind his desk and stood next to her with his arms crossed. "He won't tell me what happened." He pulled Vida closer to him so Kasra wouldn't hear him. "The teacher brought him in here and said, 'All of a sudden he wouldn't talk.' Does he have psychological issues we should know about?" he whispered.

"I better take him home." Vida clenched and unclenched her hand, placing it on Kasra's back and lightly pushing him forward so they would quickly exit the building.

The heavy assistant, sneering at Vida, held the double doors open.

Vida gave her a half-smile back, her pulse elevated for having been ignored earlier by the mean woman.

Kasra crawled into the backseat of the car, crossing his arms. When she glanced at him, his face looked more relaxed. He wasn't clenching his teeth, but his eyebrows were still pushed together, small wrinkles lining his forehead.

"Do you want to talk about it?" she asked.

He didn't respond.

She got into the front seat and peeked at him through the rearview mirror. He looked the same. She inserted a cassette tape into the car stereo. The tape played Perry Como's "It's Impossible." She sang along, eyeing the mirror and hoping the music would calm her little boy. He had recognized the song the week before on the way to baseball practice and reminded her it was his daddy's favorite song.

Finally, without lifting his head, Kasra burst out, "She called me stupid."

Vida slowed down the car and tried to catch his eye through the rearview mirror again, but he wouldn't return her gaze.

"Who called you stupid?" She gripped the steering wheel, her shoulders tense.

"The teacher," he said. Then he lifted his head. "She gave me a book and asked me to read out loud—in Farsi. I couldn't read it. I didn't know what to do. So then… she yelled at me in front of the whole class and called me stupid." His voice escalated, and he began to cry. It was a sob, like the one Vida had broken into in the hospital room in London.

She stopped at a red light. "She what?" Vida's voice was cracking. She eyed him again from the rearview mirror. She had already informed the school principal Kasra only spoke a few words of Farsi and certainly could not read it. She had told him Kasra was an introverted child who had just lost his father. *What was the teacher thinking?*

"In front of the whole class," he emphasized, sobbing. "I don't want to go to that school anymore, Mom. I hate that teacher. And I don't want to see the other kids. I want to go back to America." His words became loud and forceful. She had never seen him this angry, not even the week before when Roya had accidentally stepped on and crushed into pieces the toy airplane Kamran had brought him from Germany.

A bald truck driver with a dark mustache honked his horn loudly. He leaned out of the front window of the four-wheeler, one hand on the horn the other pointing at Vida. "*Boro-dee-ge,*" he complained.

She stared at the driver, uninterested in engaging with him. She rolled down her window and motioned for him to pass her, and he veered off.

She put the car into gear and kept driving. Turning down the radio, she said, "You're the smartest person I know. The principal must have forgotten to tell your teacher you haven't learned Farsi yet. She probably didn't know."

"But, Mommy, I want to read. I just can't," he cried. "And now... now..." He sniffled. "I'm not going to have any friends because they're all going to think I'm stupid."

She felt her stomach drop, aching for her son, and still she was furious. *How dare anyone insult Kasra? After everything he has been through,* she thought. "Don't worry, *azeezam*. You don't have to go back," she consoled him.

When she got to Pahlavi Avenue, she pulled the car over to the side of the road and parked the car. "Don't worry. You *will* learn Farsi, and I'll find a good school with nice teachers. You'll make lifelong friends. I promise." She climbed into the backseat, wiping his tears with the sleeve of her shirt and running her hand through his hair. "I promise," she repeated.

His breath was short and shallow, and he seemed to be settling down.

She got back into the driver's seat and drove back onto the road.

"Come on. Let's get out."

He climbed out of the backseat, and the two walked over to a street vendor. She didn't trust food from the peddlers because they weren't clean, but she figured a sealed bag of *Pofak Namaki*, cheese puffs, couldn't hurt. As they drove off, she watched him dig into the bag, reaching for the crispy cheesy treats. She knew he was feeling better when he bit into one and then licked his fingers to wipe off the orange specks.

When they arrived at the house, Kasra ran to his room with a burst of positive little-boy energy.

Vida tossed her purse on the front table and reached for the phone. When the principal picked up, she took a deep breath and hollered at him.

"His teacher had no right to put him on the spot. Do you understand? She knew he doesn't read Farsi. It's your job to teach him. To call him stupid? In front of his classmates? And to say he has a psychological disorder without any basis? What kind of a school are you running anyway?" Her voice was loud and forceful.

"But Mrs. Shamsa, we..."

Then she slammed down the phone. Her hand was shaking, and she felt a pounding in her head. She felt angry her husband had died, angry she had to move to Iran, and angry to be dealing with this school situation.

She looked up, and Homa was standing in the doorway, drying her hand with a dishtowel hanging on her shoulder.

Vida said nothing at first, her heart still pounding.

"Who was that?" asked her stepmother. She took a seat next to Vida and gently held her hand while Vida recounted the story.

"Are you finished?" said Homa in her regular sweet tone.

"Yes."

"Keep him at the TAS for now. There have been too many changes in the last few months. He needs stability. After he learns Farsi, you can enroll him in a bilingual school. Maman can tutor him," Homa added.

Vida's heart had stopped its irregular pounding. "Maman?" asked Vida frowning.

At the time Maman was married off to Agha Joon she had not finished high school, even though she had wanted to finish her education. In fact, her conflicts with Agha Joon arose when Maman's brothers were sent to Germany to pursue higher education, and she expressed a desire to do the same. After she filed for divorce, not only did she finish her high school degree, but she got her teaching credentials with the Ministry of Education and was now a fifth-grade teacher.

"I don't want her here every day." Vida worried Maman would meddle in her life. She had lived her life up to now without any advice from her mother, and she wanted to keep it that way.

"Don't be so hard on her. She's a grandmother and wants to do what's best for you and the kids. I'm sure of it. Let her do it."

Vida stared into Homa's eyes, deep in thought. She appreciated her stepmother's suggestion but had concerns.

The next day, at the insistence of Homa, Vida called her mother.

"Of course I will do it. This is what I live for," Maman said enthusiastically.

Vida didn't want to admit to herself that secretly she admired her take-charge mother.

* * * * *

The following day Maman arrived at Vida's father's house at 4:00 p.m., when Kasra was already home from school. Vida came home early that day to monitor the situation. Maman sipped a cup of tea and nibbled on sweets with Homa while Vida folded laundry in the next room. Finally, Maman started her work with Kasra.

This routine continued for a few weeks. Sometime in late October, Vida came home early from the library one afternoon and found Kasra doubled-over the kitchen table, leaning on his arm, as if he was falling asleep, a pencil in hand, writing from right to left—as Farsi is written. Maman was reading from a folded newspaper and pacing the length of the kitchen floor, one arm behind her back, enunciating with authority each Farsi word as she read out loud, "*Vo-ka-la-ye... daaaad-gos-taree...*"

Kasra kept his head down, writing effortlessly.

"Ba-ra-yehhhhh…"

"Maman," Vida protested, "why are you reading *that* to him?"

"It's a dictation," her mother said matter-of-factly.

"But he doesn't understand what it means… 'the lawyers in the courtroom'?" Vida raised her voice.

"It doesn't matter *what* I read. The point is he's writing down the letters. See…" she said, pulling the paper from underneath Kasra's hand. Kasra nearly bumped his head on the table.

Vida examined the dictation, her eyes popping out. She couldn't believe her son had such beautiful handwriting and an ability to write the Farsi alphabet, which was like the Arabic alphabet and unlike the American one in so many ways. A smile spread across her face. "Oh, Kasra… I can't believe it." She laughed. She reached for her son's head and kissed him lightly. "I'm so proud of you."

The little boy looked up and gave a half-smile. Learning to read and write in Farsi seemed so effortless for him.

"See, I told you," said Maman. "He's a genius." She squeezed Kasra's little chin. "A genius, I tell you."

Vida paused and stared at the back of Maman's head. She lowered her gaze, touched by what her mother had done for her. "Thank you, Maman *jan.*"

Maman turned around and leaned her head to the side. "What are grandmothers for?" Then she lifted the newspaper. "Come on, we're not done," she barked at Kasra.

The next day before Vida walked into the kitchen, she could hear Maman's dictation,

"*Karmand-haye... dolatee... bayad... beeshtar... pool dararan.*"

Vida listened and rolled her eyes as Maman read about government workers needing to make more money. Kasra wrote down each word.

By the end of the month, Kasra was reading and writing Farsi. He may not have understood the meaning of all the words, but he could write them down. It was a huge accomplishment. When Vida took him to the Ministry of Education to take the official test for the second grade, he earned a perfect score.

* * * * *

She arrived at home ready to celebrate the good news. As she walked into the house, the phone started to ring.

"I'll get it," shouted Vida to her stepmother. "*Allo.*" She pulled off her blazer.

"Dr. Vakeelee."

What was this about? She hadn't heard from him in months. She inserted her finger into the coil of the telephone cord until her finger got stuck.

"Don't worry. It's good news," he said. "Your custody. It's been renewed for another year."

"I thought the hearing would take place in December." *Oh my god, is that possible?*

"The judge pulled in the date. Didn't I tell you the judges in Iran are progressive?" He sounded proud.

Vida sank into the chair. "But the hearing was supposed to take place in a month?"

"I was at the court for another matter with the same judge, so I asked him off the record. He decided to extend it right then and there."

This legal system makes no sense, she thought. *But it doesn't matter.* She was pleased her custody was extended. "What about the lawsuit?"

"I'm working on it. It's going to take a while."

She needed the money. Recently she had fantasized about wiring the funds back to the US once she got the money and smuggling the children back to America, despite the custody laws.

"Remember, we're running a marathon. This will not get resolved quickly," he said.

She pulled at the telephone cord again. She was reminded of how angry she was about her situation and the lawsuit.

"You should give *sheernee*. This is good news," he said, referring to the traditional Iranian way of sharing good fortune, the offering of sweets to friends and family.

"*Sheernee*? It will have to wait until after the marathon," she said sarcastically. She was grateful the custody was extended but annoyed about the situation. She was not going to celebrate anything until all the issues were resolved.

CHAPTER 10
December 1972, Tehran

———

It was early December, close to a year since Kamran's death, when Vida arrived at the school parking lot on a bright sunny day. At the recommendation of Mrs. White, and after visiting and interviewing several international schools, Vida had found the one.

The principal of the new international school, Mrs. Balazadeh, was waiting for her at the entrance with her hands locked behind her. She was a heavy-set jovial British lady with short blonde hair and blue eyes. Mrs. B, as she called herself, reminded Vida of Kasra's nursery schoolteacher in New York, and she instantly took a liking to her.

"Your children's teachers will both be American ladies who are married to Iranians. Both have children of their own here at the school. None of the children could speak Farsi when they first moved to Tehran. The kids learned the language at this school." The principal stuck her chest out as they walked the grounds.

Vida did not reveal the details of the incident at the first school a few months earlier. The international community in Tehran was small, and she didn't want word, especially the unfounded comment the other principal had made about Kasra's psychological disorder, to get around. It was comforting to know other parents shared the same challenges in raising bilingual children. As Mrs. B showed Vida the school, she wanted to tell the principal about the tragedy that had happened to her, especially about the fear of having her children taken away, but she held back. It wasn't the right time to get into it.

Vida and Mrs. B strolled into one of the classrooms. The letters of the English alphabet in small and large capital letters, in block and in cursive underneath, were lined up against the front wall. The sidewall had numbers posted in various colors. It reminded her of Kasra's school in New York.

The back of the room had a large glass window and a door facing into a courtyard. Children were playing outside. In the courtyard Vida saw slides, swings, and curved metal ladders bolted into the dusty ground and a basketball court off to the side.

"We recently installed those monkey bars," announced Mrs. B, pointing at the curved metal ladders.

"I've never seen them," Vida said, thinking back to the park near her old apartment in America, not remembering having seen anything like it.

"The children are having so much fun playing on the fixture."

"Is it safe?" Vida asked.

"Sure. You Iranian mothers are so protective of your children." Mrs. B tapped Vida on the shoulder, in a "don't worry so much" kind of way.

"The kids could get hurt if they fall off those monkey bars," Vida insisted.

"Oh no, everything is so low to the ground," she said, pointing at two boys about Kasra's age who were climbing the bars. When they reached the top, they swung back and forth until they dropped to the ground, landing on their feet. Vida observed the boys laughing as they fell, but still, she felt a quivering sensation in her stomach.

The two women continued walking. Once they got to the loud cafeteria, Vida observed the boys and girls sitting on long benches, each with a tray of spaghetti, a piece of French bread, and an apple in front of them. An intense noise took over the lunchroom.

"Excuse me for a moment. I need to make an announcement," Mrs. B said to Vida.

In a loud voice, Mrs. B called out, "Children, children, quiet for a moment." She spoke into the crowd. The general chatter continued. Then in a commanding voice, she shouted, "Chiiiill-dren."

Vida was taken aback and surprised to hear Mrs. B belt out her voice at such a high volume, but instantly the students became silent. The kids sat straight up. Most had their hands planted in between their legs.

Mrs. B patted her shirt and touched the back of her hair, ready to take charge. "Now listen, if you don't stop the *shoolooki poolooki*, there will be no *bastanee*. Do you hear me? No more *bastanee*," she said with her British accent, waving her finger in the air while threatening no ice cream unless the chaos came to a halt. The children settled down.

Vida remembered her own school and the discipline used by the British administrators back then. She smirked at Mrs. B's use of the Farsi language and liked the authority the principal exercised over the children.

On the way back to the main office, Mrs. B introduced Vida to the school nurse, an American woman. "She's very experienced," added the principal as they walked. "American educated. We're lucky we haven't needed her for anything more than a few sniffles and an upset stomach."

Vida was impressed by what she observed that morning. It was a safe and comfortable community. She decided to enroll the children in the school right away so they would get used to their new environment before summer vacation.

By the second day, Vida put the two kids on the school bus together. She felt comfortable doing that. She hadn't told Mrs. B about the issues with her in-laws, but at some point, she knew it would come up.

* * * * *

After a few weeks, at the beginning of a two-day weekend, Vida and Roya went to the school while Kasra stayed home doing homework. During a previous visit, Mrs. B had told Vida the School PTA raised funds to open a school library. She asked Vida to lead the project, and Vida agreed.

Two American women were already in Mrs. B's office. A little girl and boy were coloring at a round children's table in the corner of the office. At first Vida felt vaguely isolated, knowing the ladies probably knew each other well.

Roya tugged at her mother's long black and gray striped cardigan, curled her little index finger, and motioned for her mom to come closer. When Vida bent down, the little girl cupped her tiny hand around her mother's ear and whispered, "That's the girl... Sandy."

"What girl?" Vida couldn't remember all the things she heard about the children at school. "Roya *joon*. I told you it's not nice to whisper in front of other people," said Vida, half-smiling at the other ladies.

"But it's not a secret, Mom," the little girl protested. "The twins, remember?"

"Oh right." Vida remembered Roya telling her about the fake twins, as her daughter called them, at school, how they looked nothing like each other, how they were a boy-girl combination, and how their American mother was a teacher at the school. "Go on... sit with your friends," she said, tugging at Roya's arm.

The little boy, Sam, had blond hair and blue eyes, his face covered with freckles, and he looked a lot like one of the women in the room. Sandy had dark brown hair, brown eyes, and no freckles, more Iranian looking than the boy. Her brown curly pigtails were held together with elastic decorated pink plastic sparkling balls. Sandy put her arm around Roya and kissed her on the cheek. Sam looked up hesitatingly and continued drawing in the coloring book.

"Why don't you kids go on outside? The weather is beautiful," said Mrs. B.

Without hesitation, Sandy took Roya and Sam's hands and led them outside.

So cute, thought Vida. *Her little friends.*

The office window overlooked the courtyard, and Vida watched with trepidation as Sam sprinted in front and the two girls followed. It hadn't snowed, but it was cold outside. *The boys are always running. They are so different than girls.*

"Is it safe for them to be outside alone?" Vida asked. She didn't like Roya being out of her sight.

"Don't worry. This is a secure property. See… it's enclosed." Mrs. B pointed at the low cement walls along the back perimeter of the school.

The walls were low enough someone could jump over them.

"And there's nothing around this property for about a mile," added Mrs. B. "Look out there. See? Nothing. Just dirt."

"It's safe," said one of the women.

Vida's gaze was on the children when she took a seat at the table with the ladies, still worried about Roya wandering off.

The two other ladies were teachers at the school. One of them, Linda, was Kasra's teacher, the mother of the twins. The four women sat around the square table in Mrs. B's office, at first drinking coffee and nibbling on pastries and then strategizing about which books to buy. The *farangee*, foreign, ladies were curious about Vida's library experience and asked lots of questions, their energy and excitement infectious. Vida could hear the passion in their voices, and it reminded her of the American moms like her neighbor Rosemary. They were genuinely interested in advancing the school and creating a more solid learning experience for the children. *These women are so different than Iranian women. They dress simple. They don't seem interested in the Gucci-pucci stuff Iranian women talk about. They're not dripping in jewelry and wearing a pile of makeup. They are more my style.*

"What about The Hardy Boys collection?" asked Linda.

"How about *Anne of Green Gables*?" Mrs. B interjected. "Remember when little Anne had surgery?"

Linda protested, "That wasn't *Anne of Green Gables*."

Suddenly Doktor came to mind. Without much thought, Vida ran to the window again. "Where is Roya? I don't see her," she said.

"I'm sure they're playing somewhere," said Mrs. B.

"I don't see her," insisted Vida. *Mrs. B is so relaxed. What's wrong with her? I guess Americans don't care about their children as much as Iranian mothers.*

"Is something wrong?" asked Linda. The thin woman, with her auburn hair held back with a clip, sat calmly.

"I just need to find my daughter," said Vida running her hand through her hair but not wanting to look panicked.

Mrs. B walked to the window, resting her chubby fingers on Vida's shoulder and pointing. In a soft voice, she said, "There they are. See? They're fine. If you want, I can ask them to come inside," offered the woman.

Vida's heart was pounding. She dug into her fingernails. "I'll go with you. How do you get out of here?" she said, pushing her chair aside.

Linda and the other mother stood aside, looking confused as Vida followed Mrs. B. They rushed out without their coats. Outside Vida hugged her arms close to her chest, cold, scanning the area.

"Do you see them?" the principal sounded relieved.

"Yes," sighed Vida.

"They must be playing with something on the ground."

Vida could see the children sitting in the back corner of the yard. She sat on one of the stairs by the door. She could feel the cold stone through her pants. She tried to compose herself. *Roya is going to catch a cold sitting on the ground.*

Mrs. B kneeled beside her. "Do you want me to get you anything?" she asked.

"No. I'm fine. It's... It's my children."

Both women were hunched over to stay warm.

"What's wrong?" asked Mrs. B.

"It's just... I'm... I'm worried my children will be taken away."

"Taken away?" asked the principal. She sat up, her eyes wide. "But why?"

Vida gazed into Mrs. B's eyes. She felt she could trust her, and so she told her story and shared the situation with her in-laws.

At first, Mrs. B plopped herself down on the cement stairs. She was quiet. She had her hand to her mouth in disbelief. She kept nodding like she could not believe Vida's story. After a few minutes she took a long, deep breath,

"Now I know why you are so worried about your daughter. It makes sense," she said.

Mrs. B was taking her seriously.

"I know things are difficult for you here in Iran. But don't worry. At school the children will be safe. I will personally keep an eye on them. I will not let anybody take them, and nothing is going to happen," she said reassuringly. "Now, come on. Let's go inside before we freeze."

Vida's shoulders dropped. The two got up and walked back into the building.

Linda was at the doorway with a worried look. She didn't say anything when she saw Vida. The woman simply handed Vida a glass of water.

Tears gathered in the corner of Vida's eyes, but she didn't say anything. *What a nice woman*, she thought.

* * * * *

During the drive home, Roya talked the entire time about her new friends and the pebbles they had found in the backyard of the school and the rubber ball that bounced high and the small metal crosses called "jacks." Roya announced she would call the kids that were half American and half Iranian "half and half."

Vida partially listened as the radio played at a low volume. She was deep in thought about Linda and Mrs. B and how she felt so lucky to have found such a supportive community. The sky was gray, and it looked like it might start to snow. When Roya rolled down the window Vida felt a cool breeze.

"Don't stick your hand out the window," she yelled. She felt on edge.

"I'm not," the little girl complained.

* * * * *

Vida thought her heart skipped a beat, and then she saw an ambulance parked in the street in front of her father's house, the siren twirling silently, the red light moving in a rhythmic, methodical way. At first, she thought she was on the wrong street. The front door was open. She pulled on the emergency brake and slammed the car door as she got out. She rushed into the house with Roya behind her.

"Where's Kasra?" she called out.

Homa walked out of the bedroom, hunched over, holding a tissue against her nose. "It's your father. Vida *joonam*, it's Agha Joon."

"What?" Vida's jaw dropped, and her purse fell to the ground. "What happened?" What could have happened to her seventy-five-year-old father? *He's healthy.*

The paramedics wheeled him out of the living room with an oxygen mask to his face. He was fully conscious but in his pajamas. He raised his arm and waved at Vida in a "don't worry about me" way. The paramedics stopped.

"Agha Joon, are you okay?" Vida asked, leaning in close to her father. She felt disoriented. *What's happening?*

"I'm fine," he muttered.

His voice was faint, and Vida could tell he was struggling to breath. "You're going to be fine," she said rubbing his arm. She was scared he wasn't.

"Make sure you…" he mumbled.

Vida couldn't hear him. She leaned in closer. "What did you say?"

"Resol…"

Still, she couldn't understand what he was saying. "What did you say?" she repeated in a frustrated tone. She felt a lump in her throat and thought she might burst into tears.

The paramedics hovered over the older man as they removed the oxygen mask.

He spoke slowly. "Resolve your issues quickly. It's not worth it. And find a good man. You shouldn't live alone."

Vida's father looked pale, and his eyes started to roll back.

"Take care of him," she said to the paramedics. "I'm right behind you."

Then she looked down at her father. "We don't need to talk about this right now." She wiped a tear with the back of her hand. "Go with him in the ambulance," she shouted at Homa. "I'm right behind you."

She felt guilty. *Had her legal issue caused him so much stress that his life was now in danger?*

The paramedics wheeled Vida's father out of the house.

Vida went to the phone and dialed. She needed someone to stay with the kids. When Maman finally arrived, she rushed out of the house, speeding to the hospital. She gripped the steering wheel so tightly her thumb ached.

"He's my father," she yelled out of breath at the information desk in the emergency room.

The nurse at the desk simply bowed her head. "I'm so sorry. He didn't make it," she said.

Vida held her stomach and then sat and put her head down between her legs. She started wailing.

Homa slowly walked over to her and lifted her face. "Shshhh. At least he didn't suffer," said her stepmother. "It was quick."

Vida looked up at her.

"It was his time," said her stepmother. "Everybody has a time."

*   *   *   *   *

Vida spent the next several weeks comforting her stepmother during a time that was so emotional for her. She called her half-siblings in America to share the news and arranged for the burial, the *hafteh*, and all the other family gatherings. She knew what to do now. At nights she stayed up late in silence, looking blankly at the wall in her bedroom. When Maman volunteered to move in with her in the flat above her father's house, she accepted the offer. Her mother was finally taking care of her.

CHAPTER 11

January 1973, Tehran

During the last two months of the year, the court called a status conference three different times to discuss the lawsuit. Each time, Vida's lawyer and the judge waited for Doktor and his attorney, but neither showed up. Each time, the enraged judge ordered Vakeelee to find Doktor and to arrange a new meeting with the court clerk, as if Vida's lawyer had any control over Doktor's actions.

Frustrated, Vida didn't understand why the judge did not penalize Doktor for not showing up. Even Vakeelee did not have a good answer. The only thing that was clear was the laws of Iran were not as precise as Western laws when it came to court procedures, and the issue was out of their hands.

On a Tuesday morning the phone rang at Vida's work desk.

"I need to meet you. Today," said her lawyer. "I want to discuss the lawsuit against Doktor. I will give you details when I see you."

They planned to meet at Café Voltaire, near her office, where they had met once before to discuss her legal issues.

After the call, Vida sat distracted. It had been almost two months since the death of her father, and life had begun to finally feel normal. She continued living in the upstairs apartment of her father's home, and Maman had moved back to her own place. Roya and Kasra continued to adjust to life in Iran, and Vida worked well with her boss at the library. Life was busy, filled with the routine of school, work, birthday parties, and after-school activities.

Now this meeting. *More issues on the lawsuit?* Vida didn't have the support of her father to make any decisions. *What is this meeting about? Vakeelee has been giving phone updates so far. Why a live meeting?*

Vida rearranged her desk, shifting the stapler from the right side to the left, as if she was reorganizing her closet. She put her hand in the paper clip holder, adjusted the clips, positioning the larger ones on one side and the smaller ones to the other. At one point all the paper clips splashed across her desk. She went to the bathroom three times. She thought she had to pee, but she didn't. Afterward she glanced at her watch. Each time, it was too early to go. The restaurant was only a five-minute walk from the office.

Finally, at noon, she set out. She was wearing a black-pleated skirt to her knees and a maroon silk blouse with material flowing from the neck, tied in a bow. She wouldn't have worn the two-inch heels if she had known she was going to walk down the street to Café Voltaire. On the way, she walked past a man who was selling fresh roses. She stopped and smelled one of them. The florists paid a lot of attention to the flower arrangements in Tehran, and Vida appreciated that. When she walked into the restaurant, she eyed the tables to make sure she didn't recognize anyone. She didn't want anyone at the office to see her speaking with an attorney. She didn't want anyone to know she had legal issues.

Vakeelee, wearing a suit with a pink bowtie, was seated when she arrived. A carafe of red wine sat on the table, and he was sipping from his glass.

When she approached, he walked to her side and pulled out the chair for her. She made quick eye contact with him; he was smiling. *What is wrong with this guy? He looks silly in a pink bowtie. Does he wear this when he goes into the courtroom? No wonder we're not making any progress on this case.* Vida could tell he was in a good mood.

"Why don't we order, and then I'll tell you the fantastic news," he suggested.

What fantastic news?

"Can I pour you a glass of wine?" He lifted the carafe.

"Sure," she said reluctantly. She didn't drink much, and certainly not at lunchtime, but she wanted to be agreeable. She would take a sip and leave the rest in her glass, as she did at the American Embassy cocktail parties she attended when a dignitary was in town.

The waiter took their order. Vida rested her hands in her lap, pushing her hands hard against each other. "So, what's the good news?"

"I found a hook for the lawsuit."

"A hook?" She raised her eyebrows in surprise and remembered him using the word, but she couldn't remember the context or what he had meant by it.

"Remember when I told you we could win the lawsuit if we found *a hook* in the case?"

She straightened the tie fabric hanging from her neck. Her hands were fidgeting. "Oh yes."

"Well, we are going to win this one." He held his chin high and thrust out his chest, nodding as if he was about to declare victory in wartime.

She picked up the glass of wine and took a big gulp. "Well... please, by all means, tell me," she said.

She set the glass back on the table. It practically fell over, but she caught it before that happened.

"Did Kamran ever give Dr. Shamsa a power of attorney for anything?"

Vida felt annoyed he had referred to Doktor as Dr. Shamsa. Her husband was the only Dr. Shamsa as far she was concerned. She resented hearing the same name used for her despised brother-in-law.

She narrowed her eyes, angling her body away from the table. "Yes," she said, "after we moved to New York, we kept a bank account in Tehran. Kamran had given his brother a general power of attorney to manage his finances in Iran, specifically to manage the sale of a piece of land their father put in their names."

Slamming his palm on the table in excitement, Vakeelee said, "I knew it. I knew it. That's what I thought."

It sent a ripple across the surface of her wine. She fixed her eyes on the glass. Again, she was afraid it might topple over.

Vakeelee picked up his wine glass, examined the wine before taking another sip, and then smiled as if to say, "Don't you worry. I have it all figured out."

"Are you going to tell me what that means?" Vida asked. She was getting impatient with his dramatic delivery and worried he might be holding back important information.

"Do you think Dr. Shamsa might have used the power of attorney for anything else?" asked the lawyer.

"You mean Doktor." She pinched her lips together.

"Yes, yes, Doktor."

"Probably to sell the Mercedes."

Vida reminded him the car had been missing, that she had seen it at the burial and the *hafteh*, and later her father-in-law had told her the car had been sold. She explained they had kept the proceeds from selling the car.

"Interesting," he said, scratching his head.

"What's interesting?" *It takes this guy a long time to get it out. Get to the point!*

"It turns out Dr. Shamsa..."

"Doktor. You mean Doktor," she said, frowning. "Please. Please don't call him Dr. Shamsa."

"Right, Doktor. Doktor, your brother-in-law, has used that power of attorney illegally."

A deafening silence hovered over the table.

"What?" Her voice softened.

"He used it to get the funds from the children's bank account. He probably used the power of attorney to sell the car too."

"Doesn't the power of attorney give him the right to do that?" she asked.

He smirked. "Let me explain," he said, rubbing his hands together and then adjusting the bowtie.

Her eyes narrowed as she looked at the lawyer.

Vakeelee continued. "A power of attorney is void when the person who granted it dies. It's a crime to use a power of attorney once the person who gave it passes away. If the public prosecutor learns Doktor used an expired power of attorney to take money from the children's accounts, the authorities will not only force him to return the money, but Doktor will go to jail."

Vida took another big gulp of wine. Her glass was nearly empty now. A sense of relief and excitement rushed through her entire body, and she leaned back in her seat. "Now what?" she asked. She felt dizzy yet powerful.

The waiter brought the food. She looked down at her plate. She couldn't think of eating.

Vakeelee cut his steak into small pieces and dipped one of the French Fries into the sauce on the side of his plate.

Vida sat gazing at him and then down at the salad in front of her. She had no appetite. She had a passing thought about getting her money back and being in her own home with the children.

"If I tell the public prosecutor about this abuse of power, Doktor will be arrested and put in jail. I'm not suggesting we do that. I don't want to send him to jail. I do have a reputation to uphold."

She didn't hear the last part of the comment. She had to be firm with Doktor to send a message. But jail? Did she want her children's uncle to be imprisoned? What would people think of her? Her colleagues at work and the parent community at the school? "Really?" she said, leaning in, her voice a whisper.

"Yes."

"Jail?" she repeated in a hushed tone. She wanted revenge, but this was too much.

"Yes… yes." His voice escalated. "The real question is—what do *you* want to do?"

Of course she wanted revenge. She wanted him to be put away into the bottom of a *chah*, so he could not crawl out of the well.

"What kind of a question is that?" she asked reluctantly. She wanted her lawyer to know she was firm and decisive. But was she?

Vakeelee laid down his fork and knife.

"If Doktor is threatened with an arrest, I know he will return the money. He's not going to want to go to jail. He has a reputable medical practice. He has *a-be-roo* in this town, in this country," he said, referring to Doktor's reputation. "Once he returns the money, we can ask the prosecutor to drop the charges."

She took a sip of her glass of water, thinking. She had to send a strong message to Doktor. "I want to do it," she said.

The lawyer looked away, rolling his eyes. "Are you sure you want him to go to jail?"

Vida paused. She fingered the knife to the right of her plate and then squeezed it. Then she raised her voice. "Why do you keep asking me that? Why wouldn't I want him to go to jail? He stole my money, and he wants to take my children. It's been hell. With the cost of living rising, soon the insurance money will not be worth half of what it was."

"Keep your voice down, please," her lawyer implored, surveying the restaurant to make sure no one he recognized was in the vicinity. He replenished Vida's wine, and she took another sip.

"Don't worry about what the money will be worth. Given the interest rates, your money has no doubt grown."

She looked down at the fork in her place setting and then continued stroking the knife. "If putting him in jail is the quickest way to get the money back, let's do it."

He continued chewing. "Hmm… here's another thing we can do," he said as he swallowed. "The other option is to keep the public prosecutor out of it." He wiped his mouth with the napkin on his lap. "I can call his lawyer, explain what we have learned, and threaten to go to the authorities. You know, pretend. I'm sure he'll return the money."

"You mean a bluff?"

"Yes… a bluff."

"And if he doesn't return the money, would they still send him to jail?"

"Yes. They would."

What would Doktor do to her once he got out of jail? He would make life miserable for her.

The lawyer sighed, shaking his head in disagreement. "Don't forget, he is the uncle of your children, after all. The kids will know you put their uncle in jail. Maybe not today or tomorrow, but someday."

She lifted the knife and held it firmly in her fist. "Uncle? What uncle?" her voice was shaking. "He hasn't done a thing for my children, especially since their father died. Not a gift, a lunch, nor a dinner. He hasn't even made one phone call on either of their birthdays." She could feel her face heat up.

"Okay, okay," said the lawyer, gesturing for her to keep her voice down. He slowly motioned for her to put down the knife and adjusted the pink bowtie. "What do you want me to do, then?"

She thought she might be scaring him. *He must think I'm crazy.* She took a deep breath to calm herself. She put the knife down in its place and wiped her clammy palms on the cloth napkin on her lap. She straightened the fabric hanging from her blouse and sat up straight. "I want to you to report him to the public prosecutor and have him arrested. As soon as possible."

"Are you sure?"

She hesitated. *Am I sure? Am I really sure? Yes, I'm sure. I'll have him exactly where I want him on the lawsuit.* "Yes. Do it."

"Then that's what I'll do."

Staring down at the salad, she pushed her fork into the hardboiled egg. She couldn't eat and finally lightly shoved the plate toward the middle of the table. The wine was affecting her.

She put a small crumb of crust from the bread into her mouth. "How did you find out he used Kamran's power of attorney anyway?" she asked.

"I have friends at the *Bank-e Markazi*," he said about the central bank. "I don't want to give you the wrong impression. If I followed a formal process, I would have gotten the same information. But we'd be having this conversation three years from now. So, I bypassed the entire process. I made phone calls. You know," he winked at her, "I know how to get things done."

CHAPTER 12

January 1973, the Next Day, Tehran

———

The Ice Palace was on the second floor of a building in the middle of Tehran. On Wednesday afternoons, the last day of the workweek, Vida left work early. She and several other families from the school took the children ice skating. She longed for Kamran's home movie camera so she could capture these moments, but Doktor had not returned the camera since he borrowed it.

When Vida and the children arrived at the rink, Linda was already sitting at a table by the window in the adjoining restaurant, watching children clumsily glide across the ice. Once Roya and Kasra got situated, Vida poured herself a cup of coffee from the self-service station. She walked slowly not to spill the drink. She had been busy all day and hoped to relax with the cup of coffee and enjoy watching her children skate.

"Is everything okay?" Linda asked. "You seem preoccupied." Linda spoke quietly so the other ladies couldn't hear her.

The prior month, on Christmas day, the *saal*, the one-year anniversary of Kamran's death, after congregating at Nasreen's home for a late lunch, a gathering like the events of the previous year, Vida had done something against the Iranian norm. It was too depressing to go home as the community expected of her, and at the last minute, she and the children went to Linda's home to open presents and celebrate the holiday. At Linda's house, Vida recounted her entire story to her friend. It felt like someone had turned on the faucet, and the whole story poured out of her—the death, the custody issues, and the lawsuit regarding the insurance policy proceeds. She didn't cry but simply recounted the events. Her hands had trembled, but she felt relief talking about her situation.

"Don't mind me," Vida now said, examining the coffee.

Although Vida had recounted the legal issues, she was uncomfortable telling Linda she was about to have her brother-in-law arrested. She didn't want to get into it, not now, not in front of the other mothers. It was all so embarrassing.

Out on the ice, a girl slung her long wool scarf around her belly and then handed the ends of the scarf to Kasra. The girl skated ahead, pulling Kasra with the scarf while he held on. *If the girl stopped, Kasra would fall and hit his head against the ice*, Vida thought. She put her coffee down on the table and was about to head over to the rink to tell them to stop. When she stood up, she saw Nasreen, her sister-in-law, in dark sunglasses and a floral scarf wrapped around her head, rush into the restaurant and scan the room.

Vida knew the plan had been initiated. She looked at the rink and saw Kasra skating on his own now, away from the girl who had been pulling him.

Involuntarily, Vida whispered. "My sister-in-law. I need to go. I'll be back in a few minutes. Please make sure Kasra doesn't fall playing with that scarf." She pointed at the rink.

"Sure. Do what you need to do." Linda stood up. "Kaaaasra, Kasra, honey…" she yelled, walking out close to the rink.

Vida grabbed her purse and intercepted Nasreen, turning her away and walking her out of the cafeteria. Nasreen's voice was hoarse, and she wore no makeup, her red eyes puffy. It was clear to Vida her sister-in-law had been crying.

"What are you doing here?" asked Vida, trying to look puzzled.

"It's Doktor. He's been arrested!" Nasreen burst into tears.

"Oh no," Vida said, keeping her voice level. Deep down she felt strong and confident. *He got what he deserved.*

"It has to do with your lawsuit," her sister-in-law blurted out. Her voice was not accusatory, but then again it wasn't Nasreen's style to be outwardly confrontational, even if deep down she was angry with Vida.

Vida led her by the arm to a corner in the hallway by the stairs. "How do you know?" she asked.

"His secretary said they mentioned something about your lawsuit when they came for him. Vida *joon,* you must do something. We have *a-be-roo...* This is an embarrassment to the whole family and to you too. His career and his patients... Please, do something!"

An embarrassment to me? Vida's face lit with fury. "He's going to have to release my money," Vida said. "Otherwise, it's in the hands of the prosecutor."

"Anything you want. I'll talk to him. Just get him out. Please," Nasreen said, her hands clasped begging.

"Let me call my lawyer."

"Is he involved?" asked Nasreen.

Of course he is involved. Vida was suing Doktor for taking her money. *How could Vakeelee not be involved? Is Nasreen trying to get more information out of me?*

"I don't know anything about this," Vida lied. "Go home, and I'll call you later tonight."

"Vida *joon,* thank you. I'll make sure we make this right. I don't know how this *jarian* got so out of control."

"I don't either," mumbled Vida. Deep down, she was rejoicing.

The two women shuffled down the stairs to the first floor. Vida stood and watched Nasreen go through the glass doors onto Pahlavi Avenue. She had parked right in front of the building. She ducked into her mint green car, checked her face in the rearview mirror, and wiped her eyes with a tissue.

Vida was proud of herself. Finally, what was wrong would be put right. She found a payphone in the lobby and called Vakeelee's office.

"You're calling about what happened earlier today?" her lawyer said in an upbeat voice. "I went to the public prosecutor, as you requested. They must have acted quickly."

"Hmmm," was all she could say. She imagined Doktor sitting on a bench in the jail cell, his collar loosened, his head buried in his hands, no tie, and his jacket folded off to the side. *Do I feel sorry for him?*

"You know, *you* can get him out of jail," her lawyer said.

She paused for a minute. Silence. "I want to make sure we get the money back," she said.

"Believe me, he does not want this to continue. Shall I call the public prosecutor for his release? I can do it now."

Again, she hesitated.

Vida wondered what effect putting Doktor in jail could have on her professional reputation. Her boss, the parents at the children's school, her relatives—what would they all think? Tehran was a small community.

"Vida *khanoom*, are you there?" he asked.

"No… I mean, yes. I'm still here."

"Well? What do you want to do?"

"Let him stay in jail tonight. Call the public prosecutor in the morning and tell him once the funds are returned, I will drop all charges." She worried Doktor might retaliate, but it was too late for that now. Her decision was already made.

"Okay, you got it. Try not to let this bother you too much," he added.

"Bother me? Me?" she repeated.

"I'm just saying…"

"Are you kidding? This doesn't bother me one bit." She didn't want her lawyer to think she had any doubts, but the truth was she did. She couldn't help but wonder how Doktor might seek revenge.

When Vida arrived upstairs at the Ice Palace, the kids were sitting on the bench at the side of the rink and taking off their skates. Linda was in the coffee shop with the other mothers, putting on their coats and getting ready to leave.

"Is everything okay?" Linda asked, leaning over toward Vida so the other ladies couldn't hear her.

She wanted to tell Linda what had happened, but it wasn't the right time or place to get into a long conversation about this personal matter.

Roya was still trying to take off her skates when Vida made her way over to the bench.

"Mom, did you see me skate backward?"

"I did. You were great," Vida said.

Then the little girl turned to her brother. "And what were you and that girl doing with the scarf?"

"Nothing… okay? Why do you ask so many questions?" Kasra barked back, his ears reddening.

* * * * *

The next morning the lawyer called Vida at the office. "He was released this morning. We met with the judge beforehand."

"And?"

"The public prosecutor agreed if he promised to return the funds, they would release him."

"Did he release the funds?" she asked overjoyed.

"No. The judge was insistent he be released based on his good word, given he's a doctor and all."

She slumped in her chair. *Was Doktor going to return her money?* She wasn't sure, but there was nothing to do now.

"But there's more," said the lawyer.

"Oh?"

"Doktor's lawyer requested an investigation."

Vida looked across her desk. Ali had been carrying a stack of books and dropped them.

She raised her eyebrows. "For what?"

"He told the judge he intends to present evidence that you caused Kamran's death because you didn't take proper care of him when he was in London."

"Is this a joke?" Her eyebrows crunched together as she lifted her shoulders.

"No, I'm afraid it's not a joke."

"That's the most ridiculous thing I've ever heard!" She wasn't angry. She was mystified. *How could anyone think such a thing, let alone say it?*

"That's exactly what the judge said. He said it was the most ridiculous thing he had ever heard. I told you Iranian judges are progressive."

"And?" She took in a deep, satisfied breath.

"The judge said he didn't want to hear anything else from Doktor or his lawyer about any of this. And then he ordered us out of the courtroom."

Vida's shoulders dropped, and she sighed.

"It's over. Congratulations," said the lawyer.

Vida tugged gently at the gold chain around her neck, fingering the carnelian pendant. "Now what? How do I get the money back?"

"We will go see Doktor together. Tomorrow. I know he will return the funds."

Vida paused. She remembered her father telling her to handle as much as she could without lawyers. "I'm going to call Doktor, and I will handle this," she said.

* * * * *

The next morning the kids were still sleeping when Vida rose. She called Doktor. She couldn't remember if she had ever done that.

"Thank you for dropping the charges," he said in a soft tone.

Vida was silent. She wanted to be pleasant, but how could she? She would never get over what had happened. "It wasn't my case. It was the public prosecutor."

"Let's meet at Nasreen's house this afternoon," said Doktor.

It's about time, Vida thought. She knew they would be meeting for him to return the funds.

* * * * *

Vida drove alone to Nasreen's house. She was singing along with Sammy Davis, Jr. on the radio. The gates to the front yard were open. As she drove around the gated pool and down the gravel driveway, she spotted Doktor's car, the one he had driven before taking the Mercedes. The small gravel rocks crunched beneath her tires, announcing her approach, but she didn't care. She hit the switch on the radio and stopped singing. Turning off the engine, she looked in the rearview mirror to check her hair and touched the outer edges of her lips to make sure the red lipstick was still intact.

Under the awning at the front entrance, she paused a second to smile, proud of herself for fighting for what was rightfully hers. The check would be the final detail. She gave the doorbell a strong push.

Through the ornate glass door, she could see the family room. When nobody came to the door, she entered. The house was quiet, as it had been the mornings after both the burial and the *hafteh* when she arrived early to receive mourners. The door to the bedroom shared by two of Nasreen's boys was open with nobody inside. *The children must have been sent off to play in the nearby park.*

"Nasreen *khanoom*," Vida called out as she walked through the house. She paused in the front hallway.

Her sister-in-law scuttled out of the kitchen, tying the ends of her purple and pink patterned headdress. She wore a knee-length skirt and a cardigan over a white blouse. *Very formal,* thought Vida.

"*Salam* Vida *khanoom... khoshamadeen,* welcome," she said as if she were announcing Vida's arrival to unseen people. Shaking, she grabbed Vida's arm and whispered, "He's in the dining room, waiting. I'll take your coat."

The two women stepped into the dining room. Vida recalled the *hafteh* when she saw Doktor at the door as she had carried her lunch out, how he smirked, his plans already launched while she was picking out a casket in London.

The twelve-person ornate wooden dining room table was bare. Doktor sat alone with a cup of tea in front of him. He was wearing a white button-down shirt with no tie, the top button undone and his sleeves rolled up. She wondered if this was what he was wearing when he was in jail the night before. Head down, he was reading something on a piece of stationery. Without making eye contact, he glanced up when the two women filed in, and then down again at the paper.

Nasreen pulled out a chair for Vida. "Shall I bring you *chaee*?" she asked.

"No, thank you."

Vida did not know if Nasreen would be joining them, but she hoped she would. She didn't want to sit with Doktor alone. Luckily, her sister-in-law pulled out a chair and sat next to Vida.

Doktor cleared his throat. "Vida *khanoom*, I am not at all happy about what happened…"

Vida stared straight across the table. No expression on her face. She didn't say a word. She had a warm sensation deep in her belly, like she was on fire.

"But… we don't need to discuss that right now. I think its best we put this *jarian* behind us and move forward for the sake of the family and the children."

For the sake of the family… and the children? Vida thought. *What family?* Still, Vida stayed composed. She gazed straight across the table at his face. Then she turned to her sister-in-law and said, "Nasreen *joon*, do you mind getting me a cup of tea too? A light one, please." She already felt jittery but thought the warm liquid might calm her nerves.

"*Ma-loo-meh*, of course," Nasreen said with obvious relief and disappeared into the kitchen.

Doktor sat looking down at the piece of paper, saying nothing.

"Well, where is the check?" Vida asked. What would she do if he wasn't going to give it to her?

"Let's wait for Nasreen to come back."

Vida adjusted herself in her chair, crossing her right leg over the left and then shifting to the other side. Angry. Fuming. She preferred to have a witness to this interaction. She sat patiently. *What now?*

The threat of the public prosecutor pressing charges was still alive, and it seemed to be a part of the air in the room. With each breath, she reminded herself she could not be trapped and Doktor would not dare bring her here, by herself, and then keep the money. Still, she felt unsettled that he wanted a witness before presenting her with the check. She leaned back in her chair and waited, looking down at her fingers.

"*Befarmaeed*," Nasreen said as she set the cup in front of her. "Is the color light enough for you?"

"Thank you," Vida said. Then she looked up at Doktor, cheerfully inquiring, "You were saying?"

"Yes," he said. He cleared his throat again and reached over to his coat, which was resting on the back of the chair. From it he withdrew an envelope and handed it to Vida. She looked inside and saw a check for 315,000 tomans, the equivalent of $45,000 and change.

Vida looked at the check and did a quick calculation in her head. "I had deposited 360,000 tomans in the bank account. What is this?" she said, waving the check at him. Then she threw it back across the table. For an instant the check balanced in the air, curved, and swirled before landing face up, closer to Vida's end of the table.

Nasreen placed a hand on Vida's shoulder, as if to say, "Everything will be all right."

"Vida *khanoom*. Let me explain," he said, raising an eyebrow.

"Yes, do explain," she said shaking. Nasreen's hand was still on her shoulder, offering comfort. She took a sip of the tea and felt warm liquid sliding down her throat. "Yes, explain," Vida repeated in a more relaxed tone. *How could he possibly explain this?*

He unfolded the stationery piece of paper. "First, this money was put into a checking account, so it has not earned any interest. Second, look at this list." He reached across the table and handed Vida a couple of pieces of paper, handwriting on both sides.

It was a list of food items, an accounting from a party:

45 cokes = 158 tomans

30 orders of chelokabab = 840 tomans

18 oranges = 32 tomans

30 teas = 105 tomans

Baklava enough for a count of 30 = 210 tomans

The list went on for one and a half pages, and it wasn't until the end that she realized what it represented.

Bus rental = 350 tomans

Burial stone = 1,000 tomans

Mausoleum = 22,500 tomans—The mausoleum was the most expensive item on the list.

She was being charged for Kamran's funeral expenses. She had not asked for a mausoleum to be purchased for the entire family, nor asked for a busload of people to be taken to the funeral followed by lunch. Why did she have to support the burial for the entire family? Anyway, it wasn't customary for the widow to pay for these charges. What bothered her the most was the presentation of the expenses, now, after all this time. She remembered the day at the burial and sadness returned like a dark black veil, as if she was in Qom at the funeral all over again. She couldn't swallow her own saliva. It felt as if she might choke. If she let herself go, tears would stream down her face. Sadness. Frustration. Anger. *What is it?*

Her sister-in-law leaned over to touch Vida's arm as Vida flipped the pages back and forth. She stared at the entry that read "forty-five cokes." Finally, she pushed Nasreen's arm aside, not wanting to cry.

"This is not okay. It's not okay," Vida yelled. She was furious with him for withholding her money. She felt an urge to reach across the table and strangle him.

"Nasreen *joon*, where is the phone? I'm calling Vakeelee. He needs to notify the public prosecutor."

Nasreen's face got pale. She eyed Doktor.

Doktor cleared his throat and stood. "Um, I mean…" he said.

Vida stood up and pounded the table. "I want the phone," she said.

Doktor sat back down and reached for his coat pocket and patted his shirt trying to find something. "Wait," he said. "Wait."

"Wait for what?" she screamed. She was still standing.

"I'll write the balance. I… uhh… need to find my checkbook," he said. Doktor wrote the second check.

Vida pulled it from his fingers, scooped up the first check lying on the table, and marched out of the room.

Nasreen followed, pulling at the ends of her headscarf and tightening it. "Are you okay? Are you okay?"

"I'm fine." Vida smiled at her as she stepped outside, though she felt herself on the verge of tears. She did not want Nasreen to see her cry.

The sister-in-law followed her to the car.

Vida dug in her purse for the car keys.

"Are you going to call Dr. Vakeelee?" Nasreen asked, pushing back her headscarf.

Vida wondered if Nasreen knew about all the deductions before the meeting.

"I need to go home," she said. Her heart was racing, and she couldn't think. Not now.

"I understand," said Nasreen.

Vida looked at the gravel and remembered the *hafteh,* when she had walked over to the Mercedes and noted the scratch from the time they dropped off the movie camera at Doktor's house. When she got into the car, she rolled down the window and said, "Nasreen *khanoom,* one last thing."

"Anything."

"Can you please get back the movie camera from Doktor?"

"What movie camera?" Nasreen asked.

"Kamran's movie camera. Doktor has it. Inside the case, we have all our home movies. I need it back."

"Sure, of course. But please, please, whatever you do, don't call Dr. Vakeelee."

Vida didn't respond. She rolled up the window and smiled. As she backed out of the gravel driveway, Nasreen, looking worried, waved at her.

Vida would have told her how much she had grown to despise Doktor, but the meeting had exhausted her. She could hardly feel her hands on the steering wheel, and her legs were numb. When she lifted her foot off the clutch, the car stalled. Anger had crept into the crevices of her body.

Doktor had charged her for the coke and the kababs at the funeral, for his own brother's funeral, a grand funeral he had planned and one she could not afford. He'd charged her for the cost of a mausoleum to house the bodies of the entire family.

The gate was still open. Vida backed out and drove to the end of the street, the wheels screeching as she took the left turn. At the traffic light she saw a woman holding a little boy's hand and a young girl leaving a pastry shop with several stacked boxes tied with pink ribbon. She wished her life could be about such mundane things instead of family wars and grief. Still, she had two large checks in her purse, and before long, she found herself gazing at the blossoms on the trees and the men perched on a half-built new structure rising in an alley.

Turning on the radio to the American station she heard the upbeat voice of Casey Kasem announcing the Top 40 popular records.

The music started to play, and her mood lifted. She had a satisfying job with the American Embassy, her children attended a great school, they were healthy, and she had a supportive family—one that even had a place for Maman. At least now she had recovered her money. What else could she ask for? When she heard Ray Charles, she adjusted her sunglasses and rolled down the window. The air was warm. It was spring. At first, she hummed and then shook her head from side-to-side singing, "Hit the Road Jack."

She was screaming out the words of the song, tapping her fingers against the steering wheel with the fresh air against her face. She felt liberated. She had taken care of herself in a way she had never done before, and she was proud of herself.

* * * * *

A few days later, Nasreen called. At first it was the pleasantries and then a pause.

"I'm calling about the movie camera."

Vida did not respond.

"You're not going to believe it, but... um... Doktor's house was burglarized last night," she said.

An expected silence fell on the line. Vida did not say a word. Her jaw dropped.

"The movie camera was sitting in the entryway by the front door. Doktor was going to return it to you. *Khodaro shokr, khodaro shokr,* thank God, the burglar just got through the front door and must have realized the family was home. Nobody was hurt."

"Did he take the camera?" asked Vida.

"The case and everything in it. Thank God the family is safe."

Vida took a deep breath. She couldn't tell if Nasreen believed the lies or not, but it didn't matter. She was done with all the problems. She remembered her father's dying wish for her to resolve the issues.

"Thank God nobody was hurt," repeated Nasreen.

Vida did not respond. She was sad to think she would never see the home movies, the baseball games, and even Roya naked in the bathtub in New York. She didn't care if anybody had gotten hurt in the burglary. All she knew was her family history had vanished. Wiped out.

PART II

PART II

CHAPTER 13

Summer 1975, Tehran

——

"Are we there yet?" Seven-year-old Roya bounced up and down on the backseat of the car as they drove through the parking lot to the country club. Birds were chirping, and it was a comfortable, dry seventy-five degrees. Linda had invited Vida and the children to join her family at their fancy country club. Vida had been there once before with Linda and her husband for dinner.

The place was exclusive and reminded Vida of a country club in Westchester she once visited when Kamran was invited by a doctor friend. A formal dining room occupied the second floor of the clubhouse with a more casual restaurant and informal sitting area on the first, where oversized paintings with English-equestrian settings hung from the wall. In the gift shop on the first floor, a wide variety of imported European and American gum, candy, and chocolates were stacked on a rack next to *Time Magazine*, *International Herald Tribune*, and other foreign publications.

From inside the clubhouse Vida could see an Olympic-sized pool with two-tiered diving boards and a separate children's pool with a perfectly maintained golf course in the distance. Club members sunbathed on lounge chairs with lime green and orange cushions. The club was a patch of modernity and luxury in the middle of Tehran. The guests dressed in Western attire, veil-covered women outside its exclusive gates.

Vida and Linda stretched out on lounge chairs in their one-piece bathing suits, over which they wore loose cover-ups. Leaning on their elbows, they monitored the kids through oversized sunglasses, while Roya, Kasra, Sandy, and Sam climbed the diving boards and did cannonballs into the pool.

A tall handsome man wearing a tight racing Speedo and orange tinted sunglasses waved at them from a distance—no doubt at Linda, since Vida did not know him. He was sitting with two chunky, longhaired Iranian women, bleached blonde, string bikinis with small bows holding their lumpy bottoms in place and their tops barely covering their breasts.

Linda gave a half smile. "Those two women are something," she said.

Vida glanced over at the man, careful not to move her head too much in his direction. One of the women flipped her hair to the side, handed the man a bottle of suntan oil, and sat crossed legged facing away from him. He rubbed the oil over her back, at times lifting the strap of her bikini top with one hand while rubbing underneath the strap with the other. Then the three of them huddled, bursting out laughing.

Vida was not shocked to see Iranian women behave like this. Even Linda, a California native, was more conservative than these women.

Vida thought about her father telling her if it wasn't for Reza Shah forcing women to rid themselves of the veil in 1936, these uneducated women would still be at home, praying and doing *namaz* five times a day. She felt a revulsion toward these women who lived such contradictory lives, so different than Vida. Her father would have labeled them as hookers. Vida recognized politically Iran had come such a long way from when she was growing up.

"That man over there," said Linda nodding in his direction. "He's a good man."

Vida's pulse increased. She perked up a bit. She thought him a playboy but found him attractive. She didn't want to admit to herself she could possibly find another man attractive. It had been four years since Kamran's death. *Is it time to move on?*

In late afternoon, Vida, Linda, and the children wandered back toward the clubhouse. Vida's fashionable sunglasses rested on top of her head. She had changed into a pink and orange striped buttoned-down shirt with a big white collar and dark bell-bottomed pants. She undid the top button of the shirt.

Roya and Kasra ran behind Sam and Sandy, who apparently knew where they were going. The two mothers strolled behind. Vida didn't notice where he came from, but the tall man from the pool appeared and kissed Linda on both cheeks. He was wearing an untucked button-down shirt, and a tuft of soft salt-and-pepper chest hair was visible where the first few buttons were left undone. He wore a thin gold chain, his wet hair slicked back. Vida could smell a trace of fresh and spicy cologne.

"Linda *joon,* where is your *agha*?" he asked, referring to her husband.

Vida shaded her eyes with her hand, paying him little heed as she pretended to look uninterested while searching for her children who had run off ahead.

"My *aga*?" she said, pronouncing her Farsi word with a heavy accent. "He's in the clubhouse playing backgammon."

"Is that where you ladies are heading?" the man asked, glancing in Vida's direction.

"Yeah…" Linda giggled, tugging at Vida's arm and turning her back to him.

Why is Linda giggling, and why is she dismissing the man so quickly? "A friend of yours?" Vida asked.

Smiling, Linda said, "His name is Cyrus. He's a friend of ours… my husband's. I'm not sure he's your type."

Vida raised her eyebrow, embarrassed and a bit hurt Linda would make such a judgment about her as if she was going to pick him up. *What is my type?* She couldn't fathom the idea of a man in her life.

"He's single, a lot of fun, and a successful businessman. I'm still trying to figure out if he would ever commit to any *one* woman."

Vida moved her arm away. She pulled at the strap of the purse on her shoulder, crossing her arms. *I shouldn't be thinking of another man. It's too soon.* She didn't want Linda to know secretly she thought this man was handsome. She touched the back of her hair, straightening strands that may have strayed out of order. She wanted to say something to set Linda straight. *It's not the right time,* she reminded herself.

The two continued climbing the white marble stairs. In the club house, the grand leather-studded couches were arranged around dark wood coffee tables, like miniature living rooms. Men played backgammon as they nursed cocktails, and the ladies lounged, legs crossed, and leaned in close to each other, examining their surroundings and chatting. It was a loud space, and Vida felt uncomfortable not knowing anyone, but she surveyed the room, thinking she might recognize a face.

The two women wandered over to Linda's husband, who was sitting on the corner of one of the couches with his finger pressing on a checker piece as he pondered the next backgammon move.

Kasra and Roya begged for money to buy Butterfingers and Cadbury chocolate at the gift shop with the other kids.

As he was rolling the dice, Linda's husband looked up at Vida. "Do you think you might want to join the club?" he asked, looking back at the backgammon set.

Joining the club was far beyond her budget, but he didn't need to know. "The kids have had such a great day here," she said.

"Well, I wouldn't bother trying, if I were you. The club doesn't allow single women to join," he said.

Vida tugged at the carnelian necklace, sliding it back and forth. *What an ass. Typical Iranian male chauvinist who thinks a woman can't support herself.*

"Can you imagine? All the older single women would join to pick up rich men," he replied matter-of-factly. Then he stood up and yelled, "Yes... *joft sheesh*," before playing out his double sixes.

Vida wondered if the comment was directed at her. She didn't consider herself old at thirty-five. After all, she was not looking for a husband, rich or poor. Then she remembered the two women sitting at the pool. *Maybe he was referring to those women?* Vida thought.

Linda, who was standing, touched Vida's shoulder. "Do you see that woman there in the corner? Her kids go to our school."

Is she trying to change the subject? Vida glanced up and noticed the handsome man from the pool enter from another entrance. He shook another man's hand and began to look out into the crowd of people. Her heart started to beat faster.

He spotted Vida. At first he meandered then walked over and took a seat next to her on the couch.

Linda smiled and looked the other way.

"Cyrus," he said as he held out his hand.

"Vida," she responded, shaking his hand. She was taken aback by how close he sat to her. Her palms felt moist. He had large fingers with bunches of tiny hairs above his knuckles and a warm firm handshake. She wasn't used to an Iranian man shaking her hand. Iranian men who knew her well, relatives, would greet her with kisses on her cheeks. Others, like Linda's husband, might say hello and look the other way.

"Linda tells me your children go to school with hers," Cyrus said.

Linda tells me you might be a playboy. She was giggling inside. She glanced at him and smiled. She couldn't help wondering what kind of a man he was and whether he was a ladies' man or whether that was his reputation.

"Yes. Our kids go to school together," she said.

"I understand you work at the Abraham Lincoln Library?" he asked.

Though surprised by his forward questions, she appreciated his directness. She wondered how he knew anything about her. Most Iranians were not direct and would draw out answers by firing off questions, but Vida could tell this man was not typically Iranian.

"I…" As she was about to answer the question, Vida noticed her cousin waving from across the room. She stood up and smiled, a familiar face. He wandered over, kissed her on both cheeks, then shook Cyrus's hand.

He turned to Vida. "How are the kids? How did the move go?"

How does he know Cyrus? She felt relieved to see a family member and happy to know the cousin knew Cyrus—an instant connection. "They're running around somewhere," she said, surveying the room. "What are *you* doing here?"

"I'm a member. Are you having fun?" He had a big grin on his face.

"Love it," she said.

Standing next to her, he leaned close and interlaced his arm with hers. "Yes… and if you're interested in joining the club, let me know. You know, *Amoo Soli* is the president," he boasted, referring to his wife's uncle. Vida glanced over at Linda's husband. She wanted to strike him, the way her father used to smack their gardener in the back of the head when the poor man made a mistake, but she held back.

Right then Linda's husband looked up from his backgammon game. He must have heard the cousin's comment.

"*Salam… chetoree,*" he said to the cousin, nodding but not getting up from his seat.

The cousin nodded back. "Hey," he said and then turned his back the other way and rolled his eyes. Vida could understand why they weren't friends.

The cousin turned to Cyrus. "How is business?"

"We just finished the nursery for the factory."

"Is the nursery on the property?" the cousin asked.

Overhearing this conversation, Vida was enjoying learning about Cyrus.

"Yes, right on the premises. I figure if the women can have their children close by, they will be much more productive and less distracted. It takes one worry off their minds, especially with the newborns. The mothers can be available for regular feedings."

"*Afareen*, forward thinking. If only we could get our government to be as open-minded as you are," said the cousin.

"I'm being practical. By putting in a nursery I can hire husbands and wives together. I don't have to rely on foreign labor."

"That's terrific, man. With the amount of construction and factories around here, I imagine it's tough to find good workers these days."

"Yes, for sure. With unemployment next to nothing, it *is* tough to find good help. Building the nursery has become quite political. I got a lot of resistance from the Iranian board members. What a headache," he said rolling his eyes. "I'm glad the German members were able to convince the others it was the right thing to do."

"Fantastic," said the cousin.

It was rare for an Iranian businessman to be concerned with hiring women and especially mothers. She was happy to hear the German government was so influential on the Iranian one. Although she wasn't politically active, how could she ignore all the political advancement in Iran? She wondered what Cyrus would think about her situation with the custody battle.

"Speaking of nurseries," her cousin said, "I have to go find my kids, the little rascals… They're taking tennis lessons."

Cyrus turned to Vida. "Do you…" It seemed he was about to ask Vida a question when they were interrupted again by swarming children.

Sandy and Sam climbed on Cyrus's lap, touching his hair and talking over each other. "Uncle Cyrus, Uncle Cyrus… remember when… and can you make the trumpet sound?"

Vida couldn't quite make out what they were all talking about, but she noticed Roya standing to the side, intrigued. She remembered Kamran used to make a trumpet sound when Roya would sit on his lap.

During all of this, Kasra leaned on the couch next to his mother and studied the continuing backgammon game. He was so reserved.

Roya sat on Vida's lap and observed the other kids, as if she was planning to get in on the action with Cyrus. Finally, she interrupted them. "What's your name, Uncle Cyrus?" she asked.

The adults laughed, Linda's kids looked at her, and Kasra rolled his eyes.

Roya ignored them in her usual focused and determined way. "Oh yeahhh," she said in a long-drawn-out way, peeking at her mother, as if she was embarrassed but unwilling to admit it. Roya paused for a moment, looking down. Then she whispered, "It's Uncle Cyrus." With a puzzled look, she turned to him. "Are you *really* their uncle?"

Cyrus continued to make the trumpet sound while he stared at Roya. The little girl watched him in amazement, her jaw wide open. It was fun for Vida to watch Roya interact with this handsome man. Still, her shoulders felt tight. She couldn't imagine a man in her life, living with her and the kids, ever.

He held Roya's little fingers in his wide palm. "Well… you see… I am a close friend of those two," he said, pointing in the direction of Linda who was listening intently. Her husband was focused on winning the game; most of his opponent's checkers were off the board.

"Can I call you Uncle Cyrus too?" Roya asked in a sweet soft voice. She was blinking as fast as she could.

"Sure you can," he said, rubbing her tiny fingers.

Vida wondered how much Roya must be longing for a father figure and was curious as to whether Roya remembered Kamran making the same trumpet sound. She felt a heaviness in her chest and looked down. Her little daughter missed having a male presence in her life. Vida did too.

Sam suggested Kasra go play ping-pong, and the two ran off. Roya stayed behind. First, she stood up from Vida's lap, and then she squeezed her little body between Cyrus and Vida, making herself comfortable in the middle of them.

"Can I ask you another question?" she asked, gazing up at Cyrus.

"Sure, anything." He put his arm around her.

"If you're my uncle, then how come you never come to our house?"

A flush crept across Vida's cheeks. She cleared her throat.

Linda was deep in conversation with another lady and was no longer focused on the little girl's conversation.

"Roya. Stop asking so many questions," Vida said, gawking at her daughter.

Cyrus smiled confidently and peered into Vida's eyes. "I've never been invited."

Vida blushed. She wondered what Cyrus would think of her house. When Vida got her money back from Doktor she had bought a duplex, moved in upstairs with the kids, and rented the downstairs unit.

"Can you come to our house today? Mommy, can Uncle Cyrus come to our house today? *Pleeeaaaase*?" she said, bouncing up and down on the couch in between the two adults.

Reddened, Vida stood up and said, "Roya…" *She is so fixated on this man*, Vida thought.

Roya hopped off the couch and tugged at Cyrus's fingers. "Uncle Cyrus, come on, let's go to our house. I want to ride in your car."

Vida asked Roya to stop, but a part of her was glad her daughter was being so persistent. She got up and placed her purse on her shoulder. "Actually, we'd better go home. It's getting late."

"I have to go too," he said. "I'll walk you out to the parking lot."

Not knowing what to think, Vida gave Linda a hug. "Thank you so much for a great day. I'll call you later," she said.

Kasra skipped over after he saw the group get up to leave, and the four pushed through the glass doors and strolled out of the clubhouse.

When they got to the parking lot, Roya was still insisting Cyrus come to their house.

"I'll follow you home. Okay?" he said.

Vida had a wide grin, but she clenched her jaw.

I don't want him to come into the house. What if the neighbors see him? Or what if Doktor or one of Kamran's other relatives drops by unannounced? They never do, but with my luck they will today. It could be dangerous. And I don't have anything to make for dinner. Her thoughts were firing away. She wanted to invite him over, but she hardly knew this man.

Roya asked to ride in his mustard yellow Ford Mustang, but Vida refused. *How can I let Roya sit in a car with a stranger?* Cyrus looked like a race car driver with his leather gloves and the brown leather wrapped steering wheel.

At the traffic light, he pulled up next to Vida's green Iranian-made Paykan and revved the engine. Roya leaned forward, grinning broadly and waving at Cyrus. Kasra gave a half-smile, seemingly uninterested in his sister's enthusiasm. Vida felt her cheeks flush again.

When they got to the house, Cyrus came to the passenger's side and lifted Roya out of Vida's car.

"I'll come over another time, Roya. I promise," he said.

The little girl jumped toward Cyrus and gave him a lingering hug around his legs. He shook Vida's hand lightly, struck Kasra's back, locked eyes with Vida, and then drove off.

Unable to focus, Vida's palms felt moist again, and her heart was racing. She had expected him to invite himself in and was disappointed when he didn't. But she viewed the gesture as a sign of respect for her.

CHAPTER 14

Summer 1975, the Next Day, Tehran

––––

The next morning Cyrus called Vida at the office and asked her to lunch.

What if this turns out to be a romantic relationship? What if one of my in-laws sees us together? What will happen to the children? What about the custody laws?

Nasreen, who had lost her husband at a young age, never looked at a man after her husband died. At least, that's what the family said. In the same way, it would not be acceptable for Vida to have a male friend, even if she didn't have any pending legal issues. Then she recalled his smile and fingered the back of her hair.

After the call, Vida stepped over into the kitchen. Ali sat in front of a large glass of tea, a small plate with a block of feta cheese, a sheet of *lavash* bread, and an open jar of honey. Looking quite focused, he had a spoon in his hand. He had scooped a healthy portion of honey into his mouth when Vida arrived.

"Good morning. You're here early," she said, reaching for her coffee mug in the cupboard.

Ali swallowed hard. "Good morning, *khanoom*," he said, referring to Vida in his usual formal way. He was squinting as if he had downed a spoonful of awful tasting medicine, but he reached wrist-deep into the jar for another scoop.

"Ali *agha*, you're eating an awful lot of honey. You're going to get sick."

"I know. I don't like honey." He coughed.

"So why are you eating so much of it?" Vida hovered over him.

"*Khanoom*, my wife is pregnant again," he said in a disappointed tone.

"Congratulations," Vida offered.

"It's only good news if it turns out to be a boy."

When Vida had interviewed him for the job at the library, Ali already had three daughters. His first born, Ayshe, was named after the prophet Mohammed's controversial wife, whom the prophet had married when he was fifty-three years old and she a mere nine-year-old girl. Shortly after he was hired, his fourth girl, Asieh, was born, right behind Atefeh and Afsaneh. The following year, his twin girls, Azita and Azadeh, were born.

"And, well…" he continued, "my neighbor told me if I eat honey, it'll be a boy this time." Ali looked like he might burst into tears.

Vida had seen this many times before. She wanted to chuckle, but she wanted to respect him in this moment.

Ali's ignorant comment about the honey made Vida laugh. It was so ridiculous. "Ali, for God's sake, stop eating it…" She took a sip of her coffee. "You're going to get diabetes. And you don't really believe the nonsense about having a boy. Do you? Your wife is already pregnant."

Ali crossed his arms, pushing out his chest. He was wearing an Adidas T-shirt, a hand-me-down from one of the library staffers. "*Khanoom*, my neighbor is the son of an imam. He knows these sorts of things."

Vida figured this must be coming from religious ignorance, but she didn't want to be rude to him. She walked out of the kitchen and over to one of the male staff members in the library. "You have to tell Ali to stop having so many children. He's never going to have a boy," she said. She told him the story, and the man smirked.

"I'll talk to him," the staffer promised.

Vida went back to her desk, and about an hour later her employee rushed over to the desk.

"You're not going to believe this," he said laughing out loud.

"What's so funny?" asked Vida. She rested her elbows on the desk, anxious to hear the story.

"I pulled Ali aside." The employee was laughing so hard he could barely speak.

Vida smiled. "What did you say?"

"I suggested a vasectomy."

Vida blushed. "And?"

"He got teary-eyed and grabbed his private parts and said, 'Such things are against God's will. All you people travel and have entertainment. This is the only thing I have. And now you want to take it away from me? It's against God' will... *panah bar khoda*,' And then he wept and walked away with one hand raised above his head, looking up at the ceiling as if toward God, the other hand firmly holding on to his crotch."

Vida remembered the heavy winter snowstorm after she had hired Ali, when he complained of a leaky roof. She collected money from her staff, and together they hired a contractor to put in a new roof for him. Then that spring, when Ali mentioned his wife's only wish was to travel to the holy city of Mashhad for *ziarat*, Vida funded the pilgrimage for the whole family. She was always thinking of ways to better Ali's life. She felt badly when he complained of the difference between his life and that of the others in the library, not having any entertainment.

Still, despite what Vida had done for the janitor, she knew when it came to devouring the honey, the son of an imam would be more convincing than she or anyone else at the library.

When the phone rang a few minutes later she picked it up.

"Excuse me," she said to her colleague. Vida cleared her throat.

It was Cyrus on the other end of the line. No pleasantries. "There is a problem."

Her palms got moist at the sound of his voice.

"The driver took the car for an oil change an hour ago and hasn't come back. I hate to ask this of you, but can you pick me up? I had made reservations at La Residence near the library," he said with a French accent, "but I'll have to cancel it."

The restaurant was located on Boulevard Elizabeth, named after Queen Elizabeth, a wide French-style boulevard lined with trees where many posh restaurants and nice shops had recently been built. She was excited to try the new restaurant, but it was too far for her to pick him up, drive to the restaurant, and then back to his office. It would take too much time. So, La Residence would have to wait for another time, and she was disappointed.

"That's not a problem," she said. Any typical Iranian woman might have felt awkward about picking up a man, especially one she didn't know well, but she didn't mind. She didn't think of herself as typical.

In the car she turned on the radio, and the American station was playing "Let's Get It On." Lightly tapping her fingers on the steering wheel and humming as she drove, she couldn't help but remember the fake blonde women at the country club. *Does Cyrus prefer those types of women? If he was with one of them, what would I do if I got pregnant, like Ali's wife? Has Cyrus gotten a vasectomy?*

A cat was lazily crossing the street. By the time she saw the creature and slammed on the brakes, Cyrus was already stripped naked in her mind's eye, and Roya was poking her head into the bedroom saying, "Can I ask one more question?" She missed the cat and laughed at herself. *How can I be thinking these things about him?*

Vida thought she knew the general neighborhood when she headed toward his office, but distracted by her thoughts, she ended up taking a wrong turn into a one-way alley. She drove down several narrow lanes, leaning out the window to read the street signs, careful not to fall into the *joob*, the ditches on the side of the road. Finally, she found herself on a narrow residential path—lost. She was angry with herself for running late, really late. She searched for someone, anyone, who could give her directions.

Finally, she spotted a short bald man in loose pajama pants and plastic slippers using a hose to water down a driveway. When she stopped to ask for directions, he had his head down, his finger on the hose, spraying the water.

"Excuse me, do you know where I can find *Takh-te Jamsheed* Avenue? I'm looking for—"

The man turned. He must have forgotten he had the hose in his hand, and as he started to say, "It's in that direction," instead of pointing with his finger, he pointed the hose at the car.

Before she knew what had happened, Vida was sitting in a puddle, water dripping from the tip of her nose. Too shocked to say anything, she listened to his directions and then rolled up the window. She was soaked. She turned off the radio and drove off. *What now?* Her hair was ruined. Her first reaction was to go home, but she changed her mind. She wanted to see Cyrus, she had to get back to work, and she was already close by. She made a quick decision to pick him up anyway.

When she drove up, he was standing in front of his office building. He grinned as he got into the car, probably holding back the chuckles, and didn't say anything at first. They both exploded in laughter.

She drove them to her house, and while he waited in the car, she went upstairs to change and fix her hair as best she could.

They ended up at an Indian restaurant close to her house.

"I had a lot of Indian food when I went to boarding school outside London. Love it," she said.

"Boarding school? How did that happen?"

"After my parents got divorced, my father thought it would be good for me to get out of Iran to study. I wanted to go to school in Vienna. I love music."

"So why didn't you?" Cyrus asked.

"You know how it is in Iran. It's not the right thing to be a musician."

"The ridiculous ideas Iranians have. And how did you end up with the library job?" he asked.

The waiter came by to take their order. Cyrus was polite with the waiter, asking about his day. She took mental note of this. *What a kind man.* Many Iranians were unkind to hired help.

The conversation grew serious fast, and she heard herself telling him more than she had planned, about Kamran, life in American, his death, and then the custody issue. For some reason she trusted this man. She didn't elaborate on the lawsuit regarding the money. She didn't want him to think she had financial problems.

"What about you?" she asked, hoping to get information on his personal situation.

"I want to know more about this custody issue," he insisted.

Vida looked back at him. It was his turn.

"Me? I run a telecommunications joint venture between the Iranian and German governments, busy running the factory."

He hadn't answered her question about his personal status. She wanted to know whether he had ever been married and if he had any children. But she didn't want to press the issue, not this early.

"A joint venture with Germany?"

"I travel quite a bit to Munich."

She wondered what it would be like to date a man who was away so much, but she tried not to let her mind wander too far. She was getting ahead of herself. Dating would be complicated, after all, and would have to be a secret. She thought maybe it was for the best he traveled. "Any other interests?" She didn't want to get too personal.

"I'm active with the government," he said.

She took a gulp of water and started to cough. Some of the water dripped on her skirt. She patted it down with the linen napkin. Vida's father had been a government employee.

"Are you okay?" he asked.

"It went down the wrong way. You were saying?" she prompted, dabbing the napkin on her lips. She coughed a bit more.

"I am head of a political committee in parliament. I've been involved in Shiraz, where we run the joint venture. We've initiated a lot of changes," he said.

"I can imagine. I heard you talk about the nursery you put in place at the factory."

"That's only part of it. A lot more needs to happen at work and in this country," he offered.

He chose his words carefully and didn't share any details about his personal life. Based on how involved he was in his work, Vida figured he was single, but she did wonder whether he had been married and if he had any children.

"Your issue with custody of your children... it's an interesting one," he said.

"It is what it is," she said, shrugging her shoulders. "It's the law. We've been fighting this battle for four years. My lawyer keeps getting an extension of my temporary custody. There is nothing I can do." She was interested in his opinion and his political views, but she thought the conversation was getting serious. Fast. She scooped up more rice.

"The Iranian government has been changing since the late 1960s with the rise in the reform movement."

She poured the yellow curry over her rice.

"And the Family Protection Laws changed a lot of things... but not enough," he continued.

She remembered her first conversation with her lawyer. Vakeelee had told her about the Family Protection Laws parliament passed in the late 1960s. The laws created significant advancement for women's rights, but the legal system was hard to update because it was based on ancient Islamic laws, which were not friendly toward women.

"There has always been serious opposition to the regulations by the clergy. The religious figures don't like the liberal rules because they conflict with strict *shi'a* laws and the Koran."

She had heard this and was interested in learning more from this man.

"In the mid-sixties, the first female senator in Iran proposed a forward-looking bill for women's rights. Unfortunately, her bill was rejected. In fact, her life was threatened. After that, in 1967, the Family Protection Law passed, partly because of her efforts but mostly because of the influence of the more open-minded leading clergy."

How interesting a female senator proposed change. I didn't even know we have female senators?

"The laws are still backward in this country. I can't imagine ever getting guardianship of my children, even in these modern times," said Vida.

"This is where you are wrong. I think *never* is too strong a word." He leaned back on his chair, rocking on the two hind legs of his seat.

"It's the law. Iran is a tribal country, and the laws don't recognize a mother as the official parent of her own children. I can't even take my children on vacation outside the country without asking for permission." This was such a personal issue, and Vida was getting uncomfortable with this conversation. *He probably has no children and does not understand my situation.*

Cyrus broke off a piece of the naan and dipped it into the curry sauce. Without looking at her, he said calmly and in a low voice, "I understand. But my point is there are people out there who, in the background, have been pushing for more forward-looking women's rights, and things *will* change."

She wanted to end the conversation. She sat back staring at him, unconvinced. On the wall she saw a poster of Indira Gandhi surrounded by children. Finally, she asked, "What do you mean?"

"There has been a lot of discontent within the government with the passage of the 1967 law because it did not advance women's rights enough. It simply didn't go far enough."

"How do you know?" She played with her food and looked up at him. Now he had piqued her interest. She tried not to lose her composure.

"Well, let's just say I hear a lot of things at these political meetings. In my line of work, we need women in the factories. We need women working, not distracted by family issues. If they can't focus, it has a direct impact on my business. I must be vocal and get involved in these issues. Plus, I care. I have sisters, I have nieces. I know what it's like for women in this country."

"What exactly do you mean by *things will change*?" She leaned into the table.

"There are rumors the Women's Organization of Iran is pushing for total equality." He gazed into her eyes. "Mark my words. When it comes to women's rights, this country will be more modern than Germany, France... even America. A lot is going on."

In her left palm she held the *aghigh*, the carnelian necklace, rubbing the smooth side. She didn't believe the laws in Iran could change, but she believed this man. Modern laws in Iran, the way Cyrus described them, sounded too good to be true. *He probably knows something*, she thought.

"Don't worry," he said, placing his hand on hers.

She took a quick breath.

"Believe me, things will change, and you'll be the first to know," he said.

Gently, she pulled her hand away. She hadn't felt this kind of attraction in a long time.

When she drove him back to his office, he kissed the back of her hand. "Let's do this again... soon," he said.

She looked at the back of her hand. A thrill, like a spark, ran up her arm.

* * * * *

A week later, Vida heard her lawyer's voice on the other end of the phone.

"I have good news. We must celebrate. Now it's time for *sheernee*," he said.

"Oh?" She hesitated to hear what was next.

"The newly amended Family Protection Laws, granting widows the right to guardianship of their children, just passed. It hasn't been announced yet, but it will."

Vida covered her mouth with one hand.

"What does this mean?"

"The new laws mean Roya and Kasra can live with you under the same roof, without the threat of losing them hovering over your head. And you can travel with them, outside the country if you want."

She looked up to the heavens. She felt blessed knowing Iranian lawyers and politicians had pushed for the enactment of modern family protection laws, and now she was the legal guardian of her children. *How much did Vakeelee have to do with changing the laws? And what did Cyrus know that he did not share when we had lunch?* She wouldn't be stopped or questioned at the border to prove she was the mother of her own children, the mother who had already transported Roya and Kasra back and forth between Tehran, London, and New York so many times.

"What now?"

"That's it. There's no formal meeting to finalize the custody issue. We're done," he said.

Vida looked up again and mouthed... thank you. She couldn't believe it. Her children were hers. She was free to move back to America, but now she wasn't sure she wanted to leave. *Maybe I'll stay here after all.*

CHAPTER 15

Spring 1976, Washington, DC

———

In early 1976, Mrs. White was promoted to head of the US Information System, USIS, in Tehran and recommended Vida as her replacement to take over as chief librarian. For the first time since Kamran's death, Vida felt a sense of belonging and accomplishment, an opportunity to build a career. The USIS libraries were each led by Americans, and to Vida, it was an honor they trusted a non-American for this position in Tehran. Family members had said she could be accused of being CIA since she was moving up the ranks within the US Embassy system. *There's no way anybody would think I'm a spy.*

In Tehran, Vida's new position at work included managing a growing staff, traveling within Iran to the satellite offices, attending training and conferences outside of Iran in countries like Israel, and participating in protocol activities when diplomats visited. When she needed to travel within Iran, she took the kids with her. They snapped pictures in front of the *Takht-e Jamshid* ruins at the Persepolis in Shiraz. At the *Chehel Sotoun* Pavilion in Isfahan the kids pretended to be ambassadors, receiving dignitaries in the stately reception halls. The first time the children entered a mosque was when they visited the Imam Reza shrine in Mashhad. Kasra grabbed his nose and complained of sweat and body odor stench. When they left the mosque, they discovered Roya's shoes had been stolen—it was required to take off your shoes before going into a mosque—and the little girl asked if God had taken her shoes to give to the poor.

During the weekdays, the children's guitar, piano, soccer, and ballet lessons consumed Vida, and in the evenings she engaged with work-related cocktails and dinner parties. When Cyrus was not traveling for work, he would invite her to lunch. Eventually, lunches became long dinners that ended with a glass of port and more than a kiss at her place. On those evenings when he came to pick her up, as she climbed into his Mach 1 Mustang, she looked in all directions to make sure nobody saw them.

At times the two of them would go to evening parties together, but only with a close group of friends. Even though the laws in Iran had changed, Vida felt it was inappropriate for her to advertise having a male partner. She couldn't erase from her mind the many months of intense fear she'd experienced when she thought she would lose her children. It didn't feel right to flaunt such a relationship because the laws had changed.

When she got promoted, she hired a maid, Zahra *khanoom*, a strong-willed, heavy-set older woman from Shiraz, to come to the house to cook and clean. The maid's thin black hair was regularly worn in a long braid, stuck out from beneath her multicolored *roosari*. Vida trained the maid to prepare larger portions of Persian stews and to freeze the *khoresht*. On longer workdays the maid would defrost the frozen meal and start the rice cooker before Vida got home.

When Vida had evening plans, the maid was happy to stay with the kids, entertaining them and recounting tales like the one about the time she was shot and her father threw her on the back of a horse and rode seven hundred kilometers from her village near Shiraz to a hospital in Tehran. The maid ran the household as if it was her own, and that gave Vida the peace of mind to invest the time she needed at her job.

After being promoted at the library, Vida was invited to Washington, DC, for a week-long training session on "push button education." She pondered leaving the children in Tehran with Homa or Maman, but she couldn't. The memory of the custody battle was still raw, and she wanted to be close to the children, so she reached out and decided to leave the kids with Rosemary in New York, a short flight from Washington, DC.

*   *   *   *   *

After the nine-hour flight, Vida and her children landed at JFK airport. Vida walked by a newsstand and picked up the latest *Newsweek* magazine, flipping through the pages. Jimmy Carter had won the Iowa Democratic Caucus, Diana Ross and the Supremes had completed their farewell tour, the first 4.6 miles of the Washington, DC, metro underground system had recently opened, and the

US Treasury Department had reintroduced the two-dollar bill as part of the upcoming US bicentennial celebration.

As she strolled toward baggage claim, she saw a poster with a giant apple striped with different colors with a bite taken out of the side, underneath it the words "Personalized computers by Apple."

It had been more than five years since Vida had been in New York. The airport was calm and organized compared to what she had left at Mehrabad Airport.

Exiting customs, Vida worried she might not recognize Rosemary, but there she was, the same Rosemary, just an older, heavier version. Her rich black eyes shone, and her straight, shoulder-length hair was still jet-black and cut like Jacqueline Onassis. She wore checkered bell-bottom pants with a black long-sleeve shirt.

Her friend beamed when she spotted them and cried when she bent down to kiss the children, holding each of their faces in her palms. When she hugged Vida, it was warm and familiar, and Vida realized how much she had missed her close friend.

During the ride home, Rosemary asked the children about school and their activities. Kasra was reserved, but Roya responded with her usual chatter, giggling when Rosemary asked if she took cute pills. When the family walked into the house, Vida noticed the *Kashan* carpet she had sent Rosemary from Iran many years before. On the bookshelf was a picture of Rosemary, Carlo, and their children when they were little. The picture reminded Vida of the afternoons she spent at Rosemary's, when her friend would teach Vida to cook Italian food the way Carlo's mother used to make it.

After the children settled into the guest room, the two friends sat on the living room couch, Vida in her comfortable pajamas, yawning from the long flight and nine-hour time difference, folding her legs beneath her. Anxiety about her trip to DC was trumped by the comfort she felt in this house and her relief that the children would be cared for.

"You look as gorgeous as ever," said Rosemary, handing Vida a mug.

They shared their personal traumas. They went into the story of the custody and the family issues, and after that Rosemary shared the details of her failed marriage to Carlo. When Vida had called Rosemary a couple of weeks before, Rosemary shared this news.

"He was traveling for work and had affairs," Rosemary said with teary eyes.

Vida squeezed her friend's hands.

"The last time he had an affair it was with a much younger woman. By the time I found out, the woman had already given birth to his child."

"Oh my gosh," said Vida. It was hard for Vida to believe Carlo would do that. Vida remembered hearing about a distant relative in Iran having an affair with the family maid, impregnating her, and later throwing the woman out of the house but raising the illegitimate child. The man's wife and relatives mistreated the child, but at least the child had a place to live. The child would have been put up for adoption otherwise.

As difficult as it must have been for Rosemary to know Carlo had an affair, now dealing with the difficulties of being single, Vida still couldn't understand why Rosemary had not held the marriage together.

"The worst part is he won't pay me alimony," said Rosemary. "According to the divorce settlement, we agreed he would pay child support for the kids and alimony to me. He will not send the money. He wants to punish me for demanding the divorce."

Child support and alimony were new concepts for Vida. When Vida's mother divorced her father, she had lived with her father so her own mother was not entitled to any payments, only the return of the dowry contributed by Maman's father on their wedding day. How difficult it must have been for Maman. This was one of the first times Vida had felt sympathy for her own mother.

"Can't you get a job?"

She thought of Maman who had gone back to school for her teaching credentials and later gotten a teaching job through the Ministry of Education.

"I could, but then he won't have to pay me if I get a job."

"But at least you will be independent," Vida said. *Why doesn't Rosemary want the financial stability?*

"What kind of job could I get? I've never worked, didn't finish college... I could never get a job that paid enough to manage this household." She explained how many times she had to call her own lawyer demanding payment. "It's been stressful and lonely," Rosemary explained.

Vida's heart ached for Rosemary. *Strange she has had her own legal issues.* "What can I do to help?"

"Nothing. It's just nice to be able to talk about this."

"I know. I'll do anything, anything to help you," Vida insisted. "Here I am leaving my kids with you when you have so much on your mind. Are you sure you want to do this?" For a moment, Vida regretted she had brought the children here. *I should never have agreed to attend the seminar.*

"Your kids are no bother. I love them, and it's a good distraction for me."

"How much can I pay you for watching them?"

"I didn't tell you all this for money. You know that," she said, placing her hand on Vida's.

"The kids are going to be here for a week. I should pay you something. For their food... and the activities at least."

"You're my guest. After what you've been through, I wouldn't think of it," said Rosemary standing and hovering over Vida.

The next morning Rosemary called a taxi for Vida for the flight to Washington, DC. Vida left her friend three hundred dollars in traveler's checks in an envelope on the kitchen counter with a note, "Thank you for being a friend."

When the taxi arrived, Vida held the kids tightly, squeezing their cheeks next to hers. "Be good for Rosemary," she whispered in their ears. It reminded her of the day she hugged them as she left for London to take Kamran for his last surgery. Now Vida was leaving them to advance her work, her career, to be able to give them a better life. Kasra was twelve and Roya was eight.

"I'll call from the hotel," she said before she shut the door to the taxi and waved from the backseat as she drove off.

* * * * *

When she checked in, the receptionist at the Hilton Hotel handed her a packet and told her about a cocktail reception in the main lounge that evening.

In the hotel room Vida unpacked her luggage. She turned on the television, propped up a pillow, and lay down, her eyelids heavy. When she woke, she sat up in bed, not knowing where she was at first. She called out for Roya. The white numbers on the alarm clock flipped over—5:16 p.m. She had slept for three hours. Her body was limp with jet lag, and she wanted desperately to go back to sleep but forced herself to get out of bed. She was excited to meet new people at the event.

A small reception desk with name tags placed in alphabetical order stood at the entrance to the grand ballroom. Vida scanned the table and located hers. Right below her name the words read, "Tehran, Iran," in capital letters. The tag looked official, and she studied it for a few seconds before pinning it to her jacket. She ran her hand over it, proud of herself and how much she had accomplished with her work and grateful for having met Mrs. White. When she walked into the lounge, a few hundred guests mingled, nursing their drinks. It reminded her of the few American Embassy cocktail parties she had attended in Tehran.

Vida surveyed the room, hoping she might recognize a face but knowing she probably wouldn't. She knew she would be the only person from Tehran. She had been told there would be one library representative from each country. She studied the name tags—Caracas, New Delhi, Istanbul, Abuja. It could have been a meeting of the United Nations, except everybody was American. She remembered when she was promoted, she was told she was one of the few locals in her position, and now probably one of the only non-Americans at this event.

The bar was located along the back wall, and she asked for a glass of red wine. A tall man wearing a gray and white pinstriped suit, a receding hairline, blue eyes, and glasses on a chiseled face stood beside her. He leaned over the small bar area and in a deep voice asked for a "martini up with a twist." Then he shook her hand and introduced himself.

"Bill Todd," he said. He was older than her, like a father figure. He reminded her of one of her uncles, her father's brother.

"When did you arrive from Tehran?" Mr. Todd asked.

She glanced down at her name tag and touched it. "A few days ago. Where are you from?" she asked.

This man had barely said anything, but she felt he knew her.

"Washington... I'm with the State Department. I am one of the organizers."

They strolled through the crowd. Mr. Todd stopped in front of a short stocky man with no name tag. His brown hair was on the longer side and looked unwashed. He wasn't wearing a tie, and his belly strained against his white button-down shirt, which had come untucked. All the other men, including Mr. Todd, were wearing three-piece suits.

Mr. Todd shook the other man's hand. "Glad you could make it, John. We've got people here from over one hundred different countries. It's going to be a great week." Then he put his hand on Vida's shoulder. "Let me introduce you to Mrs. Shamsa."

She wasn't used to non-family members being so forward, except Cyrus, and now she was dating him.

The short man extended his hand and shook Vida's vigorously and clumsily.

"Nice to meet you. I'm John Palmer. Voice of America."

"Nice to meet you," she said reluctantly. She had heard of Voice of America, the US government-funded news agency. One of their employees visited the library in Tehran regularly.

"Mrs. Shamsa is here from Tehran," Mr. Todd said.

The short man glanced at her name tag. "Right," he said without looking up at her.

Why didn't he make eye contact? Maybe that's how journalists behave, or maybe he is with the CIA? Wouldn't he be better dressed if he was secret service? She wasn't political and didn't quite know what people who worked for the CIA did. She had heard about the Shah's secret police, SAVAK. It was a feared organization and had a reputation of torturing and imprisoning citizens.

"Abraham Lincoln Library, right?" asked Mr. Todd.

"That's right," Vida responded. Mrs. White had told her she had to get a security clearance for her position when she first applied. Maybe Mr. Todd had read her application?

The short stocky man proceeded to scan the room, not focusing on any one thing. Then he blurted out to Vida, "Have you met Mr. Chester Harris?"

"Chester Harris?" Vida repeated. She recognized the name momentarily but couldn't place it.

"The US ambassador to Tehran," he announced. The Voice of America employee sounded irritated.

"Oh yes, I've met him. Once," Vida said nervously. Mr. Harris had been at one of the USIS cocktail parties she attended in Tehran. Mrs. White pointed him out from a distance at the two-hundred-person event.

"You know, he's an important man," said the journalist.

She was angry this journalist was testing her by asking direct questions. *Is he trying to embarrass me?*

"She's a librarian, John," Mr. Todd jumped in. "Now, why would Mrs. Shamsa be expected to meet Ambassador Harris?" Mr. Todd narrowed his eyes, and his face turned red as he spoke while sipping from his martini glass. His hand trembled a bit. Vida thought he looked as though he might throw the drink at the journalist's face.

"I'm just saying it would be nice for her, in her position, to meet the ambassador," replied the journalist.

"Of course, but I don't see why I would have the pleasure of interacting with someone in that position," she said as politely as she could, trying to make up for blanking on the ambassador's name and feeling emboldened Mr. Todd had stepped in to protect her.

The journalist then turned his head and introduced himself to the delegate from Caracas.

Mr. Todd leaned in close to Vida and in a low voice said, "Harris used to be the director of the CIA. After Watergate, President Nixon suggested he become ambassador to Iran, probably to get him out of the US. Ambassador Harris has good relations with the Shah."

The journalist rejoined. "I have recently read disturbing material about the Shah. I hope it's not true," he said, looking Vida in the eyes as if she knew what he was talking about. "There are reports of torture by the Shah's regime."

"Don't be ridiculous, John. Don't believe what you read," said Mr. Todd, as if Palmer's comment made no sense. "Iran is a forward-looking country. The Shah is a modern man." Mr. Todd forcefully grabbed John's shoulders.

"I'm just saying. You know, I hear things, Bill."

"John, go get yourself another drink," said Mr. Todd. He put his arm on Vida's shoulder. "I am so sorry about John's behavior. You know journalists. They read something and then run with it. I hope he didn't offend you. He can be annoying."

"No. That's fine," said Vida. *Wow. Mr. Todd is such a nice man looking out for me.* Vida felt lightheaded from the little bit of wine, and she hadn't eaten anything all day. "Mr. Todd, I am feeling jet lagged. I'm going to skip dinner."

"We'll see you in the morning, dear," he said, smiling at her in a fatherly way.

Vida was glad to get out of the conversation and felt good Mr. Todd had helped her out. In the elevator she leaned back against the brass railing. Her head started to throb when she thought about Watergate, Ambassador Harris, the CIA, the Shah, and what she had heard at the cocktail party. She slid her hand against the floral wallpaper in the hallway as she made her way back to her room. She hoped the rest of the week would not focus on political issues.

* * * * *

The week in Washington, DC, went quickly with interesting meetings, training sessions, and tours of the Smithsonian, the Library of Congress, and the cherry blossoms. The evenings were filled with parties, dinners, and conversations about government officials, most of whom Vida had never heard of.

Mr. Todd introduced her to practically everybody that week. He sat next to her or at her table for all the dinners. When she was talking to other people at the table, she would catch him observing her, studying her. At times, from a distance he waved, and she waved back. He knew more about her than she had shared. She felt somehow he was observing her yet was comforted that he was looking out for her.

At the end of the week Mr. Todd walked Vida to her taxi at the entrance to the hotel.

"Here's my office number," he said, handing her his business card. "Please call me if you ever need anything. You are working for the US Embassy, and you are working in a country where the politics can be delicate. Just know you have a friend in me here in Washington."

Vida looked at him. She wasn't used to this kindness. She felt good he had watched over her at the seminar and was a resource if she ever needed him.

On the flight back to New York from Washington, DC, Vida stared out the plane window and thought about how nervous she had been, leaving the kids with Rosemary. She smiled when she remembered Rosemary asking Roya if she took cute pills.

When the cab dropped her off in front of Rosemary's house, the kids dashed up to her, talking over each other. "...and then there was the Empire State Building... hot dogs at the baseball game... the parade..." Their excitement was infectious, and Vida was glad to know they had had such a great time.

Two days later, Vida and the two kids flew back to Tehran.

CHAPTER 16

Summer 1976, Tehran

———

After hesitating for a moment, Linda said, "I need to tell you something. I don't want you to panic."

Roya's birthday party was planned for after school. The night before the party, Roya and Vida stayed up placing rubber balls, sweetheart candy, and stickers from the American commissary in the goodie bags they tied with pink ribbons, the ends curled with the edge of a sharp pair of scissors. Vida had asked Linda to bake a two-layered chocolate cake. When Linda called, Vida thought she was on her way to the house to help set up for the birthday party.

Vida felt weak in her knees. "What happened?"

"Stay calm," she said softly. "There's been an accident."

"What accident?"

"Kasra. He was on the playground. He fell off the monkey bars... hit his head..."

"Is he okay?" Her heart raced faster than ever before.

"Well… I mean… I don't know. There was blood on the ground. He wasn't breathing. The gym teacher gave him mouth to mouth and resuscitated him. The ambulance took him to the hospital. He's unconscious."

"The ambulance?" Vida's thoughts were racing as fast as her heart. "Which hospital? Oh my god… Which hospital?"

"Tehran Clinic on Boulevard Elizabeth. Vida… don't… please…"

Vida threw down the phone before Linda could finish the sentence, grabbed her car keys and purse, and dashed out of the library.

She drove through red lights, her hand on the horn as she wove through Tehran traffic. The hospital was closer to her office than to the school.

When she arrived, the paramedics were slowly pulling her son out of the back of the ambulance, and then the gym teacher climbed out. Kasra's head was strapped to the gurney, and he lay perfectly still, his eyes closed.

"Is he breathing?" she asked, hovering over him and out of breath herself.

She touched her hand to his forehead, gently brushing aside the black bangs. He was warm but unconscious.

"He's going to be fine," said the gym teacher.

Vida tried to catch the gym teacher's eye, and he looked the other way, not making eye contact. She could tell he didn't believe what he was saying. He wore a bleak, worried expression.

They wheeled Kasra into the emergency room, his arm loose and warm, hanging lifelessly from the gurney. Vida prayed this might be a bad dream, a nightmare.

Doctors poured in and out of the room and lifted her son's eyelids while pointing a small flashlight into his eyes, taking his pulse, and writing things down. They sent him for an X-ray and then wheeled him back up. Throughout all of this, Vida circled the hospital bed aimlessly. Kasra remained unconscious the whole time.

Finally, Hassan, now the children's pediatrician, marched into the room.

"I came as soon as I heard," he said. He turned to ask one of the doctors several questions and pushed aside another hovering doctor. "I'm his pediatrician. I've got this," he said.

He lifted Kasra's eyelids with both hands and then put the stethoscope on the boy's chest. He held the results of the X-ray against the window, examining the dark shadows. He took a long time holding the film against the light, moving it in different directions. When he finished, he grabbed Vida's hand and led her out of the room.

"He's going to okay. But we're not going to know exactly what's going on until he wakes up," he said, arms crossed against his chest.

"Know what?" She held her purse tightly against her chest, as if it were the newborn Kasra she had clutched on to years ago at Rosemary's house.

"He's in a coma. We won't know the extent of the damage until he comes out of it, but he should be okay." Vida dropped her head down. *A coma?* She remembered when her husband went into a coma after the last surgery and when the surgeon told her she was lucky if he died quickly.

She tried not to compare Kasra with her dead husband, but how could she not?

"You'll take care of him?" she whispered to Hassan. She felt tightness in her chest, as if her lungs might collapse at any moment.

"Of course. He needs time. That's all. We need him to wake up," he said. "Go home. Get rest."

"I can't. I need to stay," she mumbled.

Hassan stood in the hallway, his arms crossed and his head bent down as if something tragic was about to happen.

Vida stumbled back in the room and reached for her son's hand, holding it and stroking his hair where dried blood was next to his left ear. From the box next to his bed, she took a tissue, wet it in her mouth, and then she tried to rub away the blood, as if removing it would change things.

When she looked up, she saw Linda in the room, breathless, leaning against the door.

"I came as fast as I could," she said.

"He's in a coma," Vida blurted out, feeling like she was going to fall over. Up to now she had held herself up unsteadily, like the house of cards the kids put together, ready to crumble with one strong blow of air.

Linda wrapped her arms around Vida. Vida collapsed onto her friend's shoulder, crying silently.

"We're going to call the parents to cancel the birthday party. Okay?"

"No, no… don't cancel it." Vida separated herself. "Roya will be disappointed. I know Kasra will be okay. Don't change anything." She wiped her tears, using the same tissue she had used to remove the dried blood from her son's ear.

"Okay, whatever you want," Linda said confidently. She gave Vida a warm hug, and Vida tried to hold herself together to control her tears. Then Linda left the hospital room.

* * * * *

After several hours, Vida slipped off her shoes, pulled an extra blanket from the nurse's closet, dropped into the chair next to the hospital bed, and rested her feet on the corner of the bed. She wanted to feel as close to her son as she could. She hoped she wouldn't fall asleep, but her eyes closed. She wanted to be there when he woke up. She remembered the few days she sat beside her husband in the hospital in London after his surgery. *This is different. My son is going to be okay,* she told herself.

She dozed and then fell into a heavy sleep. She dreamed of the school playground. She could see Kasra and others climbing up and down the monkey bars, each time going faster. She wanted to yell, "Stop!" but no sound came out of her mouth. In her dream she surveyed the playground, and in an instant all the children were gone. She thought they might be playing hide-and-seek. Suddenly, she felt a finger tapping her shoulder.

"Excuse me… excuse me."

With a sudden motion, Vida turned her head. When she opened her eyes, she saw Doktor. She sat up in her chair. *What is he doing here? Am I still dreaming?*

"I came as soon as I heard," he said.

Vida figured he had heard from one of the other doctors. The medical community in Tehran was small. Suddenly she was afraid. *What is he going to do?* She slipped her shoes back on and sat up in her chair.

"What did they tell you?" he asked. "The doctors."

"We have to wait for him to wake up," she said, her voice shaking.

"Of course, he will." He put his hand on her shoulder. "Boys fall. It happens all the time."

She felt relieved. For an instant she thought she was talking to Kamran. For the first time she saw a resemblance between Kamran and Doktor, their hazel eyes.

"But after he wakes up, you should take him to America for a checkup. As soon as you can, take him this summer."

"Why?" she said. *Did Doktor know something she didn't?*

"We don't have the most up-to-date equipment in Iran."

"Do you think it could be serious?" she asked. She couldn't believe she was having a normal conversation with this man.

"I don't know. I'm sure he will recover. But these falls can have a long-term effect. You will want to be sure," he said.

"Yes, I want to be certain there are no problems for him in the future," she whispered. This was the first time she had seen any sign of compassion from Doktor. She had a knot in her stomach. Was he going to come down hard on her later?

"Do you want me to stay here with you?" he offered.

"No. But thank you," she said, looking down.

"You have been through so much. I am so surprised by your resilience. You are a strong woman, Vida *jan*."

She couldn't believe she was hearing this.

"I hope you realize I am not a monster. I am just looking out for the children's welfare. Let me get you something to eat," he said, wiping tears streaming down his face.

"I don't have an appetite. Not now," she said, feeling badly for rejecting the offer. "But I will call tomorrow. I will let you know how he is doing."

He nodded, looking down.

"Anything I can do to help with Roya?"

"It's her birthday today, and there's a party for her."

"Oh." Doktor's eyes lit up, and he smiled.

She wondered if he might have been embarrassed that he didn't know.

"Her friends are at the house with a couple of my friends." Then she remembered Linda telling her Roya, Sandy, and Sam had gym class that afternoon, and Linda was going to pull them out of class early for the birthday party. For gym class they would have been on the basketball court near the playground, maybe at the same location where Kasra had fallen. *Had Roya seen Kasra fall?*

Vida held her stomach, thinking how worried her daughter could have been, and now she wished she had canceled the party so Roya could be with her at the hospital. Her eyes filled with tears.

"Everything will work out," Doktor said. He again placed his hand on Vida's shoulder.

Vida pulled the used tissue resting on the corner of the hospital bed and dabbed the corner of her eyes. She nodded, lowering her head.

"Let me know how I can help," he repeated. He tapped her shoulder. "He's going to wake up. Don't worry."

"Okay," she mumbled as he left.

She rested her feet on the bed again. She remembered the day Kamran received a letter from Doktor where he had mentioned the power of attorney Kamran had given him. Kamran had not shown Vida the note, but Vida remembered sneaking downstairs after he was sleeping and curling up in the corner of the couch to read the letter. She remembered most of it because she had saved the letter and come upon it when her things were shipped back to Tehran from the US It read:

My dearest precious brother,

I hope you, Vida jan, Kasra, and little Roya are all well. I imagine Kasra is getting older, getting good grades at school. He is such a smart, serious boy. He is sure to become a doctor like us. And my little Roya... she must be saying cute things. I miss them so much.

All is well here in Tehran. Maman and Baba joon are well, busy with the garden, planting tomatoes, cucumbers, eggplants, and those hot green peppers you like so much. Remember those?

We still get together on Fridays for lunch at their house. After lunch Baba joon takes a nap but the rest of us play Rumi. Navid hid one of the cards last week, and it angered me and caused us to break up the game early. You know Navid, always a kidder and always trying to get a good laugh out of us.

We all miss you. When do you plan on visiting? I hope soon. I so much wish I was there with you or you were here with us so the whole family could be together again.

I am worried about your health and hope you are continuing to stay well. I imagine you are continuing your monthly visits for blood tests and scans to ensure the awful disease is out of your system and does not return. I imagine after the excellent treatment you received in London you are totally cured, but it's best to continue your doctor's visits in America for a good five years.

The rest of the letter was about the property he had sold. She remembered how angry she was when she found out Kamran had given Doktor the power of attorney. At the time, she'd thought the letter was a scheme for Doktor to dominate control over Kamran. All those issues seemed so insignificant now.

Vida looked up and saw Kasra lying on his back, the white sheet covering him up to his neck, a blanket on top of the sheet, a thin tube rising from underneath the sheet that led to an IV sack, the clear liquid nearly gone. She couldn't be bothered thinking about Doktor anymore—not at a time like this.

All night she sat beside the bed, dozing off and on.

* * * * *

The next morning when Linda returned, she noticed Kasra moving his fingers. Vida fixated on his fingers. When he finally woke up, he cried at first and then leaned over and threw up into the bedpan. The boy did not know where he was and couldn't remember his own name nor the fall. Vida talked to him slowly. She pulled out a tissue and handed it to him so he could wipe his mouth. She ran out to get the nurse and then came back and talked to her son, reminding him of what had happened. He started to talk and sounded normal. Linda rushed out of the room and called the nurse again.

"He's awake! He's awake!" she shouted out loud.

The doctors poured into the room.

Vida stood by the bed with her arms crossed, weeping and staring at her son, not knowing what would come next. *What if he has lost his memory? His vision or hearing?*

Linda joked with Kasra and told him about a pretend conversation she had with him when he was asleep where he admitted to having a girlfriend. Kasra blushed, and Vida knew then he was fine. Within a few minutes, he regained his memory and was laughing at his Auntie Linda's jokes. They brought him a soft-boiled egg, a piece of *sangak* bread, and feta cheese. He cracked the top of the egg with the back of the miniature spoon, the way Vida had taught him, sprinkling salt and pepper on top, the yolk dripping on the side of the white shell. He finished the whole thing.

"Cyrus came by late last night. He asked about you," Linda said.

Vida perked up. "He did?"

"He didn't want to come to the hospital. He thought it might be awkward."

He does care for me, she thought.

Later that morning, Hassan came back with a neurologist who ordered another X-ray.

"The second X-ray shows no damage," the specialist said.

The neurologist looked young, as if he had recently graduated from medical school. "It was a bad fall. But he's going to be just fine," he said. "You have nothing to worry about. Make sure he gets a good night's sleep tonight. He can go back to school in a few days when he's ready."

"Should I take him for follow-up visits?" Vida whispered to Hassan in the hallway.

"You can, and you should. But for now, he seems fine. And the specialist will be releasing him."

Vida felt relieved. She couldn't wait to take Kasra home, to cook for him and sit by his bed, and for her to take a shower and feel refreshed.

* * * * *

She kept her son home for a week. The first two days she and Roya stayed home, her daughter offering her brother sweetheart candies left over from the birthday party. He picked out the green ones. In the afternoon, a few of his classmates dropped by and brought an oversized card with drawings, stickers, and handwritten notes from his classmates. The school principal telephoned and promised the monkey bars would be taken down. Linda came over with a Boston fern plant. The two talked over a cup of coffee and a slice of the leftover birthday cake. Vida couldn't believe just a few years before she had thought of fleeing Iran.

On the third day when Vida went back to work, Maman came to the house to stay with Kasra and played cards with him on his bed. She told him *Rashti* jokes and made him laugh. After a week, Kasra's coloring was fine, he was eating, sleeping well, and anxious to get back to his friends. He finally went back to school, and the family got back to their regular routine.

* * * * *

About a month after Kasra's accident, the USIS announced the completion of the newly constructed library building. Vida was asked to manage the move of the library over a two-week period and to help with the opening celebration on the Fourth of July, to coincide with the American bicentennial.

Packing the thousands of books and periodicals in an organized way would not have been possible without Ali, who stayed late nights working with other staff members.

He complained of an aching back, but Vida's promise to make sure he got cash for his extra efforts was enough to convince him to stay late. She put in place an aggressive schedule and drove the group to meet deadlines. For the next two weeks, Vida and several of her staff, including Ali, went in, even on the weekends, to set up the new library. By the end of June, they were fully operational in the new facility.

Boxes of banners, flags, and red, white, and blue balloons were delivered to decorate the library for the grand opening. The day before the celebration, a courier brought a large-framed photo of Gerald Ford with instructions to hang it in the library entrance. They placed the photo behind the front reference desk, next to the picture of the Shah, which was in an ornate gold-trimmed frame.

The team posted ads at the universities and sent out invitations to dignitaries and professors about the opening.

On the day of the celebration, Vida wore a black pencil skirt. Her red silk blouse matched her nail polish and lipstick. Her employees wanted her to wear the tall red, white, and blue-striped hat that was included in the package from the USIS, but the silly Uncle Sam hat would have made her elegant outfit look like a Halloween costume. She didn't want to mess up her hair, either, which, the night before, had been in rollers for two hours and teased afterward.

Instead, Ali wore the hat and stuck out his chest, not appreciating or grasping its significance but knowing it was American. It made him stand out from the rest of the staff—in a good way.

Vida stood at the front door, greeting visitors as they walked in and handing out miniature US flags. By midmorning she had shaken hands with all four hundred guests.

Late morning she was talking to a student when one of her employees motioned for her to go to the front of the library. Visitors from the embassy arrived, and Vida squeezed through the crowd, making her way toward the entrance.

Mrs. White stood with several other men dressed in navy-blue suits, white starched shirts, and red ties. They reminded her of the US Olympic team at the opening ceremonies she had seen on television with Kasra. Oddly, a few of the men in the group, looking serious, wore dark sunglasses and were surveying the room.

Mrs. White waved and motioned for Vida to come to the front.

"Mrs. Shamsa is the chief librarian here at the library," she said proudly, turning to the men.

The men with the dark sunglasses continued scanning the room.

"Vida… this is Ambassador Harris," she said.

A tall man with a receding hairline shook her hand. His smile was warm when he fixed his eyes on her. She tried not to show her nervousness. She couldn't believe she was shaking hands with an ambassador.

"You've done a nice job with the library," the ambassador remarked.

She clasped her fingers and stood straight. "Thank you." She was indeed proud of all her hard work. She remembered Bill Todd and how nice he had been to her that week in Washington, DC.

Suddenly, a photographer came from behind. "Smile for the picture," he said, holding up the flash. He must have been part of the navy-blue suit group because Vida had not hired a photographer for the event. His shirt hung out from his pants, and his oversized belly stuck out. He reminded Vida of the Voice of America journalist she met at the cocktail party her first night in Washington, DC. The photographer held a large flash in one hand as he took the picture. Ali stood behind the photographer wearing the oversized hat, half-smiling at Vida. The ambassador faced the photographer with a gracious and practiced expression. Facing him, Vida held out her hand, careful her fingernails would not scrape into his palm. *I don't like this,* she thought.

"That's a beautiful blouse, Mrs. Shamsa," the photographer said.

Vida straightened her back and lifted her chin. "Thank you."

Then the flash went off. For an instant she couldn't see anything but white light. When she was able to focus, Ali was gone.

Immediately afterward, Mr. Harris gave his speech about the opening of the library and the significance of the bicentennial.

"To celebrate the two-hundredth anniversary of the US Declaration of Independence, Gerald Ford, our president, has said peace overseas will depend on peace in Iran. I am proud to be the US Ambassador to one of our closest allies here in the most important region of the world, the Middle East..."

With his speech, the crowd in the library put down their drinks to applaud him. The clapping lasted for three minutes. Ambassador Harris raised his drink as if toasting the crowd. The group cheered, and a few whistled loudly, as if they were at a soccer match.

Afterward, the ambassador wandered through the crowd, shaking hands with visitors, smiling, and throwing out a few Farsi words. Vida was proud to be a part of this library and this Iranian American community. She was making a difference, and it was appreciated.

At lunchtime, Ali, who had placed a charcoal grill in the courtyard of the library, was blowing onto the fire with a straw fan. The grill was normally used for Iranian-style kabobs, but instead he cooked hamburgers and hot dogs and served them buffet style for lunch in the audio-visual room.

Vida had ordered an oversized cake in the shape of an American flag from the French bakery next to the library. Sliced strawberries and blackberries arranged for the stars and stripes.

When the day was over, Vida was relieved. It had been a long day in her high heels. After two hours of cleanup, when Vida was leaving the library, one of her employees whispered, "You're going to be famous. Your picture was taken with the US Ambassador," he said.

"Don't be silly. Do you know how many people get their pictures taken with him?"

"I'm serious. This was a big event. And you did a great job. You should be proud," he insisted.

Vida put her hand on her staff member's back and smiled. She didn't care about the picture. She was simply relieved the opening had gone well.

* * * * *

A week after the celebration, Vida had an appointment to see Mrs. White at the embassy. Behind the desk was an oversized leather chair. Vida was appreciative to see Mrs. White, a woman, in this position. Her boss got up from behind her desk when Vida entered the office.

"Quite a party last week. How did you manage the move in such short a time?"

"We couldn't have done it without Ali."

"Well done. And Ambassador Harris was impressed."

Vida was relieved she had orchestrated such a smooth-running event.

"Did you see the picture?" Mrs. White asked.

"What picture?"

"The one they took of you shaking hands with the ambassador. It was printed in *Time Magazine*."

"What?" Vida was shocked. Hanging on the wall behind Mrs. White's chair was a picture of Ambassador Harris shaking President Ford's hand. "I didn't know," she said.

"I'll send you a copy, but you should be getting a copy at the library in a few weeks. I was on a call with Washington earlier today. You know Bill Todd? I had a call with him, and he mentioned seeing a picture of the ambassador shaking hands with 'our beautiful lady at the Bicentennial Celebration at the library.' I assumed it was you."

Vida smiled. *Should I be worried about this photo? In* Time Magazine? *Should I pay attention to my intuition this time? I never do.*

"He mentioned the publicity. He said he didn't think you would like the limelight or that you would appreciate having your photo taken with a politician," she said.

"It's okay," Vida said. "It's just a picture. I'll look for it."

When Vida finally walked out of Mrs. White's office, all she could think of was how proud she was of herself and Mrs. White for what they had accomplished—in Iran. When she got to the car, she was still thinking about the magazine photo. This time she grinned. *I wonder how my hair turned out.*

Since her meeting ended early that day, instead of going back to the office Vida went straight home, arriving a little earlier than normal.

* * * * *

It was now eighteen months after Kasra's fall. It was late, close to midnight, when Vida woke up to a banging sound. It was a monotonous tone, and with it she heard a hissing like a whistle. She got out of bed and opened her bedroom door. The sound was coming from Kasra's room. When she rushed in, she found his head banging against the headboard, his mouth foaming, his eyes rolled back in his head. *Oh no, a seizure.*

For a moment she thought she might be dreaming. "Kasra…" she whispered. She rubbed her eyes in disbelief, but what was happening was real. She tried to grab his arm. His body jolted back and forth. She had seen this before. She put her hand on Kasra's head so it wouldn't bang against the headboard, but the force of his body pushed her down, and she tripped over her nightgown. She caught her breath and got up, trying to hold him, but she couldn't do it. His body was shaking. Assuming Roya had gotten up from the loud noise, she yelled, "Roya… Roya… get the bottle of perfume."

When Vida held the bottle beneath Kasra's nose, his body stopped moving, and he fell limp into her arms. The noise stopped. Vida turned her head, and Roya was standing in the doorway, just as she had during Kamran's seizure. Except this time, she was standing alone, and she was older.

"Roya *joon*, call Uncle Hassan. Tell him to call an ambulance."

* * * * *

When they examined him, the doctors said Kasra had a hairline fracture in his skull, behind his left ear, where he had fallen.

"I thought you said it was nothing?" Vida protested to the neurologist.

Hassan stood beside the doctor, his arms crossed, looking down at the ground.

"It didn't show up then. But there's really nothing to worry about. It *will* heal as he gets older," said the neurologist.

Raising her voice, Vida demanded, "What do you mean, it will heal? And in the meantime, my child will continue to have seizures?"

"It's possible." The neurologist shrugged as if he wasn't sure of himself. He exuded no confidence.

She was furious. "Is there anything he can take for it?" she asked.

"No. Just keep an eye on him," the neurologist told her.

Hassan continued to look down, his nostrils flared as he breathed. He looked like he might explode.

When the specialist marched out of the room, Hassan turned to Vida. "Take him to America right away. They have more advanced doctors." He clenched his fist, and his eyes were piercing when he added, "And this doctor… we will fire him."

Doktor told me the same thing when Kasra fell, to take him to America. He is looking out for my son's welfare.

* * * * *

For the next few days, Vida stayed home from work. Maman moved in with her. Zahra *khanoom*, the maid, did all the cooking.

Late at nights, when it was morning in the US, Vida called the neurology departments at various hospitals in America. She called Rosemary to help her with the search. She got an appointment with the head of the neurology department at the Albert Einstein College of Medicine, where Kamran had done his residency, for the following week. The doctor was an expert in child neurology.

During the next few days, Maman slept on the floor in the living room in case there was another seizure. But nothing happened. No seizures. Vida was worried out of her mind and paced in her bedroom after the kids went to sleep until finally, on the last night before they left the country, she passed out from exhaustion.

In New York, Vida and the children stayed with Rosemary.

* * * * *

The doctor confirmed the hairline fracture when he pointed to the X-ray. He prescribed medication, phenobarbital, a barbiturate. He said the medication would make Kasra sleepy and his hands might shake.

"And your son should not drink any alcohol while he is on this medication."

"Drink alcohol?" Vida said. "He's only twelve."

"I understand... I mean later... when he's older."

"How long does he have to take the medication?"

"It depends. He'll need to take it until the fracture heals. And I don't know when that will be. Maybe when he stops growing." The doctor placed his hands in his coat pocket.

"Is he going to have another seizure?" she asked, eyeing Kasra who sat with his arms crossed like he didn't trust the doctor.

"Not if he takes his medication," he said. Then he gently smacked Kasra on the back. "You'll be fine."

After they left the office Vida made a promise to herself: *I'm not letting him out of my sight. I'll watch him to make sure he has no more seizures.*

PART III

PART III

CHAPTER 17

Spring 1978, Tehran

———

The sheep was tied to a tree in Vida's father-in-law's backyard. The shepherd stood next to the sheep, scraping two oversized knives against one another to sharpen them, preparing to slay the animal. Mahmoud stood next to the shepherd with a hose ready to spray the blood clear from the patio with water, after the killing. Vida's mother-in-law and Nasreen were in the kitchen preparing plastic bags for the distribution of the sheep's meat. Kasra hid in his grandfather's room with the door locked, refusing to come out. Roya sat on the couch, her knees bunched up to her chest, pale, her hazel eyes round like they might pop out.

"It's just going to take a few minutes," Vida said.

"There's no way. I can't do it," Kasra yelled from the other side of the door.

"It'll be quick. I promise. Unlock the door."

"No. I can't watch them kill a sheep," he complained.

"You don't have to watch. You just need to stick your finger in the blood. It'll take a second. It'll be over before you know it."

"There's no way, Mom. I'm not doing it," he yelled.

A couple of days after Vida and the kids returned from New York from visiting the neurologist, Vida's father-in-law announced he would pay a shepherd to sacrifice the animal in his backyard. The shepherd would cut the meat off the bones and put portions into plastic bags tied with a knot. Afterward, Vida, her mother-in-law, and sisters-in-law would drive to a poor neighborhood in the northern suburb of Tehran and distribute the meat to the poor. The custom was meant to result in a quick recovery from Kasra's near-death accident. Part of the ritual required Kasra to stick his finger in a pool of the sheep's freshly slain blood.

Vida was familiar with this Islamic custom. Her father and Maman had made fun of people who engaged in this rite, and the idea of her son sticking his finger in the dead animal's blood made her want to vomit. All that aside, she liked the idea of giving to the poor, and what better way than to put food in their mouths. *Maybe something about this ritual will benefit Kasra.* She didn't believe Kasra sticking his finger in a pool of blood would necessarily help the healing process, but it certainly couldn't hurt.

All of a sudden, a screeching sound from the backyard echoed through the house.

"See, it's done. They're finished," Vida announced. "Come on. Open the door."

A heart-breaking silence lingered between Vida and Kasra through the locked bedroom door. After a few seconds, her son slowly opened the door.

"Where do we go?" he said, looking down at his shoes.

Vida interlaced her fingers with Kasra's as they wandered outside. His hand felt clammy.

The sheep lay on its side in a pool of various shades of blood. *Poor thing*, Vida thought.

"Give me your finger," said Mahmoud.

Kasra kneeled at the edge of the puddle, placing his hands on his knees. He studied the blood.

"Are you okay?" Vida asked.

"I'm fine," he said without lifting his head.

But Vida could tell he wasn't and thought he might pass out.

"Put your finger in the blood. Quickly," she said.

Kasra sat staring at the dead animal. Then frowning, he quickly put his index finger in the pool of blood.

Vida thought he might fall over. "Okay. That's enough. Let's go inside," Vida said.

"Very good," said the father-in-law as he proceeded to hose down the blood and carcass.

Vida and a pale Kasra strolled back into the house. Vida's mother-in-law brought him a glass of ice water mixed with sour cherry syrup. *This is crazy. It's not worth all of this*, thought Vida.

"Here, drink this." The grandmother placed the tall thin glass in front of him. "You look pale, and it's hot outside." Then rolling her shoulders and making a pained expression, she mumbled, "You're definitely not going to be a doctor like your father," as she headed back into the kitchen.

Vida was annoyed at the woman's obvious display of disappointment. She was glad this ritual was over. If she had known it would cause Kasra so much angst, she would not have agreed to it.

*   *   *   *   *

The American neurologist had explained people who suffered from convulsions could choke on their tongue or saliva while they were sleeping. So, during the first couple of weeks back in Tehran, Vida would tiptoe into her son's room and put her hand on his back while he slept to make sure he was breathing, just as she had when he was a newborn. Even though he adjusted well to the strong medication, he didn't experience side effects or any more seizures. She started to think he might lead a normal teenage life.

Up to now, Vida had planned on sending her children abroad to boarding school. *They will have a better chance of getting into an American university if they go to high school abroad,* she had thought. But Kasra's fall changed all of that. Now she was worried about sending him away. She worried about him taking his medication on time and the risk of having a seizure when he was alone.

* * * * *

By this time, Vida's relationship with Cyrus had started to grow. She had told him about her own upbringing, living with her father and stepmother, spending weekend days with Maman, her Venezuelan roommate in boarding school who showed her how to smoke in front of a mirror, and Queenie, the cleaning lady in boarding school who brought her tea when she got homesick in London.

He told her about his love of race cars, his poor grades in high school, his longtime pals from high school, and how his grandmother who lived next door when he was growing up spoiled him. He finally explained how his marriage had failed due to their inability to conceive. He had also lost a sister at an early age and took solace in his own childlessness by staying involved in the lives of his niece and nephews.

Vida and Cyrus were now fully involved in a construction project on the piece of land Vida inherited from her father. She made him an equal partner in the project when he provided the capital for construction. He was often away on business travel, so Vida met with contractors and visited government offices to seek permits for phone lines, water, and electricity.

One Friday afternoon, when Cyrus was in Tehran for the weekend, she took him to see the property. The construction was in its final stages.

"The tiles in the bathrooms and kitchens are so well done."

"Do you like the balcony?" she asked, walking outside, careful not to get too close to the ledge, which was not yet enclosed with a proper railing.

"I do, nice for a cocktail party. And nice views of the *bashga*," he said, referring to the perfectly manicured grounds of the country club adjoining the apartment building.

Without any warning, she asked, "What do you think about selling these units?"

Cyrus slowly walked into the kitchen. "Now? Are you kidding?" he asked. He was running his finger along a seam of grout on the kitchen counter and looked up at her. "This complex is a goldmine. And prices are rising. It's a perfect location."

"I know, but… I am going to need the money soon," she said.

"It's not the right time. Maybe in a few months, after you've gotten all the permits, and the units are polished."

Vida ran her fingers along her necklace. She was disappointed by Cyrus's reaction.

"What do you need the money for?" he asked. He walked closer to her and lightly touched her neck, caressing the pendant.

"I'm thinking about sending Kasra to boarding school."

"*That's* a big move." He turned his back to her for a moment and paused.

"I'm worried about his health. But I think he'd get a better education." Talking about the prospect of being separated from her son was scarier than just thinking about it and flipping through brochures of European international schools late at night.

"What's holding you back?" He stood close to her. She pulled back a little.

"You know he's taking medication for the fall he had a couple of years ago?"

"So?"

She could feel her face turn red. Her gaze bounced from the back wall to the kitchen counter and then back to the light switch. *Is he not taking Kasra's situation seriously?*

"If he forgets to take the medication, he could have another seizure. I mean... he could die," she said, her nostrils flared.

Cyrus didn't say anything. He just looked at her.

She planted her eyes on him for a few seconds and then looked down.

He tipped up her chin and peered into her eyes. "Nobody's going to die. Do you hear me? And... I don't mean to be insensitive to the medication and the fall. Stay positive, and stop worrying all the time."

She pulled away from him.

"Sending him to Germany will be good for him. A learning opportunity. He'll learn the language, discipline... And he won't have to do military service in Iran."

"He's exempt from military service because of Kamran. You know how it works. Right?" Kamran's death made Kasra the only son in the family, and because of that he was exempt from serving. She was surprised Cyrus did not know this.

She turned to walk back to the car and then swung around. "And wait a minute... who said anything about Germany?"

"Where else would you send him?"

"I don't know... There are a lot of places. He could go to school in London or Paris."

"Oh no. Not France." He rolled his eyes. He marched down the unfinished stairs.

"Why not?"

"Tell me one thing the French are known for besides wine and chocolate. Not even chocolate, the Swiss have better chocolate," he said, laughing out loud.

She didn't like the sarcastic cackling. "Very funny." She had several family members who had studied in France.

"Think about *his* future. Technology is taking over the world, and the Germans are going to be at the center of it. Imagine... he'd learn German." He raised his voice.

She could tell he was frustrated with her. His anger and tone reminded her of her own father, how he would swear and bang his fist whenever he failed to convince her of his viewpoint on a particular subject. She knew Cyrus favored Germany because he had finished university there, and she knew his negativity toward the French had everything to do with the fact that his ex-wife was French.

She slowly descended the half-constructed stairs and kept going toward the car so her heels wouldn't get caught in the dirt.

He unlocked the car door for her, then got into the driver's side. "The French..." He smirked and nodded. "No sense of time or commitment... and arrogant. And peef... peef..." he said, waving his hand back and forth in front of his nose. "Their body odor. He'll have to pack *Peef-Pawf* from here." He smirked again, referring to the common air deodorizer manufactured in Iran.

Kasra was overly clean and sensitive to smell, and the comment caught her attention. She found it amusing their conversation had turned to body odor when they started the conversation talking about her son's future. That was how her father would have argued. Cyrus's logic was familiar, and she couldn't help enjoying that he reminded her of Agha Joon.

"If you're serious, find a good school in Munich. I'm there once a month… I'll visit him and look out for him."

That would be nice, she thought.

He put on his leather gloves hidden in the middle compartment and revved the engine. "You cannot run over there if something goes wrong."

Distracting herself from the conversation, she started looking through the tapes he kept in his dashboard.

"And if you're worried about his medical situation… he doesn't have to board. He can live with a family." Cyrus put on his sunglasses. "I'll help you find the right family."

Vida inserted the cassette tape into the deck, rolled down the window, and lit a cigarette. She leaned her arm out the window and looked out. She could smell the jasmine in bloom on the warm spring afternoon.

He put his hand on her thigh and sang along with the music as he drove.

She continued looking out and wouldn't turn her head, but she was smiling. The song reminded her of a recent party they had attended together where he got down on one knee in front of his friends and sang to her.

She could see from the corner of her eyes he was leaning over the steering wheel, trying to catch her attention. He sang a little bit louder.

She turned her head, held his hand, and sang with him, at first softly, and then she belted out the words with him, each of them swaying back and forth in their seats, holding hands tightly.

When the song was over, Cyrus was smiling and shaking his head. "France… huh… Those *pedarsookh-deh's*… with their escargots…" he said with a French accent, sticking his nose in the air like he was imitating a snob. "Who eats that stuff?"

Vida looked out the window and saw a sheep at the side of the road. *Should I be sending Kasra away? With a head injury?*

CHAPTER 18
Summer 1978, Munich

—

Vida pulled at her T-shirt, glued to her chest with sweat, as she tried to breathe in the mid-August Munich humidity. The sun popped off the cobblestone and shop windows around the Marienplatz, melting the makeup she could feel sliding down her face as she tugged the kids across the plaza. Roya's little starfish hand kept slipping out of her hold.

Kasra had folded his arms when she tried to grab his hand, so she handed him the shopping bags to carry instead. The puffy ski jackets bulged out of the sacks, filled with sweat suits and Adidas soccer cleats, still impossible to find in Tehran. She had taken the children on vacation to America. On the way back to Tehran, she planned a two-day layover in Germany before flying back to start the school year.

* * * * *

The second day they met Cyrus at the fancy hotel where he stayed during his regular business trips to Germany. He was on his way to the south of Spain the next day for a weekend trip with a group of childhood friends. Vida pulled out a fistful of change and Deutsche marks and handed them to Kasra.

"Take Roya and go buy some of those gummy bears you like," she said.

Vida sat at a low table next to the bar, her legs sticking to the leather on the ottoman. It had been a few months since she had seen Cyrus, and she hung on his words. She admired his dimples when he smiled and longed to remove his glasses, touch his face, and give him a long-lasting kiss, but it wasn't the right time or place.

"I've missed you." He removed his glasses and gazed into her eyes.

"Me too," she said, blushing. She looked away and then behind her to make sure the children were not close by. She didn't want them to hear her talk like this. They didn't know the direction her relationship with Cyrus had taken, and she wanted to keep it that way.

"I'm telling you; things are *shooloogh pooloogh* in Tehran."

Why is he talking about chaos in Tehran? She had quit smoking earlier that summer and pulled out a piece of Trident gum from her purse. She had bought several packs at the duty-free shop at the JKF airport to curb her urge for a cigarette.

"There's been a lot of civil unrest. Demonstrations in the major cities," he said. "Did you not hear about the fire yesterday?"

She spindled the gum wrapper between her fingers, embarrassed she was so out of touch.

"The Cinema Rex in Abadan was set on fire... The doors were locked, and nobody got out... Four hundred people died."

She pressed her palm to her mouth. "Oh my god. I didn't know that." When she was little, she remembered her stepmother talking about her father traveling to Abadan, the port-city near the Iran-Iraq border. She didn't know anyone who lived there. Violence like this was rare in Iran.

"Islamic radicals," he said.

She stared at him, not knowing what to think.

"They say Khomeini is behind it." He glanced down at the Dewar's in the short round glass in front of him, swirled it around, and then took a sip.

She had heard of Khomeini but didn't know too much and didn't want to sound ignorant. "Oh, right," Vida said.

"Ayatollah Khomeini... you may not remember. You were probably in New York with Kamran then. Right?"

Listening intently, she rolled the gum wrapper back and forth between her fingers. She had difficulty swallowing.

He reached over to his jacket and unfolded a copy of the *International Herald Tribune*. The title of the story read, "Cinema Rex in Iran Set on Fire." She scanned the article.

"You might remember in 1963 when the Shah announced the White Revolution? It was a program that provided for land reform, gave women more power with electoral change, and allowed non-Muslim's to hold office. The Shah started a literacy campaign. At the time, Khomeini got a group of imams together, in Qom, to get them to vote against the White Revolution, and publicly insulted the Shah," said Cyrus.

Qom is the holy city where Kamran was buried, thought Vida.

"The Shah then made a speech attacking the clergy, which got a rise out of Khomeini and his group. They then claimed the Shah had violated the Constitution, and he was responsible for creating a puppet government at the beck and call of America, Israel, and other Western countries. In June 1963, Khomeini gave a speech claiming the Shah had to implement change in Iran and that the people would overthrow the Shah."

"In 1963? I was living in New York then. I remember this," she said. A newlywed, she had traveled to America the year before to be with Kamran.

"After, this Khomeini was arrested and released. Then in November of 1964, when he denounced the Shah again, Khomeini was banished from the country. First, he moved to Turkey and then to Najaf in Iraq," said Cyrus.

"I can't believe Khomeini wasn't killed," said Vida.

"Well, the rumor now is Saddam Hussein has asked him to leave Iraq, and some people say he's in hiding in Neauphle-le-Château because he's afraid of being killed."

"Where is that?"

"Your beloved France," said Cyrus, pursing his lips and shaking his head, once again demonstrating his disappointment in the French. He looked at the glass bowl and picked out roasted almonds from the mixture of nuts placed on the bar table. He was in deep thought, and so was she.

"And what did you decide about sending Kasra to school?" he blurted out.

"Nothing for now." She looked at the bowl and put a broken piece of walnut in her mouth. She could barely taste it. "What does that have to do with Khomeini?" she said, looking up at him.

"I wouldn't take Kasra back to Iran... not now."

"You mean... *tomorrow*? I shouldn't take him back?"

"Yes, tomorrow."

"What do you expect me to do with him?" she said, shocked at his radical suggestion.

He continued looking in the bowl, picking out the almonds. "I'm serious. If things don't settle down in Iran, there's no saying what's going to happen. And you never know. He could get drafted. If things get bad, he might not be able to get out." Cyrus popped a nut into his mouth and chewed before licking the salt off his thick fingers.

Her plan was to wait another year before sending Kasra out of the country. "I already told you. He's exempt from military service," Vida said frustrated. She felt overwhelmed with information. She picked up the glass, jiggling the ice unintentionally. Her hand was shaking.

"It's up to you. All I'm saying is things are not right in Iran and... things could go from bad to worse fast. You never know. Laws could change, and who knows what might happen."

"So maybe Roya and I shouldn't go back either?" she asked half-sarcastically.

He looked away. Once before he had told her he didn't like sarcasm.

"I got applications in the mail, but I haven't made any decisions. And I was going to wait a year. I can't just show up tomorrow at the Munich International School, for example, enroll him, and then leave him here."

"Sure you can. Call and change your flights. Stay here a few extra days. I told you before, if the school doesn't find him a family, I'll find one."

"This all sounds rushed," she said. She felt the urge to pull out a cigarette.

"Think about it," he insisted. He got up and searched for the pen, hidden in the inside pocket of the jacket folded over behind his chair. Then he lifted her Seven Up off the table and wrote something down on the napkin beneath the glass. "It's going to be fine. I'm not trying to scare you."

Deep in thought, she didn't stand up when he kissed her on the cheek. Her knees were locked.

He handed her the napkin. "Look, I'm heading to Marbella for a few days. Here's the information. I'll be back in Tehran the following weekend. I'll call you for lunch. We'll go see the property."

"Sure." She felt numb.

Digging for her sunglasses in her deep purse, she imagined Kasra in a military uniform. She remembered the time when her cousin, a doctor and living in France, had visited Tehran during the summer. Her uncle had sent that cousin a newspaper clipping announcing men born in certain years were exempt from military service. The cousin had gone to Iran on vacation, relying on that information and believing he would not be drafted. But then after his arrival in Tehran, he learned of a follow-on article announcing no doctors were exempt. Unplanned, her cousin had left his belongings in France and stayed in Iran for two years.

What if the laws suddenly change and Kasra gets stuck in Iran? she thought.

That night, first she called Homa and then Maman. Both confirmed the national state of panic apparent on the news and in the local newspapers. She consulted with them on whether she should leave her son in Germany. Maman thought it was a good idea. Homa thought it was an extreme move to leave Kasra, but if it made Vida feel at ease, it was a good idea. Homa explained Munich was a short flight away, and she could visit him often and bring him back quickly if she needed to.

* * * * *

The next morning, Vida called the Munich International School and made an appointment with the principal for that day. At first Kasra complained of the sudden decision. "What about my friends?" he had whined.

"We'll just take a look," she explained. She didn't want her son to know how serious she was about the decision.

She and the kids took a taxi to Starnberg, outside of Munich. The three-story white castle-like building was in the middle of a Bavarian Forest. Ducks floated on a lake next to the school. When the taxi pulled up, Mr. Cade, the principal, was standing in front of the school, his hands tucked in the pockets of his blue pants, talking with a few others. He was thin with hair down to his shoulders. He reminded her of some of the people she saw strolling the streets of New York back in the early 1960s. The principal wore round metal glasses like the ones her father had worn.

"Mrs. Shamsa, so nice to meet you," he said. He shook her hand by holding it in between both of his as if they knew each other well. Based on his accent, she could tell he was an American. *Maybe from the Boston area?* She wasn't sure why she thought of Boston. She had been told they had a funny accent.

They walked into the building toward his office.

"It's a twenty-six-acre property built in 1968," said the principal. "We have an international curriculum with students from all over the world. Have you and your husband already relocated to Munich?" he asked.

"No," she said. She bit her lower lip.

As he was walking, he stopped and turned around, looking confused.

"No," she said.

He stared into her eyes. Then he started walking again. "We'll take the stairs to my office." He led the family down the hall and into his workspace. Unlike his casual personality, the principal's office was old-fashioned with a high ceiling and dark wood paneling. It was dim, except for the lit lamp leaning over his desk in the shape of a question mark. He walked to the oversized leather chair behind the desk, similar to the one Mrs. White had in her office.

Kasra walked over to the tall shelves and pulled out a book, studying the inside jacket.

"Don't do that." whispered Roya, now standing next to him.

"I'm just looking," he said, glancing up at Mr. Cade as if asking for approval. "Do you mind?" the boy asked.

"Go ahead, son," said the principal. Then he sat at his desk and leaned forward to Vida sitting across from him. "Are you living in Munich now?"

"No, we are not." She cleared her throat. *What am I doing here?*

When she had called earlier in the day, Vida did not explain her situation about wanting to leave Kasra with a family. Maybe she should have explained. It was all happening so fast. She had simply said she was seriously considering the school.

"I know its short notice, but I need to enroll him right away. He can take whatever admission test he needs to... today, even," she said, passing the principal Kasra's transcript. She happened to have it with her because she had considered enrolling him in summer school on their US trip earlier.

Mr. Cade removed his glasses and leaned back, crossing his leg. He held the pages close to his face and studied the document.

Vida bit her fingernail. She looked over at the kids. Kasra appeared preoccupied with the book, and Roya waved at her. She noted quite a distance between the desk and the bookshelf in the long office. She was sure the kids could not hear the conversation.

"His grades are impressive. And I see his school has a British curriculum?"

"That's right," Vida said.

"We like the idea of having more foreign students, especially from a country like Iran. Such a rich culture," he said. He flipped back and forth, studying the pages without looking up. "If you are not planning to move to Munich... where is your son going to live?" he inquired in a low voice.

"I'll need to arrange that," she said, reaching into her purse as if she was looking for the answer.

"A minor detail," he said, leaning back in his chair. He looked over at Kasra and then at Vida. He must have known the conversation was about to turn serious. "Maybe the kids can go outside... and check out the grounds... I can arrange for ice cream later."

Roya, who had been looking at the book jackets, turned around when she heard the word "ice cream."

Mr. Cade meandered over to the office window, which occupied the entire length of the wall, and gazed out onto the lake. "It's safe here."

"Of course," Vida said. It wasn't like her, but she did feel safe on these premises. *Maybe I feel secure because we are in Germany and bad things won't happen here.* She felt protected being outside of Iran. She always had. After all, it was Europe. So many family members had studied here.

"Why don't you kids go outside?" Vida told the children.

"Come on," said Roya, pulling her brother's hand.

Kasra, looking at the principal, rolled his eyes begrudgingly and followed her outside.

Vida explained the loss of her husband and the situation in Iran. "I could be wrong, but it would be best for Kasra to stay in Munich for the time being based on the political situation we might be facing in Iran. I need to find a family for him to live with."

"Let me tell you a bit about myself. I'm from Oklahoma," he said. "My wife and I, we've traveled all over the world, especially the Middle East. In fact, we traveled in Iran by backpack several years back."

She was impressed this man had been to Iran and knew about her birthplace.

"We know how things can change in these countries. We might be able to help. We have taken boarders into our home in the past."

What a coincidence, she thought. *And they've been to Iran.*

"That would be a huge help, and it would be temporary," she said, carefully choosing her words so as not to appear as though she was making any assumptions.

"Let me check with my wife before I finalize the offer," he said.

She liked that he respected his wife enough to consult her ahead of time. It wouldn't have happened with most Iranian men.

"Of course. That makes sense," she said.

Even though Vida wasn't sure about leaving Kasra with the principal and his wife, she felt disappointed that she wouldn't get an answer right away. She didn't have time and needed to know her options quickly. "Do you know other families that take boarders?" she asked.

He inched over to her side of the desk and sat on the edge facing her. He was holding his unfolded glasses, twirling them when he said, "I don't want to disappoint you, but just about all the students at this school live with their parents. Let me talk to Paula and get back to you."

She was nervous and unsure. What would they think if they learned about Kasra's fall and his medication? Leaving Kasra was a big commitment and a big responsibility for the family. Out of habit, she reached for the gold chain with the carnelian pendant she normally wore around her neck. It was gone. For a moment she thought it had fallen off her neck, lost somewhere in the streets of Munich. Then she remembered leaving it on the nightstand at the hotel.

Just then the kids came back to the office. The conversation was over, so they walked downstairs. Mr. Cade led them to the school kitchen, and Roya and Kasra picked out prepackaged ice cream cones.

Outside the building as Vida and the children were getting into the taxi, the principal said, "Why don't you and the kids come over for dinner tonight?"

She still couldn't believe she was thinking about leaving Kasra on such short notice. She felt rushed and had a knot in her stomach when she thought about it, but Cyrus had worried her so much about the current situation in Iran she figured leaving Kasra was the logical thing to do.

On a small hotel room notepad, which she had stuffed into her purse earlier in the day, she wrote down the directions and phone number for the principal's house.

In the taxi, leaning forward toward the cab driver, Kasra asked, "Is this a Mercedes?"

"Ya," answered the man with a heavy German accent.

"Wow…" Kasra gave her a big smile. "Mom, I really liked the school," he blurted out.

Roya was looking out the window humming.

"I'm so glad," Vida said. "What would you think about going to school here?"

"You mean I can?"

She was surprised to hear the enthusiasm in his voice. She had expected him to resist the possibility of changing schools.

"What about Iran and my friends?"

"You'll see them during vacation. You'll be home several times a year."

"You know what, Mom, I would love to go to school here. And later I can get a job in Germany and buy a Mercedes." He smirked. "Mom, when I'm rich and famous, I'll even buy you a Mercedes."

Vida slumped in the backseat of the taxi with a smile as they drove to the hotel.

"She'll be too old by then. I'll have to get her a driver," Roya chimed in as Vida laughed out loud.

"I saw the soccer field outside. One of my friends says his boarding school has a team that travels all over Europe for games," said Kasra.

"Yes, and Mr. Cade said the team here travels to other countries too," Vida said.

"Woohoo!" He sounded elated. Vida hadn't seen her son so excited in a long time. She felt an unexpected release of tension.

CHAPTER 19

Summer 1978, the Same Day, Munich

———

When they arrived back in the hotel room, Vida went straight to the nightstand to search for the chain with the carnelian pendant. It wasn't on the table where she had left it. She looked underneath the alarm clock—nothing. Then she went to the bathroom and hunted through her makeup bag and her toiletries. Frustrated, she went back to the main room and sat on the bed. She thought about calling Cyrus to get his advice about the school. She thought it was a bad omen she couldn't find the pendant, a sign of bad things to come. She wasn't superstitious, but these things had been culturally ingrained her. She picked up the phone and asked the operator to connect her to his hotel.

* * * * *

It was a short train ride on the S-Bahn to the Cades' house from the hotel. The homes on Gabriel Max Strasse were adjoined like the ones she had seen in residential areas in England. The neighborhood was quaint and quiet.

An American lady greeted them at the front door, Mr. Cade's wife, she thought. "You can call me Paula," she said, extending her hand to pat the top of Roya's head.

The principal's wife had blue eyes and straight shoulder-length hair with a bobbed haircut. The metal glasses she wore were much like her husband's. She wore slacks and a tie-dyed button-down shirt.

The floor was wooden, but the entrance was covered with a long, oval-shaped Persian-style carpet with a red-base background. It reminded Vida of the carpet in the entry to her father's house where she lived as a little girl. The house was clean, and she could smell chicken, like Homa used to make.

A warm *Naeen* Persian carpet, beige with light blue and brown designs, spread across the living room floor. The ornate silver plates on the mantel above the fireplace were empty, except the one filled with pistachios. On the coffee table was a wooden backgammon set embedded with bits of flat shiny pearl. Vida played with her grandfather on a similar set.

The wife must have noticed Vida looking at the plates. "We got those in Isfahan," she said, handing Vida a glass of red wine. "You drink, yes?"

Vida still couldn't believe this couple had been to Iran. "Yes, of course."

"How about some pink lemonade?" she said to Roya and Kasra who were dutifully standing next to their mom. They both nodded.

"When were you in Iran?" asked Vida, running her hand along the edge of one of the plates.

"We have traveled to Iran twice, mostly when we were with the Peace Corps. In our younger days…" she said, pushing strands of her salt and pepper hair behind her ear. "We were stationed in Istanbul."

After dinner they sipped Turkish coffee while Roya sat at the kitchen table leaning on her elbows, her chin in her hands, watching the Cades' son and Kasra debate the moves from Kamchatka to Irkutsk while they played Risk.

The Cades jumped from one subject to another, mostly about trips to Beirut and Alexandria.

Vida knew the conversation would turn to Kasra living with them, and she'd have to tell them about the fall. *What if they didn't want to take the responsibility of having Kasra live with them?*

When Mr. Cade went to the bar to pour himself an after-dinner drink, Paula invited Vida upstairs to see the rest of the house.

The second floor had three bedrooms and one bathroom. They went up to the third floor, and Paula showed Vida a room with an adjoining bathroom and small shower. The bed was made with crisp white sheets. A maroon comforter draped across the bed, and a mismatched set of beige hand and bath towels were folded neatly on the edge. *Clean and homey.*

"Kasra can take this room," she said.

Vida looked around the room. "So, you will take him in?" She sat down on the bed. It had a sinking feeling, and she thought she might fall on her back but caught herself.

"My husband called this afternoon. He said he had a good feeling about your son. We would love to have him live with us."

"Thank you," Vida said. She looked at the wall and noticed a poster of a soccer player Kasra had shown her in one of his magazines. "You know, I leave on Wednesday. So, I will have to bring him over tomorrow evening."

"The timing is perfect."

"There is one other thing," Vida said. She told Paula the story about Kasra's fall from the monkey bars, the seizure, and the medication. "He's not supposed to drink any alcohol while he's taking this medication. I mean, that's the big risk. But why would he be drinking alcohol? He's only fourteen." Vida laughed nervously.

"Exactly. He will be safe here with us. Don't worry," Paula said.

"Thank you. Thank you so much, Mrs. Cade." Vida wanted to reach out and give the lady a hug. *But is it too forward?*

"Please, call me Paula," she said, holding Vida's hand in both of hers, as her husband had done earlier in the day when he first greeted her.

Vida sighed.

"Come on. Let's go downstairs. My husband wants to play backgammon with you."

They slowly stepped down the steep staircase to the first floor. Halfway down Vida paused, holding on to the railing. "Mr. Cade must have told you Kasra doesn't have any of his things. I'll have to send them after I return to Tehran."

"Don't worry. We'll take care of him." Paula laid her hand on Vida's shoulder.

Vida resumed her descent. She held the railing tightly so she wouldn't fall. She was making a quick decision, but the plan was falling into place.

Downstairs, they discussed the tuition for the school and monthly payments.

At the hotel, Vida spoke to Kasra about the school and living with the principal and his wife. He put his hands on her shoulders like a grown up. "I'm going to be fine, Mom. I really am, and I'm excited about living here."

* * * * *

The next day Vida dropped Kasra off at the Cades' home. As she stood at the front door, she had a lump in her throat. How could she leave him here, in this house, on this street, in this country, so far away from Iran? Had she lost her mind?

Kasra gave Vida a distant hug, barely letting her hold him and pulling away right after she kissed him on the cheek.

My little boy is growing up.

Paula stood at the door with them, and Vida knew her teenager must have been embarrassed. At that moment, she missed him as if she was already in Tehran, four thousand kilometers away. She rolled down the car window to wave as they drove away. She wiped the tears with the back of her hand.

Mr. Cade dropped Roya and Vida off at the hotel early that night. They had a flight back to Tehran the next morning. During the car ride Vida didn't say anything. She looked out the window, rooted in her thoughts and wondering if she was doing the right thing leaving her fourteen-year-old in Munich with strangers.

After Roya fell asleep, she went to the hotel lobby. She reluctantly bought a pack of Winstons at the gift shop. She ordered a glass of red wine at one of the small low tables in the bar area. As one cigarette was about to go out, she used it to light the next one. She smoked more in the hotel lobby that night than she had ever smoked at one time.

What am I doing? What if Kasra forgets to take the phenobarbital? What if he has another seizure? What if he can't handle all the chores? I was a year younger when I left for London. He can handle it. Should I go back and get him and take him with me back to Tehran tomorrow? What if something happens to me in Iran? Will Kasra get stuck in Germany? What if we go back to Tehran, and he gets drafted? A thousand thoughts ran through her head as she lit one cigarette after another.

It was ten o'clock when she finally asked the waitress to call her a taxi. Her thoughts were a dense cloud, as dense as the cigarette smoke. In her haze, she decided to go back to the Cades and call the whole thing off.

Grinding out the last cigarette, the last one in the pack, she marched toward the lobby entrance, having made up her mind to retrieve her son. *I'll be quick. Roya can stay alone in the hotel room for an hour. She's asleep.*

As she was walking toward the entrance of the hotel, several men in suits and ties were strolling out of the hotel restaurant laughing, telling a joke in English. *Probably American businessmen, traveling to Europe for work. Kasra could be one of these people if he got the right education.*

The taxi pulled up to the front of the hotel.

"Madam," said the bellhop, holding open the door.

Vida tugged at her purse strap. She started to cough. The air was damp and muggy; it was going to rain. She looked up at the sky. It was pitch black. She couldn't see any stars.

"I will not need a taxi after all," she said, turning around and heading back into the hotel and up to her room.

When she reached out to turn off the light, she saw something sparkling on the carpet. The carnelian necklace. It must have fallen to the ground when the housekeepers cleaned the room. She placed it around her neck and rubbed the smooth side of the pendant. Then she turned off the light and rested her head on the pillow.

CHAPTER 20
Fall 1978, Tehran

———

Vida and Roya had arrived in Tehran a couple of days before Roya would start fifth grade. Deep down Vida had a visceral feeling the political situation would go from bad to worse.

"Mom, how about his ski stuff?"

"*Azeezam*... I was thinking of a small package of clothes. It's too hard to send the skis and poles."

After their arrival back to Tehran, Vida found Roya in Kasra's room, gazing at The Hardy Boys collection on the bookshelf and running her hand along the green and white-striped wallpaper and the antique desk and bookshelf that used to be in Kamran's New York office, now in their Tehran home. On the flight home, Roya had informed her mother she refused to help pack her brother's clothes to be sent to Munich. When Vida saw her daughter looking lonely in the bedroom, she suggested they pack together, and Roya quickly agreed.

"Well then… how about just the ski jacket and the gloves?" Roya asked.

Roya seemed overly concerned about her brother's well-being. She was missing him. *Perhaps leaving Kasra in Germany was a good idea after all.*

"You're very thoughtful, Roya. Why don't you fold the turtlenecks and the sweaters the way you did the T-shirts, like I showed you."

Vida had spoken to Linda earlier that day about local political events while they had been out of the country. Her friend relayed what she had heard about peaceful demonstrations that summer, some of which were close to Vida's house at a community recreational center where students gathered for discussions.

Vida didn't have much of an appetite that day. She couldn't figure out if it was because of all the cigarettes she had smoked a few nights before in Munich. Maybe she was sick or perhaps nervous about packing Kasra's clothes? Now this conversation with Linda didn't help. She had a constricted throat as she watched Roya fold the shirts.

By the end of the night, they had a neatly folded pile of clothes, ready for Vida to send off in a box.

* * * * *

Vida felt a tingling in her fingers and toes when she saw Cyrus. It was Friday, September 8, 1978, when Linda and her family invited Vida and Roya to join them at the country club.

She noted a calm buzz when they arrived at the club. Members appeared relaxed, sharing stories from summer vacations at various spots, from the Caspian Sea to Cannes. It was the last weekend the pool would be open, so families were soaking up the last bit of sunshine and perfecting their tan.

Preoccupied with the property, Vida asked Linda to keep an eye on Roya after lunch while she and Cyrus went to check on the construction.

In the car, Cyrus hummed to the music on the radio. "Does Kasra like his school?" he asked.

"I think so. He's living with a nice family."

"I told you it would all work out." He rested his hand on top of her thigh, tapping, as he drove.

She smiled but couldn't help but wonder if she had done the right thing leaving her son in Germany. When they stopped at the red light, she looked onto the sidewalk and saw a black bird, dead, its head broken off as if attacked by a much larger animal. Vida got a sick feeling and looked the other way.

"Yes. I'm glad I found the family," she said. "I'm still a little worried about the expenses, though. It would be a huge help to me if we sold the apartment complex."

Cyrus didn't respond. He lifted his hand from her thigh and placed it back on the steering wheel, focused on the road.

"There's so much going on in Iran, it might be the right time," she said.

Still nothing. *Am I talking to myself? Fine, I won't say anything else about the subject.*

When they arrived at the construction site, the tires bumped over the dried mud where the driveway would be placed.

From the outside, the building looked finished. Cyrus climbed out of the driver's seat and locked the door. "I know you are worried about what's going on here in Iran. I am too. But we have time. Nothing will happen to this government. Not so quickly," he said.

"I'm worried. You know... the protests. It could affect the economy."

She thought she may have upset him with her suggestion about selling the property so quickly.

"Strange things are happening," she explained. "People have changed."

"People we know?" he asked as he continued walking up the stairs.

"Ali, for example."

"Who?" Cyrus stopped and turned, giving her a challenging look. Clearly, he didn't recognize the name.

"You know, the janitor at the library. We were talking about the demonstrations, and he told me he had participated in one."

"So what?"

"Well, Ali… he's an ordinary guy, afraid of his own shadow. Why would he join such an event?"

"Have you ever seen birds when they migrate?" Cyrus asked.

"Yes, of course. But what does that have to do with anything?"

"When you look up, you notice they fly in the shape of a V? One bird always flies ahead of the crowd, and all the others follow."

She paused. "Why are we talking about birds?"

"Don't you get it? It's the same with people. Most people are followers. This guy Ali… he probably has a cousin or someone he knows well who's an imam or something, or someone told him to join a peaceful gathering, and so he did."

"Probably," she said, shrugging her shoulder unconvinced. She remembered Ali did, in fact, have an imam as a neighbor, the same guy who told him to eat scoops of honey to change the gender of his conceived but unborn child. "I am simply saying if people like Ali, who work for Americans, are getting involved, who knows what else is going on."

"Look... I know a lot is happening. And the situation may get worst. But we have time. Selling this property is not the right thing to do. Things may boil over even in the next few weeks. That's why I suggested you leave Kasra in Germany. We can always sell the property later."

"When things get worse, who's going to buy this apartment complex? It will never sell for the right price."

They unlocked the ornate wooden door to one of the units and walked in.

"See what we've done?" she said pointing at the living room.

"Wow..." he said. He looked genuinely impressed with all the progress.

They walked into the bathroom.

"These are the imported tiles we picked out."

"I see that," he said, squeezing her hand.

Then they walked over to the kitchen. It was completed with green counters and matching metal cabinets. All the apartment walls were painted light beige. Vida had paid her housekeeper to clean the place, and it was move-in ready.

Cyrus walked over to an electric outlet in the living room. A wire was sticking out. "What's this?" he said, fiddling with the incomplete work.

"The electrician was here yesterday and said he needed to check the outlet," Vida said.

Cyrus examined the outlet. "He should put the plate back on when he comes back."

"Okay," she said, sounding disappointed. "Don't you think the building is ready for sale?"

He was kneeling, facing the opposite direction. He stood up and looked at her, and in a calm voice, he repeated, "We have time."

She paused for a minute, gazing into his eyes, and then she raised her voice. "Time? People are angry. They keep storming the streets. The number of demonstrations is out of control. You think we have time?" She was furious with him for not agreeing with her. Nervously, Vida banged her hand against the wall, making a loud bang.

Cyrus put his hand on her shoulder and in a soft voice said, "What are you so angry about? Have you forgotten something? We have a Shah. There may be more run-ins with the military. But it will die down."

"How do you know? There's talk of martial law being imposed. Kasra is in Munich, and I'm here… How's that going to work?"

"Aren't you glad you left him?"

She looked over at his hand resting on her shoulder and moved it. "I am… but I'm worried. I don't want to get stuck in Tehran and not be able to reach him."

She walked ahead of him out toward the car.

"I don't feel good about this. I want us to sell these apartments and get the money out of the country. I have a bad feeling."

He held the car door open for her. "You can get your money out of the country anytime. Even if things go from bad to worse, your money is safe. Be patient," he said. He climbed into the Mustang.

They sat in the car, and she stared out the window. She sensed he was watching her, but she didn't want to look at him.

"Anyway, we don't have all the permits. Who's going to buy a place when its half done?"

The place was more than half done. She crossed her arms and stayed silent. He started the engine.

In a soft voice she said, "Yesterday I talked to Homayoun," referring to her architect cousin. "He says there are people who will buy the place even if we don't have all the permits."

Cyrus lit a cigarette and leaned his arm out the window. "But then we'd have to sell at a discount."

She continued gazing out the window. She noticed a bird's nest resting on a high branch.

"I can't keep running from one government office to another. I'm tired of it. We need to get rid of this property," she said in a low controlled tone.

"Look, Vida *joon*, I know what I'm talking about. If you can wait a little longer, we will get more money for these units," he said, resting his hand on hers.

She was clasping his hand and then pushed it away. She wanted to believe what he was saying made sense, but it didn't.

On the drive back to the club, they didn't talk or listen to music.

The route to the country club was a narrow two-way asphalt road. The entrance was usually guarded by a man in a booth in formal attire. Normally when a car drove up, he would step outside and release a chain to let members drive through. But this time when Cyrus and Vida drove up the chain was down, and the security guard was not at his post.

"These *pedarshookhte's...*" blurted out Cyrus, seeing the booth unmanned and the chain down. "The security guards. They get paid a lot of money to sit in that booth," he said as they drove up toward the clubhouse.

He dropped her off at the front and then parked the car.

Vida looked at her own reflection in the window to the entrance of the clubhouse to make sure her lipstick was still intact. She climbed the stairs and walked down the short hallway, instantly sensing something unusual. In the lobby area the room was crowded with people standing and talking, the chatter overtaking her. Nobody played backgammon or chess, and the atmosphere was agitated instead of relaxed like it had been earlier in the day.

Linda and her husband, standing in a corner, were talking to a group of people.

Vida scurried over to them. "What's going on?" she asked.

Her friend nodded. "They're talking about the demonstration today," she said. "A big one. Massive, in Jaleh Circle... It started peaceful but it turned ugly."

Jaleh Circle was downtown.

"What do you mean *ugly*?" Vida asked.

"I don't know... I've been hearing bits and pieces. They say hundreds of people showed up, and the military rolled out tanks, and helicopters hovered... Several hundred people were killed," Linda said, her eyes wide.

Oh my god, Vida thought. She looked across the lobby and saw a woman trying to hold on to a child stomping his foot, yelling, "I don't want to go home."

She saw Cyrus coming down the hall. He hurried toward them.

"Linda… tell Cyrus," Vida said, as if to say, "I told you so."

"Tell Cyrus what?" he asked. "Where is *Agha Mehdi* with my Dewar's?"

Vida crossed her arms. "This is serious."

"What's serious? Why is everyone in such a bad mood? It's a beautiful day… Friday afternoon. Where's the *takht-e nard*?" he asked, referring to the backgammon set.

Linda's husband put his arm on Cyrus's shoulder and whispered into his ear, pushing him into the hallway.

Vida couldn't hear, but she watched Cyrus lightly push Linda's husband's arm away and put both hands on his hips, moving his head back and forth. He looked stunned. The two men stood talking for a long time, but it couldn't have lasted more than a few minutes.

Then Roya ran up to Vida. "Mom, I don't feel good. I have a stomachache."

Vida got on one knee and reached to feel her forehead. Her own stomach ached horribly, but she didn't want Roya to know. "Did you have fun at the pool?"

"No… We wanted to play on the trampoline, but the bigger kids wouldn't let us. Can we go home?" she whined, tugging at her mother's light summer scarf.

"We'll go home soon. Go get your swim bag," Vida said, stroking Roya's curled ponytail.

When Vida stood up, Cyrus was standing beside her, his face pale.

"I must go. I'll call you tonight," he said. "Everything is going to be fine." Then he rushed away.

She thought about the hundreds of people who were killed. *Were they students? Families? Was Ali one of the demonstrators? Would he have taken his girls to the demonstration? He's stupid enough to do that.* She ran her hand through her hair. She couldn't think of anyone else she knew who might have participated in the protests.

* * * * *

At night, after Roya was tucked in, Vida sat at her dressing table. She removed her gold chain and placed it into the jewelry box when the phone rang.

"I'm going to Shiraz tomorrow," Cyrus said.

"You just got here today." She sighed. She stood and looked around her, behind her, her heart racing.

"I need you to do something. Call your cousin. Ask him to help you sell the property… with or without permits."

She sank into the bed. "Cyrus… what's going on? I thought you said we have time?"

"Some peaceful demonstrations got bloody. It's not unheard of. But the government needs to take control. Otherwise it's all going to get out of hand fast... faster than I thought."

"I didn't ask about the demonstration. The building... Why do you want to sell it now? I thought you said we have time?"

He seemed preoccupied. "We might. I don't know. I just don't know anymore. Sell the property. Whatever the price... and get the money out of the country."

The line went dead, and she could hear a beeping sound. She stared at the receiver and then gently put it down.

Even though Cyrus had put up the money for the construction, they had not altered the deed to the land, so it was still in her name. She would not have to deal with the formality of getting power of attorney from him to sell the property. The arrangement had been a friendly one. No contracts. Once they sold the building, they would split the proceeds equally.

* * * * *

The following few weeks Vida rushed from one government office to another for permits to sell the building. What they built was a modern complex with four units, and she purposely underpriced it so it would sell fast. The realtor found one buyer. Vida worried the deal would not close and was relieved when the details were completed. By the end of October, the property was sold.

She deposited her half in her bank account at the *Bank-e Markazi* and Cyrus's portion in his. A week later, at Cyrus's suggestion, she flew to Munich for a couple of days to deposit her money at Deutsche Bank. It would give her a chance to see Kasra too. She could have wired the funds, but she didn't have a bank account in her name, and it was impossible to open one remotely.

She arrived in Munich on a Friday and went straight from the airport to the branch at Marienplatz, the one near the Penta Hotel where they had stayed in August. She opened an account and deposited $120,000 in traveler's checks.

She had a passing thought. She remembered the time she went to the *Bank-e Markazi* in Tehran during her lunch break, when she discovered Doktor had taken all her money from the children's bank account. She found herself clenching her teeth. She glanced past the glass wall of the German bank manager's office. The customers in the bank were nicely dressed. The women wore neck scarves. She looked behind the manager, and on the wall was a poster of the German National Soccer Team, and underneath it said 1978 FIFA World Cup. She was in Munich now, a different time, a different world.

* * * * *

When she got to the Cades' home, Paula opened the door. As they caught up in the doorway, she heard Kasra run from the other room. She hadn't told him she was coming to surprise him.

"Mommy... what are you doing here?"

She thought she might melt when she heard him call her "Mommy." He hadn't called her that since he was a little boy.

"Kasra *joon*," Vida whispered and then wrapped her arms around him, enveloping him.

She drew back to study his face and then held him close again. His hair was cut short, and it smelled fresh. He had small hairs growing above his upper lip, and his voice sounded a little different. He looked the same, but he had changed. She couldn't quite tell how, but he wasn't the same. *Growing into a young man,* she thought. *He looks relaxed.*

Paula stood staring at Vida and Kasra in an endearing way.

"Mr. Cade… Mr. Cade… guess what?" Kasra called, running back into the house.

Vida stood in the entryway and set her overnight bag down.

"I had to come. Things are getting uncontrollable in Iran," Vida said. "Lots of demonstrations. I was worried I wouldn't be able to get any money out of the country."

"I'm glad you came. You will have to stay at the house."

"I can't. I reserved a room at the Penta."

"Then you'll have to cancel it. I insist you stay here," Paula said.

Vida looked down at her luggage. "Okay. I will."

That afternoon mother and son went to the city center. Kasra spoke German when he bought tickets at the booth for the Strassen Bahn.

"Mom... I joined the soccer team last month. We've already been to Frankfurt and Strasbourg," he said with excitement Vida hadn't heard since he was five. "I love the school," he added.

He talked more than he ever had before about friends from Milan, Vienna, and Rome. He said he was learning to play guitar from the Cades' son.

After dinner, Vida watched Kasra wash all the dishes. She would never have asked him to do that when he lived at home, but he didn't seem to mind. She liked that he had become so responsible. He seemed so grown up in only two months.

When the principal and his wife left the room, she grabbed his arm and quietly whispered, "Are you taking your medication?"

"Mom?" he said, gazing at her.

She had been caught in her rhetorical question. "I'm just asking. Can't a mother ask her son a question?" Vida said in mock protest.

"Of course. And there have been no problems. Don't worry," he said, reaching out to give her a hug. "You always worry. I'm fine. I love it here."

* * * * *

At the end of the weekend, before she got into the taxi for the airport, he gave her a reassuring hug. This time it was as if he had become the parent and she the nervous child going away. When the plane lifted off from the Munich airport, she had a strange feeling she'd be back, sooner than expected.

CHAPTER 21

Early January 1979, Tehran

———

Vida lay still on the bathroom floor with Roya wrapped in her bedspread and asleep in the porcelain bathtub.

By late fall martial law was imposed, and the prospect of violence was ever-present. The city exploded with riots. Mobs set fire to the British embassy. Roya's school, run by the Brits, was shut down "until further notice."

Earlier that night when Roya had food poisoning from tuna fish, Vida's limbs had shaken, and her hands were fidgety. Her adrenaline spiked, and she couldn't calm herself. It was time to leave the country. She didn't know where they would go or for how long, but she knew it was time to get out until the political situation calmed down.

When she heard the ringing the second time, she ran to the phone in her bedroom, hoping it wouldn't wake Roya. She gulped down breaths to stay quiet. "Kasra *joon*, it's good to hear from you. Why are you up early?" she whispered into the phone. She worried Kasra had heard about the shootings on their street the night before and somehow knew she and Roya had slept in the bathroom. *He could not have known that.*

"Mom, I don't want you to worry. Okay?" he said, sounding agitated.

"Everything here is fine," she said.

He paused.

She leaned back onto the bed, the telephone cord extended across her chest and her hand against her forehead. She felt an uncomfortable tingling in her toes.

"I don't mean in Iran… I mean I don't want you to worry about *me*," said Kasra.

She sat up. Her shoulders felt tight. "Why would I worry about *you*?" she asked. She was sure then something had happened to him. "What's going on, Kasra?"

"We went on a ski trip to Italy."

"So?"

"And everyone was drinking wine. They offered me…"

"You're fourteen, and they offered you wine?"

He wasn't listening to her. "Well, remember when the doctor told me not to drink with my medication?"

She gripped the bed, her hands bunched up in a fist. "What happened?"

"I remembered what the doctor said. I didn't take my medication with the wine."

"You didn't take it with the wine? Did you take it at all?" she spoke slowly and methodically.

"No," he said.

She stood up, resting her head against the wall.

"I must have had a seizure. When I woke up, I was in a psychiatric ward."

"Where are you now?" Her voice got faint.

"Mom, please don't get upset. It's funny."

She pulled at the roots of her hair as if she was going to pull each one of them out.

"They didn't know I had a seizure. They thought I was crazy. Isn't that funny?" he said nervously. "They checked me into the psych ward. When I woke up, I saw a man pull it out and pee on his own bed. When he saw me watching him, he told me not to tell anyone. That's funny. Right? Mom… funny." He laughed nervously.

She said nothing. Her eyes bounced from the closet to the dresser, her jewelry box, the curtains, and then the door.

"Mom, Mom... are you there?"

She was listening but couldn't believe what she was hearing. Her son in a psych ward? *I should not have left him in Munich.* "Oh God..." she whispered.

"Mom, I'm fine," he said, clearly not wanting to upset her. "I'm home now."

She swallowed hard.

"Mrs. Cade thought I should tell you."

"You weren't going to tell me?" She raised her voice. How distant she felt from her own son. "Let me talk to her."

"Okay. But, Mom, I like the school. Please let me stay. I won't drink any more wine."

"Pass the phone to her," she said. She had lost her patience.

"He's fine," said Paula in her friendly tone. "We got the call from the hospital. They didn't know what was wrong. Once he told them about the medication, they released him."

Vida sank into her bed. She thought she might start to cry. *What if Kasra wasn't okay? What if they were holding something back?*

"Is everything okay over there?" Paula asked.

"No, it's not. Roya and I are going to fly out as soon as I can get us out." She explained the events of the night before, and Paula listened quietly, not making any comments.

Vida thought she must have shocked her.

Finally, Paula said, "We will be waiting for you."

CHAPTER 22

January 1979, Tehran

In the evening, Vida turned the key to lock the door to the front of the house, not knowing when, or if, she would return to her home or to Iran. Again, she examined her oversized leather wallet, the one that had belonged to Kamran years before, checking to make sure the maroon passports, green cards, and traveler's checks were all in the right place.

They were on their way to Maman's house. She had decided to stay with her mother on the last night before flying out the next morning to Germany because Maman lived closest to the airport.

Roya sat in the backseat of the car bundled up in her purple winter coat, earmuffs, and multicolored wool gloves. The ten-year-old cradled the soft mustard yellow Samsonite carry-on bag Vida had given her for her belongings, as if it were the Mrs. Beasley doll she'd parted with the year before. It was the same bag Vida used the last time she traveled with her late husband.

The driver loaded the other two suitcases in the trunk. Vida then settled into the car, scooping up the bottom of her camel-colored winter coat so as not to slam the door on the fur swirling around the bottom.

"Go ahead." She signaled the driver.

He drove through the Tehran streets toward the John F. Kennedy Square to Maman's house. The noise of the city was dying down as the sky darkened. The curfew was about to cloak the city like the black veil women wore at burials. People hurried back to their homes. Intermission was over, and the show was about to begin again.

When the night curfew began, the number of soldiers on the city streets would increase. They hunted down violators but strangely didn't know what to do with them. It was the beginning of a revolution, but Vida did not know it at the time.

During the drive to her mother's house, she gazed out the window past the many soldiers on the road. She was staring at the reflection of herself and wondering how long she and Roya would stay in Munich. Would she leave the kids in Germany? It would cost too much to leave them both there. She could call Rosemary. But if she was going to come back to Iran, New York would be too far away. How long could she be away from her job?

The week before, Mrs. White had agreed to give Vida a leave of absence. But at the end of the conversation, she said she was optimistic "it" would all work out, whatever "it" was.

In the last few months, civil unrest had spread throughout Tehran. Bombings in public places and explosions were now a common occurrence. Anti-Shah and anti-American demonstrations, and demonstrations just to demonstrate, took over. Graffiti spread across walls like overgrown ivy with words like, "Death to the Shah... Down with Carter... Death to America." Workers at oil refineries went on strike protesting the political situation. The airport was announced as "closed" off and on. Local banks disallowed the transfer of funds to foreign banks. The USIS closed Vida's library at least once a week due to bomb threats. The staff would stand next to each other outside in the ice cold while the Marines checked for explosives. They never found anything.

The driver pulled up in front of Maman's apartment close to 8:00 p.m.

Maman ran out with a silk scarf around her neck and a long brown cardigan sweater wrapped around her. "What took so long?" she whispered to Vida as she nervously glanced up and down the street.

Vida knew well her mother's loyal neighbors from the last several years, the ones who had been like family up until then, who were so devoted, were now eager to report suspicious activity. It was as if aliens had descended and kidnapped the nice neighbors and replaced them with revolutionaries.

"The curfew is about to start. Come on. Hurry up," Maman said, grabbing at one of the pieces of luggage the driver was unloading. "Roya *joon*, what's taking you so long? Get in. Get-in-the-house, I said," she ordered, clenching her teeth.

Vida didn't say a word. She didn't want Maman yelling at her daughter, bossing her as she had done with Vida when she was little, but she knew better than to argue out in the street while the neighbors watched from behind their curtains. Roya and Vida hurried up to the second-floor apartment and dragged the luggage up the stairs.

"Leave them there," her mother ordered, pointing to a spot outside the entrance. "You're leaving in a few hours."

"I want to make sure they're out of the way," Vida protested as she maneuvered each piece so the corners of the suitcases touched and were perfectly even, as if aligning the luggage gave her control over her family's future.

The electricity went out just as Maman pulled open the sliding glass door to the apartment. She took a matchbox out of her cardigan pocket, bunched up the loose part of the sweater in one hand to keep it out of the way, and then slowly lit the candles.

When she was done, the house resembled a shrine. Vida barely noticed the electricity had gone out with the candlelight around her and wondered why she hadn't used more candles in her own home the last couple of weeks.

She hung her coat in the hallway closet and then went to the wall-mounted phone in the kitchen to call Kasra. As she circled the telephone number on the rotary phone, she figured her son and the Cades were probably getting ready for dinner. She expected she would have to try several times to get through but succeeded on the first attempt.

"Kasra *joon*... Yes... Tomorrow morning... Flight 928... That's right... Okay... We'll talk when we get there... See you then."

Vida tried to stay positive. How could she not? She considered it a good omen she had gotten through right away, a good sign everything might be going in the right direction and would turn out just fine. She kept the conversation brief, still worried about her son and whether his recent seizure was the sign of more to come.

"Is he okay?" Maman asked, placing plates and utensils on the round kitchen table for the early breakfast the next morning.

Vida remembered the night she had told her son about his father's passing, how Maman had asked about Kasra, and how Vida had snapped at her in anger. Now things were different between her and her mother.

"He's fine," Vida said. She hadn't told Maman about the wine and Kasra's convulsive attack in Italy because it would have been one more thing for her mother to worry about.

Maman had three glass mugs in her hand, and as she was setting them on the table, one slipped and crashed onto the floor.

"*Ey vay*," Vida said startled. She bent to gather the pieces of glass.

"Go out, out. I'll clean it up," Maman said loudly as she motioned for Vida to leave the kitchen. "I don't want you to cut yourself."

"Maman *jan*, I can help," said Vida with a friendly tone, wanting to help clean up the mess and feeling guilty about being at her mother's place so late in the night and causing Maman so much stress. She picked up the broken pieces.

Maman gathered the straw brush and dustpan leaning on the side of the refrigerator to sweep up the smallest of the shattered glass.

"He'll meet you at the airport?" Maman asked as she swept.

"Of course," said Vida curtly. *Why was Maman asking so many questions about Kasra?*

"*Azeez*, I'm just asking," Maman said, dumping the broken pieces into the metal trash bin.

"You're always trying to control everything," Vida said.

Maman stared at her for an instant, threw the dustpan down, and then walked out of the kitchen as Roya walked in.

Vida turned to Roya, pretending nothing had happened. "Maybe we'll even go skiing in Germany? Fun."

"That would be great, Mom," Roya said hesitatingly. The little girl paused for a moment. "But we didn't pack our ski clothes."

"We'll figure it out when we get there," Vida said, wondering if she was giving her daughter false hope.

Maman came back, trying to make eye contact with Vida, but intentionally Vida looked the other way. The years when Maman had been an absent mother had marked them both. Vida had leaned on her stepmother, and everything Maman said and did embarrassed her. Now Vida had to say goodbye, maybe for a long time.

Logistically, the details had already been arranged between mother and daughter by phone the week before. Vida had explored all the possibilities about how long they would be out of the country and given her mother specific instructions. Maman had asked questions and given Vida motherly advice Vida didn't want to hear. Vida had provided all the necessary phone numbers: Kasra' school, the Cades' home, and even Rosemary's number in New York in case they ended up there.

Maman had agreed she would go to the house on *Mirdamad* Circle once a week to water the plants. Vida gave her bank account information and power of attorney in case the stay was prolonged and affairs needed to be handled.

The three of them stood in the kitchen. Three generations of women, the two older ones filled with years of pent-up anger, the younger one probably feeling the tension but not old enough to comprehend the complexities of a mother-grandmother relationship.

Maman poured Roya a half glass of chocolate milk and filled the rest with white milk, Roya's favorite special snack, particular at Maman's house. While she stood drinking, Maman and Vida sat leaning on their chins at the kitchen table, watching the little girl. When Roya was done, Maman placed her glass in the sink. She kissed Roya and then Vida on the cheek.

"Go on, go to sleep. You have an early morning tomorrow," she said.

Vida and Roya walked toward the guest room with Maman behind them.

"I put two extra blankets in the corner in case it gets cold."

Vida stood in the doorway to the guest room. "The driver will be back at six a.m., plenty of time to get to the airport for our nine a.m. flight."

"Okay... *Azeez*," said her mother turning away. Maman seemed less agitated. Then she turned back. "Vida, come in the living room for a minute."

Vida shut the door behind her so Roya wouldn't hear them.

"What is it?" Vida asked.

Looking down, Maman had her cardigan bunched in between her fingers. "I know you're angry with me."

"I am not," Vida said, looking the other way.

"Listen, I know you've been angry with me for a long time, and I don't blame you."

"Maman, I'm sorry if I lost my temper earlier." Vida didn't want to have this conversation. Not now.

"I don't mean tonight."

She sat down and placed her hands on her lap.

"*Azeez*, listen. Listen to me."

Maman looked nervous. Vida had not seen her this way.

"I know I left you when I divorced your father. You were very little. I was young. Maybe it wasn't the right thing for me to do. But it was the law. Under Islamic law, I couldn't take you."

Vida stared at her mother, holding back emotions built up for years.

"But you are older now than I was then. Whatever you do, don't leave your kids. If you must, stay with them. It's not worth coming back. They need you. Don't make my mistake." She bowed her head down.

Vida scanned the living room and fixed her eyes on the ornate table with the small antique dishes her mother collected, one of them filled with pink and white candy-coated almonds. When she was little and her father and mother had gotten divorced, Vida's old crotchety paternal grandmother would push Vida's tiny hands away from the candy dish, telling her it was for the *mehmoon,* guests that could arrive unannounced. She was angry Maman had not apologized before and angry her mother was telling her what to do with her own children, but she understood. She put her head down and walked toward the guest room.

"*Azeez*," said Maman.

Vida turned around.

"I'm sorry," Maman said, this time gazing into her eyes.

Vida came back toward her mother.

"Maman *joon*, I understand," she said. She moved toward her mother and hugged her hard.

"What are you going to do here? Are you going to be safe? Why don't you come with us?" Vida blurted out.

"I can't leave. Not now," said Maman, stroking Vida's hair. "I'll be fine. Go on. Go to sleep now. You have a big trip tomorrow."

Vida walked toward the guest room. She turned around and said, "Maman, I won't leave them. Don't worry." She felt a tightening in her chest. She had been angry with her mother all those years growing up. It was time to let it go, to forgive and forget.

She tried to sleep, but she kept running through her mental checklist—what she had packed, what she may have forgotten. All she needed were the passports, the green cards in case they ended up in America, and the money she had withdrawn from the bank. Worst-case scenario, she figured, they would be back in Tehran in a few months in time for the Iranian

New Year, the first day of spring. She concentrated on falling asleep, knowing she would need her energy for the next day.

At 5:00 a.m. Maman knocked on their bedroom door, peeking her head into the room. The scent of Darjeeling tea with a hint of cardamom hovered over the breakfast table in the kitchen above the warm *barbari* bread, butter, and homemade *albaloo*, sour cherry jam, Roya's favorite.

After they freshened up, Vida nervously folded the pajamas, made the beds, and searched for her wallet. Through the doorway she could see her mother and Roya. Her daughter methodically cut bread, smothered it with butter, and topped it off with drops of the *albaloo* jam. Maman was staring at the floor, sipping her tea with the traditional chunk of sugar in the corner of her mouth. They exchanged few words, and they all looked half asleep.

At 6:00 a.m. the driver arrived—for once, an Iranian who went about his affairs in a timely manner. He was referred by her cousin. Vida didn't know how the driver was able to leave his house before the curfew was over, but she didn't ask. She had learned not to ask questions. She was grateful to be getting out.

The driver walked upstairs and leaned into the entryway of the apartment so he wouldn't step inside. He was probably used to taking off his shoes before entering the house. He lifted the suitcases.

Vida's mother stood by the glass door. "*Bodo-een*, it's time," she called.

The driver took the luggage downstairs, and the others followed. Vida and Roya stood on the front doorsteps, bundled up in their coats. It was still dark, the air crisp and cool. The driver slammed the trunk.

Maman was right behind her. After an awkward second, and without looking her mother in the eyes, Vida reached for her, and they hugged tightly. At first, not a peep, but as they held each other tightly they both whimpered loudly. Vida backed away as they both wiped their tears.

Her mother held Roya and gave her a strong hug while kissing both cheeks. "Take care of mommy," she said, choking on her words with Roya's face in her hands.

Vida did not look back. She couldn't bear to see her daughter and mother crying. "I'll call," she said, wiping her eyes with her finger. Then she got in the car and, looking out the window, blew a kiss. From her purse, she grabbed a tissue and wiped her tears so she wouldn't disturb her makeup, and then lightly blew her nose.

"In a few hours we'll be in Muuu-nich," she said in a singsongy voice to Roya.

Roya hugged the yellow Samsonite carry-on as she had the night before and gave her mother a weary half-smile.

Vida closed her eyes and took a deep breath.

CHAPTER 23
January 1979, Later That Morning, Tehran

———

The sun was rising when they drove past Eisenhower Avenue, nearing the airport. When they got out of the taxi, Vida looked up. The sky was turning blue with no clouds. From the outside, Mehrabad Airport looked empty, but when the sliding glass doors opened it was packed.

Did they sleep here last night?

At the ticket counter, an airline agent was standing alone. He was tall and lean with thinning hair and wore a three-piece suit with a white starched shirt.

"All the airlines are oversold, and flights are delayed," he told her. "Plus, some of the international airlines have stopped flying in because they're afraid of getting stuck here. No fuel."

Vida rubbed the back of her neck, biting her lower lip.

"I know you're on the Lufthansa flight. But they've canceled all their flights to Mehrabad until further notice," he said. "Let me check with the other airlines. It might take a few hours."

"You mean we might not be able to get out?" Vida wrinkled her eyebrows. "*Agha*, I must get out of here. My fourteen-year-old son is waiting..." She felt her throat constricting. She hadn't entertained the possibility of complications, never imagined her flight would be canceled or the airport would be overflowing with people. She might not get out, and she was terrified.

The man put his hand on her shoulder. "Let me see what I can do," he said reassuringly and then left through a door behind the ticket counter.

In the airport, men and women were standing, sitting on their bags, lying down, or using their jackets as pillows while children were crying, small boys playing cards, young girls chatting while they snacked.

Vida and Roya sat on a bench, waiting. A few hours went by.

While they were munching on the bag of mixed nuts and dried fruit Vida had brought from Maman's house, the ticket agent returned. "The KLM flight to Amsterdam leaves at six p.m., or you can take the Swissair flight to Zurich at eight p.m.," he said.

"Thank you, but is there any way we can take an earlier flight?" He had to do better. They had to get out as soon as possible.

"Look, it's the best I can do," he said. "I would take the flight to Zurich. It'll be easier to get a connecting flight to Munich." He was clearly hurried.

"Yes… the Swissair flight then." She bit her lip. This man was all she had, and she didn't want him to think she didn't appreciate what he was doing for her.

She couldn't believe how plans were getting rearranged and wondered how the masses of people in the airport were going to get out, but it didn't matter. All she cared about was herself and Roya and that Swissair flight.

The day turned into night. Vida called Maman from a pay phone a couple of times to give her updates. Exhaustion took over. Roya fell asleep in the early evening hours with her head on Vida's lap.

The two finally boarded the flight to Zurich at 10:00 p.m. Before the flight took off, Roya fell asleep against her mother's shoulder. By 9:00 a.m. local time they were in Munich.

Vida and Roya took a taxi to the Cades' home. The terrible worry of getting out of Iran, of being reunited with both her children, was over. She buried her face in Kasra's hair, smelling his scent and kissing the top of his head. She couldn't believe they had finally made it.

She and Roya would stay in the downstairs bedroom—the same one she had stayed in a few months earlier during her October visit.

* * * * *

Vida was tucking Roya into bed when Paula cracked the door open and stuck her head in. She wore white flannel pajamas covered with candy canes, a Christmas season left over.

"Come to the family room for a minute. I want you to see something," she said.

When Vida walked in, the television set was on. The reporter spoke calmly about the fact the US had told the Shah it was time for him to leave the country. The reporter said if the Shah left, he would never get back to Iran and the US's primary concern was the country's stability and independence. He mentioned a shift in US policy in that a civilian government was needed in Iran, which would only survive if the Shah left. He further indicated the future of Iran was either a right-wing military or the emergence of an anti-Western highly conservative Islamic state.

"Did you know?" Paula asked, standing next to Vida.

Vida was plunged into thought. *Time for the Shah to leave? What's going to happen in Iran?*

She looked up at Paula. "I'm sorry… what did you say?"

"Did you know the Shah might leave Iran? Is that why you left?"

"I had no idea," Vida whispered, still stunned by what she had heard on the news. "If I can't go back… I don't know what I'm going to do. My job… the house…" Thoughts were running through her head faster than she could speak to them.

Paula placed a hand on Vida's shoulder. "Well, reporters don't know. They have to say something. Maybe the Shah won't leave. It's a good thing you got out. Sounds like chaos over there."

"Yes," Vida said, her thoughts racing. "It's good we're not there. The demonstrations are dangerous." She paused, drowning in her thoughts. "But you're right, what do American journalists know? The Shah is the king. How *could he* leave?" Vida said, fighting what she feared might be true.

She went back to the bedroom, where Roya lay fast asleep, and sat on the edge of her bed. *What's going to happen to me if there is a change in government?*

* * * * *

A strong snowstorm descended on Munich, and they stayed inside for most of the next few days. At night, after the kids went to sleep, Vida would watch the news, losing hope. She called Tehran a few times during those days.

Mrs. White told her the library was shut down indefinitely, but the American Embassy expected it would reopen and wanted all the employees to come back to their positions. Vida worried she would get fired from her job if she didn't go back.

Maman focused on more practical matters on a phone call the next day. "It's cold at night, especially when the electricity goes out. But your plants are doing fine. Don't worry about a thing."

When Vida tried to reach Cyrus a couple of times, she couldn't get through. She figured he was still busy shuttling between Tehran and Shiraz.

She thought hard about whether she should return to Iran. She had left her house and her job, her income. She had money in the bank in Germany, but it wasn't enough. *How long would it last?* After a few days, she decided she would need to go back to Iran no matter what happened—back for the house to rent it, sell it, something. Then she had her job to consider. She had to return and formally resign. On the third day in Munich, she called Rosemary.

"I've been so worried about you. I called your house in Tehran twice last week."

Vida mentioned she might want to bring the kids to the United States.

"Don't think twice about it. Come," Rosemary insisted.

Initially, Vida had doubts about taking the children to New York. She would probably need to go back to Tehran at some point, and New York was that much further away. Still, it was not possible to leave both children in Germany at the private school, and Roya was too young to live with strangers. She couldn't think about being so far apart from them for an extended period, and taking the children back to Iran was out of the question. She thought about her last conversation with Maman when she promised she wouldn't leave the children. How could she? But if she was going to break that promise, leaving them with Rosemary was the logical choice.

She would stay in America until the political situation settled down. Then she would return to Tehran for a couple of weeks, rent the house, and resign from her job.

* * * * *

In the morning, she finally settled on a plan. Vida walked into the kitchen to tell Paula. The sun was shining outside, and Paula was dressed to go out. She poured Vida a cup of coffee, set the *International Herald Tribune* in front of her, kissed the top of her head in a motherly way, and left the kitchen.

Vida followed Paula with her eyes, knowing she wasn't prepared to read what was in front of her in black and white. She put down her mug. Reluctantly, she looked at the front page of the paper. Her hand hit the mug, and she managed to catch it as the coffee began to spill. She quickly mopped the spill with a paper napkin and looked back at the paper.

She noted a picture of the Shah with a stooped posture, his head down and brows bunched like he was crying. The headline read: "Iran in Turmoil as Shah Departs." Iran had been a monarchy for more than 2,500 years. *How could this be?* Her eyes were focused on the newspaper, but the words were blurred. Her thoughts jumped from the house in Iran, Mrs. White, Maman, Homa, and her bank account in Munich. *Will I have to leave Iran? What's going to happen to the house? What's Cyrus going to do? He works for the Shah's regime.*

She heard Roya in an upbeat tone. "Hi, Mom."

Vida glanced up, folding the newspaper.

"What's that?" Roya asked.

"Oh, nothing."

The ten-year-old took the newspaper and opened it. She saw the Shah's picture, and then she looked at her mother. "That's the Shah," she said.

"Yes, it is."

She put her head down and, in a soft voice, said, "We're not going back. Are we?"

Vida's knee was bouncing up and down. She noticed the rubber band holding up Roya's ponytail, a pink plastic sparkling ball on the elastic. She remembered Rosemary had bought that for her when she left the children there during the trip to Washington, DC.

"No. I don't think so." Vida held her slender fingers. Roya's palm felt moist. "Not for a little while." Vida was heartbroken to tell her daughter this way, but she had no choice. *We've lost our home and our country.*

In the afternoon, she went to the Deutsche Bank where she had opened the bank account in October. "I'd like to leave a change of address for this account," Vida said.

When he gave her the form, she changed the address from her home in Tehran to Rosemary's address in New York.

CHAPTER 24

January 1979,
New York to Tehran

"How long will you stay?" Rosemary asked as she carried
Vida's bag to the back room where the children had stayed
the last time.

"A couple of weeks. I'll leave once the kids start school and
get settled in," Vida said.

"You are welcome to stay as long as you want," Rosemary
assured her.

Vida couldn't believe she was going to leave the children in
New York for an indefinite period of time and then head back
to an Iran in turmoil.

"Are you afraid?" Rosemary held Vida's hand.

Vida cleared her throat. "Of course. But I can't take them back
with me. That's out of the question. I must go back alone and
get back as quickly as possible." She was trying to be calm
but raised her voice.

"I totally understand. Don't worry about the kids. They'll be okay," Rosemary said, squeezing Vida's fingers.

"I know. I know." Vida yawned and then rubbed her eyes. She felt comforted, knowing her friend would take care of her children, but still she worried something awful might happen while she was gone. "I want to make sure we do this right," she changed the subject.

"Do what right?" Rosemary asked.

"I need to pay you... for watching the children."

"You can pay me later. With your situation, leaving your house and your job, I don't feel right doing this now."

Vida put her hand on Rosemary's shoulder. "Look, I'm not comfortable leaving them here without paying you. We need an arrangement."

"We'll talk in the morning."

Paying Rosemary would be less expensive than leaving both children in Munich. That was why Vida had brought them to New York. As uncomfortable as it was to talk about money, she had to do it. She fingered the chain that held the carnelian necklace and scratched her neck.

The next morning, the two came up with a simple financial arrangement. Vida would open two bank accounts in the name of the children and write monthly checks to Rosemary so Rosemary could cash them regularly. If

Rosemary needed extra money, she could draw funds from one of the accounts as long as one of the children cosigned the withdrawal slip.

When Vida went to the Citibank branch to open the accounts, she remembered the day she went to the *Bank-e Markazi* in Tehran to deposit the insurance money and how easily her money had been taken away. *What happened in Iran would never happen in America*, she thought. Still, she felt overheated when she spoke to the branch manager and kept clearing her throat.

"If there is any emergency, you will have access to more money," Vida assured Rosemary.

"The monthly checks will be plenty to cover all of their expenses, and then some," Rosemary had responded.

During the next few days Rosemary guided Vida to enroll the children in their new schools, took her to buy school supplies, and accompanied them for their first day of school. The plan was Vida would return to Tehran for a few weeks, two months at most, but then she'd return to New York before the school year ended.

During this time Cyrus called Vida with updates on what he was doing. On one of the calls, he told her he was heading to Germany to look at a factory and then to Switzerland where he would be skiing.

"Business is slow, and I figured I'd take advantage while I'm in Germany. And I'm not going back with all this happening."

She knew how much he loved to ski.

They both paused on the call. Then Cyrus chimed in, "Eventually Iran will go back to normal. It's just going to take time."

"You have no idea what they're showing on the nightly news here."

"Don't believe it. American media blows it all out of proportion. They're known for that."

"What I'm seeing is scary, though." Vida knew how the American system worked, but how could she not believe what she was seeing. She had experienced the outbursts on the streets during the last few months in Iran, and now she saw the anti-American demonstrations and the protests broadcast live. She couldn't understand why Cyrus thought things would go back to normal over time. *Does he know something I don't know? Or is he trying to make me feel better?*

Despite what Cyrus thought and what she saw on ABC News, she knew the right thing was for her to go back to Iran, sell the house, and formally quit her job. She would return to be with the children in New York as soon as she could.

That afternoon she booked her flight back to Tehran.

*   *   *   *   *

After dinner, Vida was drinking coffee with Rosemary in the kitchen when Roya ran in. "Come... Iran... it's on the news," announced Roya.

The news was tracking Iran's progress, so it wasn't surprising there was an update that night. Vida went into the family room while Rosemary finished washing the dinner dishes.

The television screen showed a man with a large white turban walking down the stairs of an Air France plane. The flight had landed in Tehran.

Vida stared at the television set, not blinking, as the British announcer reported with a heavy English accent.

Finally, Rosemary walked into the room. "Vida, what's going on? You're as white as a ghost," she said.

"Ah, ah… watching the news," she said. Her words spilled out in a robotic way. "They say after being in exile, Khomeini has returned to Iran. They say the real contest will be between the ayatollah and the Shah's army. They are calling him 'the father of the revolution.' The inside of the terminal at the Tehran Airport became chaotic when he landed. More than a thousand religious leaders came to see him. Khomeini's first words were that he wants to get rid of all the roots of the old regime. The announcer says he is adored, so many people believe this frail priest can be the answer to Iran's problems."

Rosemary asked, "Who is this ayatollah?"

"A troublemaker," Roya announced. "He won't be in Iran for long. The Shah's going to come back, and we'll be home by *Nourooz*." She referred to the Iranian New Year, which was coming up in a couple of months. Then the ten-year-old turned to her mother. "Right, Mommy?"

Vida sat on the sofa and stared into her coffee mug. She didn't know what to think or say. She bit her lower lip, not wanting to give her daughter false hope.

"Right, Mom?" Roya repeated, throwing herself roughly onto the couch next to her mother. As the girl landed next to her, Vida lost control of the mug, and the coffee splashed into the air. Vida jerked her leg so she wouldn't spill the hot liquid on herself. A drop of it landed on her pants, but the rest of it found the Persian carpet, the one Vida had sent Rosemary from Tehran as a thank you gift for watching the kids when she went to Washington, DC, for her seminar.

"Roya! Now look... it's all over the carpet." She forcefully placed the near empty mug on the table.

The little girl ran into the kitchen and came back with pieces of paper towel.

"I'm sorry." On hands and knees, Roya tried to wipe the stain.

"I know it was an accident, but you need to be careful," Vida said firmly.

Rosemary reappeared with a small carton of salt and shook a thick layer of it onto the spilled liquid, the white crystals instantly turning brown.

"The stains will come out. You'll see. It'll all be gone," she said. She looked up at Vida. "I have all kinds of tricks up my sleeve."

Roya smiled, relieved Rosemary was going to clean up the mess she had made.

Vida stared at the carpet with her muscles quivering and her heart pounding. It wasn't the coffee; it was her future.

"It's all going to work out," yelled Rosemary, who was now tugging the upright Hoover from the hall closet. "I'll take care of it."

Vida took the mug back into the kitchen. Khomeini had landed in Iran. All she could think about was how she would have to distance herself from Iran as fast as she could. Her thoughts drifted to Cyrus, and she wondered if he would be able to go back now that a new regime was being put in place. She wondered if his life was in danger.

*   *   *   *   *

It was February of 1979 when Rosemary and the children took Vida to the JFK airport for a flight back to Tehran. The day before, Vida had gotten a call from Mrs. White that the library had reopened. The lady at the Pan Am counter called out Vida's row to board the plane. Vida stopped and waved at the kids before she walked down the runway to board the flight. She had a knot in her stomach.

When she took her window seat, she fell into deep thought about leaving the kids. *What if they get sick? What if Kasra has another seizure? Roya is a picky eater.* Vida held her necklace in her hand, tugging at the chain while gazing out the window. When she flew with the children, she always took the aisle. Kasra liked to sit by the window, and Roya liked being cocooned between the two. The only time Vida remembered sitting by the window was when she was sent to boarding school. Her life had been filled with so many flights, each one the end of an old chapter, launching her into a new one.

After a few minutes a man arrived to take the seat next to her.

"I'm on my way to Cologne to visit the German factory... we've just released the Ford Granada in Britain and Germany. The European Granada is barely any different than the US version. Same standards of the Ford specifications. It's a fantastic car," he proclaimed as if Vida might be interested.

She didn't care, but she didn't want to appear rude, so she nodded. Her mind drifted to the house in Tehran. She could rent or maybe sell it. But perhaps it wasn't the right time to sell. *I wonder what Cyrus would say about selling the house.*

The man next to her continued his chatter. "The Ford Granada is a fantastic car."

He just needs to shut up.

* * * * *

As the plane was about to land, Vida put on a trench coat and covered her hair with a floral scarf. Maman had told her over the phone it was now mandatory all women cover themselves in public, and most importantly their hair, in strict observance of Islamic law. It was early morning when

388 · IMPERFECT

the plane landed. Her cousin had ordered her a car, and his driver stood outside of customs holding a sign with her name. She smiled and let out a huge breath when she made eye contact with him. He didn't smile back. The driver had been an orphan when her cousin brought him into his household. Vida had known him practically his entire life. He was family.

In the car, the driver explained, "Things have changed here, *khanoom* Shamsa. Why did you come back? We've lost our Iran. It's gone," he said.

Vida looked to the side of the road and noticed a group of unshaven young men, maybe a few years older than Kasra, standing stiff and carrying machine guns.

"They're kids. What do they know about guns?" said the driver.

"Who are they?"

"They are the children of the mullahs. They are running this country now."

At a traffic light in northern Tehran, Vida saw no smiles on people's faces. Women walked on the side of the street with their hair and bodies uncomfortably covered. On the side of Pahlavi Avenue on a billboard, Vida saw an oversized poster, blood red handprints on top of a picture of soldiers and tanks. Above them a white dove hovered. *Allah o'Akbar*—God is great—had been inscribed in the dove's wings. Next to that was a poster plastered on a wall with a mother in her fur coat and jewels. She held the hands of a boy and girl, behind bars. The inscription read, "All the wealthy from Shemiran in *zendan,* jail." Shemiran was Vida's neighborhood where she lived growing up. She didn't consider herself wealthy. It had been a calm middle-class suburb of Tehran until an uprising against the whole neighborhood took place.

As they got close to the home, the driver stopped at a traffic light in front of a girl's high school, the same one Vida would have attended had she not gone abroad. School girls stood in line at the entrance, each with their hair tightly covered with a *roosari,* their faces blank. An older woman wearing a black chador was seated at the entrance. She handed each girl a tissue, and they wiped their lips with it before entering the school.

"She is checking to make sure they're not wearing any lipstick. At some of the schools, if they find out a girl has been wearing makeup, they put acid on the tissue and force her to wipe her face. We hear these stories every day," said the driver.

Vida felt a pounding in her ears. She never thought it would come to this. This was a foreign country.

* * * * *

During one of the first few days, Vida drove to Linda's house for dinner.

"It's a good thing you got the kids out. *Everything* has changed. At school the boys and girls are separated in different classrooms. The girls must cover their hair with a scarf and wear a gray *roopoosh.*"

Vida imagined Roya covering her hair and wearing an overcoat. She would never put her ten-year-old daughter through this madness.

She had made the right decision, leaving her children in New York.

"And it's not safe here anymore," Linda said. "They're arresting people all the time, for no reason. And the phones are tapped. They're listening to phone calls. Be careful what you say on the phone," Linda said.

"Who's 'they'?"

"I don't know. People say things on the phone, and then they get arrested the next day," Linda said.

Vida felt alone with Cyrus out of the country. She knew she had to act fast to get out.

* * * * *

After she arrived in Tehran, Vida went back to work. She wanted to leave Iran within a few weeks but stayed much longer than planned. When she spoke to Mrs. White, her boss assured her the embassy had strict orders to keep the library open. When Vida would buy a ticket and use up the food in the refrigerator, Mrs. White would come up with a new task that only Vida could do. It was clear her boss didn't want her to leave.

On the first day of spring, *Norouz*, the celebration of the vernal equinox and the Zoroastrian tradition that predated

Islam, the city was calm. The demonstrations had stopped and gas stations operated as normal.

Homa had a gathering on that first day, her *haft seen* table arranged with the traditional goldfish, hyacinth, and all the usual dressings. Relatives visited. Vida felt a surge of hope the political situation might stabilize and she might bring the children back.

At first it appeared as though this regime was not going to get in the way of the secular *Norouz* celebrations. But then after a week, the government issued an edict declaring the new year celebration as *taghootee*, associated with the former royal regime. *Norouz* would be banned as a secular celebration and for its lack of connection to Islam. On the thirteenth day of the new year, *seezdabedar*, when traditionally the Iranian people would picnic in parks and by rivers to celebrate the end of the holidays, the riots began again.

Vida talked to her children weekly, asking for details about school, their new friends, and piano lessons. Her body ached when she heard her children's voices. They seemed well-adjusted, but she couldn't believe it was true. Each time they spoke, Rosemary insisted Vida stay in Iran as long as she needed to take care of her affairs.

CHAPTER 25

Summer of 1979, Tehran

It was getting warm, and the air conditioning wasn't working. Vida didn't sleep well several nights in a row. It was early June when she couldn't bear to be away from the children a moment longer. She had stayed in Iran longer than planned.

Cyrus called her at home one night. He was still in Switzerland, afraid to come back to Tehran given the new regime.

Vida periodically sent him a care package stuffed with his clothes.

In the past she had phoned him from home, but now she was afraid to use the home line. They, whoever *they* were, could be listening. "I'll call you tomorrow," Vida said abruptly.

The next day, knowing it was still a risk, but hoping *they* wouldn't be listening to the phones overseen by the American embassy, Vida called Cyrus from the reference desk at the library. She looked up as Ali walked by. *Is he listening to my conversation?*

"I can't come back, not now. It's still too early," Cyrus said.

"I know. It's not safe. You should not come back. It's too dangerous for you. I don't want to be here either. But Mrs. White keeps saying all is going as planned." Vida talked fast to get off the phone.

"Things will go back to normal, but it's going to take time, longer than I originally thought," Cyrus said. "Maybe a year."

A year? He had been far more optimistic the week before.

"What should *I* do? I can't be away from the kids anymore," she whispered.

Ali was walking back down the corridor, and she swirled in her chair to turn away.

"I've contacted graduate schools in the Boston area. I'm going to enroll in an MBA program. Come with me," he said.

Boston? She had not been there and knew nothing about Boston.

"It'll be temporary," he said. "We'll come back to Tehran once things settle down."

She was still thinking, digesting the plan he had hatched without her. She tapped her finger on her desk.

"Vida? Are you there?" he asked.

"Yes. I'm here."

"I thought we got disconnected. What do you think?"

She held the phone against her chin and looked down at her gold bangle bracelets as she ran her fingers along the ridges. "I will need to take a leave of absence from my job. Do you think it's safe to lock up the house and leave?"

"Yes, Mirdamad is a good neighborhood. Just lock it all up. It will all be there when you get back. But whatever you do, act fast. You need to get out of Iran," he said.

*   *   *   *   *

The next night Vida visited Maman at her apartment.

"Don't worry about the house. It's not important. Your children are more important," said Maman.

"I agree, Maman *joon*. I agree," Vida said looking down. "I'm worried about your safety."

"I'll be fine. If things get bad, I'll join you in the US," said Maman.

For once, Vida didn't feel any anger toward her mother. She looked at Maman's hands resting on the kitchen table, and Vida noticed her fingers were long and tapered like Roya's. Vida reached around her neck and took off the carnelian necklace. She bunched it up in one hand.

"It's for you," she said, ashamed she had not thought about buying a gift for her mother before leaving, this time for good.

"It's beautiful," Maman said, running her hand along the gold chain. "But it's yours." She offered it back to Vida.

"It was mine. It brought me luck, and now I want you to have it," Vida said.

Maman looked down, the stone shining under the kitchen light. She looked up at Vida. "I will treasure it," she said.

* * * * *

The next day Vida had an appointment to see Mrs. White in her office, not knowing what she was going to ask for even though she was within days of leaving. The mental exhaustion had been building, and she couldn't tolerate it much longer. She told her boss she couldn't stand to be away from her children any longer and asked for a leave of absence for a year.

"A year?" Mrs. White repeated. "That's a long time. Things will get back to normal here. And the American Embassy doesn't want us to shut down the library," she said, leaning forward on her desk.

"Do you believe that?" Vida said.

Mrs. White leaned back in her chair and looked down. "Of course. These orders come from Washington, DC," she said.

"So you're being ordered to stay," Vida said leaning forward. "Do *you* believe things will get back to normal in Iran?" Vida asked, staring into Mrs. White's eyes.

"Vida, you're a smart woman. I can't argue with you. I don't know. I'm not sure anymore," said Mrs. White.

"Does six months sound reasonable?" Vida asked, rubbing the back of her neck. Her eyes bounced from the desk to the back wall to the stapler. She started to sweat and couldn't stare down Mrs. White any longer. This woman had been so helpful to her, and she couldn't find it in her to ask for more favors. And a part of her felt bad. *What if it's not safe for Mrs. White to stay in Iran? What if they have it all wrong in Washington?*

Mrs. White sat back in the reclining leather chair, and it squeaked as if it might be trying to tell Vida something. Her boss played with her pearls, twirling them as she contemplated the offer. *If she twisted them anymore,* Vida thought, *she might choke herself.* Her boss seemed to be struggling, holding back something important.

"Is six months too long for a leave of absence?" Vida repeated.

Mrs. White sat up. "We will manage. I will hold your job," she answered at last.

Vida's eyes were shining and locked on Mrs. White now. "Thank you so much," Vida said. Then she stood, rounded the desk, and gave Mrs. White a strong hug. It felt as though her boss might melt in her arms.

*   *   *   *   *

That afternoon Vida went back to the office. On her way, she thought about who would be in charge at the library and how she would divide up her duties. She wouldn't tell anyone about her departure until she had a plan in place.

She went into the kitchen for a cup of coffee. Ali was wiping the counter. Before she could say anything, he looked up at her, "Vida *khanoom*, are you going to make coffee?" Then he sat down at the small table in the corner and crossed his legs, leaning back in his chair like he was waiting for her reaction.

She was taken aback. It was strange he had referred to her by her first name. In the years he had worked for her, he had always called her by her last name, "Mrs. Shamsa." Usually, he would insist on making her coffee, or at least he would boil the water while she would scoop a spoon of instant coffee into her mug. That was his job. His smug attitude was new. She was surprised to see this change in him.

"Yes, I am. How are you doing, Ali?"

"What do you mean?" he asked defensively.

She shrugged her shoulders. "I'm wondering how *you* are doing. You should make sure you have enough food at your house—rice, cooking oil, milk for the girls. I can help if you want. You never know what will happen with these demonstrations," she said. "Shops could close down for a long time."

"I am not worried about it," he said, rocking on the back two legs of his chair. "If I run out of food, I'll take it from your house. I'm sure you have plenty for all of us," he said, staring defiantly at her.

Vida couldn't look at him. She crossed and uncrossed her arms, and then she rubbed her hand down her leg. She had an empty feeling in the pit of her stomach. Ali was different.

The water started to boil. She poured it into her mug and stirred. The sound of the spoon striking the mug echoed in her ear. She opened the refrigerator for milk, pouring a little bit in her mug. When she turned around, Ali was gone. She couldn't figure out what was going on with him. She put the mug to her mouth but didn't have an appetite for it.

* * * * *

That night she went home and began to plan her move. She had put on her nightgown, and her teeth were already brushed. She pushed back the bedspread, climbed into bed, and reached over and turned off the light. After a few minutes, the phone rang. When she picked up, she didn't hear anything at first. *Maybe an overseas call—America? Germany? The kids? Cyrus?*

"*Allo... Allo...*" she said.

"Vida *khanoom*?" asked the muffled voice on the other end.

"Yes," she said. Her stomach ached.

"Your library... it's a beehive... a beehive for spies like you," said the voice on the other end of the line.

"Who is this?" she asked, sitting up, reaching for the bedside light.

"You are a spy for the Americans. You will have to admit it," the muffled voice said. It sounded as if the person was covering the mouthpiece.

"Who... is... this?" she asked again firmly. She sat up in bed, the bedspread bunched in her hand. She eyed the curtain. *Was someone outside of the house?*

Then the line went dead.

She hung up the phone and stared at it for a few seconds. Terrified, she looked down at her shaking hand. She went into the windowless family room and closed all the bedroom doors. She sat on the love seat and folded her legs up against her.

The first thing that came to mind was the bicentennial celebration in the library in July of 1976. She remembered meeting Ambassador Harris and Ali wearing the Uncle Sam hat, standing in the background, grinning, while a photographer snapped her picture. Then she remembered her conversation with Ali earlier that day and how he, a servant with a newfound boldness, had shamelessly invited himself to her house to take her food, calling her by her first name, Vida *khanoom*.

The tremor of her legs rippled inside her. *I'm just imagining this*, she thought. *I need to sleep.* She remembered her conversation with Mrs. White and how her boss was not sure everything would be okay.

Slowly she opened the door to her bedroom, went inside, and stood by the edge of the window. Pulling back the curtain, she looked outside at the street and expected to see people waiting outside her front door. Nobody was there. Her heart was racing.

A few months earlier, in January, demonstrations erupted on the same street, the night Roya had thrown up and slept in the bathtub. Now that same street was quiet, as though those turbulent moments had never happened.

She went into the living room and poured herself a shot of brandy. Hassan had told her to do that once when she couldn't fall asleep. She climbed into bed and pulled the covers over her head, as if to hide from her own life problems. Turning from one side to another, lifting her head off the pillow, punching at it as if she was in a boxing ring, eventually she fell asleep.

* * * * *

The next morning while listening to a tape in her car radio, she felt more relaxed. She thought about how she would make her announcement to her staff about the leave of absence. She wouldn't say how long she'd be gone. She would only assure the team everything would work out, as Mrs. White had initially told her.

When she pulled up, a crowd of people milled around outside the library. Men stood in uniforms at the front entrance, as if blocking it. She turned off the radio and parked the car in front on the street.

For a couple of minutes she sat in the car, watching through the windshield and leaning on the steering wheel as she tried to understand what was going on. Marines were indeed blocking the entrance so nobody could get in. Through the glass doors she could see similar men in uniforms. She pulled the emergency brake and then climbed out and slammed the car door.

"What's going on?" she asked one of the men in front. "I'm Mrs. Shamsa, head librarian."

"There's been a bomb scare. We're sweeping the library to make sure we don't find anything. We don't think it's serious," he said.

Serious, she thought. She had a vision of Kasra and Roya in New York with Rosemary. What could happen if she got stuck in Iran with her children so far away? In that instant she knew. *What am I doing, taking my time? My children need me. The hell with the job and the house. I must go.*

When she met with her employees, they were clearly shaken by the bomb scare. She made a point of assuring them her leave of absence had nothing to do with the morning events.

"I planned it many weeks ago," she told them in as convincing a voice as she could manage. "The American Embassy has no intention of closing the library. We need you all to stay," she said with confidence, invoking the same tone Mrs. White had used the day before.

Her employees simply looked and listened. Nobody took notes or asked questions. Her eyes caught a glimpse of Ali in the back, and her heart started to race. He looked at her as if he was in a trance. Vida knew she wasn't convincing any of them. But what else could she do? She had to go, no matter what anyone thought.

The next evening as the plane accelerated and began to lift off the runway in Tehran, she sat by the window and gazed down on the city lights. Her eyes were sore, and she sniffled as she wiped her nose. Out of habit, she reached for the carnelian necklace, but it wasn't there. She wondered if Maman was wearing the necklace and touching it at that moment. She could hear the engines on the plane. She couldn't help but wonder when, or if, she'd ever come back to Iran.

CHAPTER 26

July 1979, Westchester County, New York

———

Vida felt safe to be in America.

By the time the taxi drove up to Rosemary's house, it was dark. She saw a brand-new red convertible in the driveway. *I hope she doesn't have visitors. I am in no mood to socialize.* She longed to see the kids and to relax with Rosemary.

Outside the air was warm and muggy. *How long will I stay in New York?* She had told Cyrus she would take the children to Boston. *What is Boston like? Will I need a job right away? Where would Roya and Kasra go to school?*

She rang the doorbell but noted the door was ajar. She peeked into the house, put her luggage down, and the kids came running. Rosemary was strolling along behind them in a pink silky nightgown, her hair up in a twist, wearing layers of foundation and large false eyelashes. *Is this Rosemary?* The kids appeared healthy and happy, chattering about going to school, camping with the Girl Scouts, and taking guitar lessons. Everything seemed normal, but something was not the same. Rosemary looked like she might be medicated. Vida wondered whether the kids had been a bother. She was tired and wanted to hold the kids for a while.

That night after tucking them in, kissing them on the cheek, something Vida longed for over the last few months, she put on her pajamas and got ready to go to sleep.

Rosemary came to the room and stood in the doorway. She was holding envelopes, many of them. "Do you want your mail?" she asked, holding out the bundle.

Rosemary's voice was harsh, hostile.

"I got a lot of mail," Vida said reaching for the stack. "I'll look at it in the morning. I'm feeling more jet lagged this time than I did before," she said.

Why is Rosemary being so distant? Setting the envelopes on the desk, Vida noticed all of them had been opened. Each letter and statement opened and unfolded and then stuffed back into the envelope. Vida's palms felt sweaty.

"Rosemary?" she called out, poking her head into the hall.

Rosemary was already down the hallway. "Yes."

"Why are the envelopes all opened?"

Rosemary turned her head, her chin in the air. "I thought I should open them," she said, her voice quivering. Then she continued down the hallway.

What's going on? Vida looked through the stack. Most of the envelopes had bank statements from Citibank and the Deutsche Bank in Munich. She found a letter from the State Department at the bottom of the stack.

The balance of the Deutsche Bank account was the same, unchanged. When she unfolded the most recent Citibank statement from her US account, she noticed the balance was far less than it should have been. She blinked because she thought she was mistaken. She examined the figures again and did a quick calculation in her head. The balance was off—by a lot.

Then she opened the bank statements from the earlier months. Withdrawals had been made in March, April, May, and June, at first for $10,000 in March, April, and May, and then $20,000 in June.

Vida marched into the kitchen. "Rosemary?" she asked, still hoping for an explanation.

Rosemary was holding the phone, its long yellow cord extending from the wall across the kitchen table. "Darling, I'll call you back."

Darling, I'll call you back? "Did you withdraw money from the Citibank account?" asked Vida.

"Yes, I did," responded Rosemary. She sat back down at the kitchen table and began flipping through the pages of a magazine. Her voice was shaking again.

"Why?" Carefully, Vida pulled a chair out and sat down, not knowing what to expect and searching her mind for reasons. *Had Kasra gotten sick and gone to the hospital? Medical bills?* Vida had bought health insurance for the kids before she left, and they would have mentioned something on the weekly phone calls if there had been a medical emergency.

Rosemary closed the magazine and smacked it on the kitchen table. "You told me you were leaving your house in Iran."

"I did," Vida said, wondering what this had to do with her question. "I locked up the house and left." *What does this have to do with my money in the bank?*

"You said you have no other money," Rosemary said accusingly.

"I did not say that," Vida protested. "I told you it was a difficult situation in Iran. It was difficult to get money out of the country and to sell my home, which is true."

"You said you couldn't afford to leave both kids in Germany," Rosemary continued.

"Correct. I couldn't leave them there," Vida said in as calm a voice as she could manage. "Roya is too young to be left with strangers. You have been like family to me."

Vida took a deep breath. "We made a financial arrangement before I left, and you insisted the monthly amount was fair," said Vida, raising her voice.

Rosemary looked down at her fingers.

"Did we *not* have an arrangement?" asked Vida firmly.

"Yes," said Rosemary in a soft voice, picking at her nail polish. "But, but... after I talked to Jimmy, we decided it wasn't fair," she said, looking up at Vida as if she was apologizing.

"Who's Jimmy?" asked Vida with a look of disgust. The hair on her back stood up.

"My boyfriend."

Vida's eyes nearly popped out, and she raised her voice. "Your boyfriend? What does he have to do with *our* arrangement?"

Rosemary looked down at the table, drawing imaginary circles with her fingers.

"If you needed more money, all you had to do was ask," Vida said, leaning across the kitchen table and staring into Rosemary's eyes where she hoped to find her old friend in there. *Who is this stranger?* "I would have given you what you needed. You took thirty percent of my savings, and it is all I have to live on now."

"When I saw your bank account from Deutsche Bank, I realized things weren't as bad as I thought... We decided

I deserved more," Rosemary said flatly. "I'm sorry, okay? I'm sorry," she whined.

"*We* decided? So, you just went into the kids' account and took the money?" Vida bunched her fingers. She wanted to pound her fist on the table. *So*, Vida thought, *this again*. She didn't want to raise her voice. She didn't want the kids to hear her.

"Your situation is much different than Jimmy and I thought. Plus, you got a letter from the State Department. You probably have a new job lined up too," Rosemary said, now crossing her arms. Vida could tell her friend was trying to get aggressive with her, but it wasn't in her nature to do that. Rosemary looked lost.

"What *new* job?" Vida looked at the envelope from the State Department. She pulled out the letter. It was from Mr. Todd.

When Vida stood up, she leaned against the side of the table, and it felt like it might flip over. "Is that it? Is there anything else I should know?" Vida asked. Heat was flushing through her body.

"No... that's it." Rosemary opened the magazine again. Her hands were shaking.

Vida was burning up inside. She went back to the room and opened the letter from Mr. Todd. It was dated from the week before, the day she had spoken to Mrs. White. She must have given him a forwarding address. He said he thought it was the right thing for Vida to get out of Iran, that he couldn't write much in a letter but invited her to call him once she got to the US. He would be a reference if she needed a job.

That night Vida paced in the bedroom. The kids were asleep. As quietly as she could, she repacked the clothes she had started to unpack a few hours earlier.

*   *   *   *   *

In the morning while the kids still slept, Vida showered, dressed, and called a taxi.

Rosemary was buttering a piece of toast when the taxi arrived. "Where are you going?" she asked as Vida swooped in and grabbed her purse. Rosemary looked like she might burst into tears.

"I have business to take care of," Vida said, refusing to look at her. She felt a tightness in her eyes.

Sliding into the backseat, Vida told the cab driver to take her to the nearest car dealer.

"There's a Ford dealership close by."

"Fine. And please, I'm in a rush." She rolled down the window, propped her elbow out, and sat back.

The cab driver, a young dark-haired man with slick hair, was still looking at her in the rearview mirror.

"Please go. I said I'm in a rush."

He was looking in the rearview mirror and drove. She knew she had frightened the driver with her rude response.

The dealership, with its red, white, and blue banners, leftover from the Fourth of July celebrations, reminded her of the opening of the library and all of the decorations they had put up for the bicentennial only three years before.

"Can I help you with something?" asked one of the salespeople as he rushed outside from the building, pulling on his blazer.

"I need a car now. I can pay with traveler's checks," she said. "What do you have?" She started to raise her voice.

The salesman looked pale and frightened and started walking to the back of the lot.

"Are we talking about a sports car, a four-door...?"

"A family car. Four doors."

"I would recommend a Granada. It's a solid car."

She remembered the Ford executive on the flight back to Tehran a couple of months before when he had given the car great reviews.

Without hesitation, "I'll take the Granada," she said.

"We have one in gold. It was just cleaned this morning, and you can drive it right off the lot."

She didn't like the color—too flashy. It reminded her of jewelry, only it was a car.

"Do you have any other colors?"

"I can get one in green, but you'd have to come back tomorrow to get it. It's a beautiful hunter green. Do you want to—"

She cut him off. "No. I'll take the gold one."

"Do you have insurance?" He loosened his tie. "Ma'am, I'm trying to help you. Can you please slow down? In the State of New York, we cannot sell you a car without insurance."

She crossed her arms and in a low voice asked, "Where can I buy car insurance?"

"Do you see the Sears department store across the street?" the man said, pointing. "There's an Allstate agency in the basement. I can get the paperwork ready for you while you go to buy the insurance. By the time you come back, the car will be ready, and you can drive it away."

"Great," she said, unfolding her arms. She felt light, like she might be able to fly over to Sears.

"Where can I get a map?" she asked.

"Where are you heading?"

"Boston."

"I'll see what I can find."

"Thank you." As she marched off, she laughed at how ridiculously bossy she had been. It was a first.

In the basement of the department store she bought the insurance. When she came back, the gold Granada was parked in front, as shiny as the chain of her carnelian necklace. She stuck her head in. It smelled brand new. It felt as though she was starting a fresh life. On the passenger seat lay a folded map, and on it the handwritten words, "Good Luck in Boston." She smiled.

* * * * *

Back at the house, the kids were eating breakfast.

"Mom, did *you* pack all my clothes last night?" Roya asked, biting into a piece of toast.

Rosemary's face went pale. "You packed all their clothes last night?"

"What are those keys for? Is that for a car?" Kasra asked.

"Yes, I bought a car. I need you to hurry up. Get your bags. We're leaving," Vida said.

"Wow, a new car." Kasra's face lit up.

"But, Mom…" Roya whined.

"Go… go… get your things. We're leaving in ten minutes."

Rosemary sat down at the kitchen table. "You're leaving? Just like that?"

Vida stared at Rosemary. She spoke loudly and firmly, "Just like that." She couldn't remember ever raising her voice like this, and it felt good.

"Vida… please don't go. Not like this. I thought you would be staying for a few more months until everything settles down in Iran."

"You thought wrong," Vida replied as she kept walking, her chin high and her chest puffed out.

"Ahh…" Rosemary caught up to Vida and placed her hand on Vida's shoulder.

Vida looked at Rosemary's hand. "Please don't touch me," she said and pushed the hand off her shoulder as if it were a piece of lint. She saw a ray of sunshine beaming through the window. "And don't try to take any more money out of my accounts, or you'll regret it."

In the process of purchasing her car, Vida had already notified the bank to remove Rosemary's access to her accounts by phone. She needed to formalize it right here and now.

"Kasra, Roya… come on. I don't have all day," she called.

In the kitchen Rosemary bent over to hug Roya. She held her in her arms, squeezing hard like she didn't want to let go. When Roya pulled away, she said, "I love you," tugging at the little girl's fingers, her voice breaking.

Kasra stood looking at the two of them.

"Love you too, Rosemary," Roya said.

"Bye," said Kasra, showing no emotion.

Vida's face felt cool from the burning sensation when she first yelled at Rosemary.

Kasra adjusted himself in the front seat with Roya in the back, leaning forward over the armrest so her face popped up in between her mother and brother.

"Where are we going?" the fourteen-year-old boy asked in a calm tone.

"Boston." She started the car and released the brake. Vida started whistling.

Kasra opened the map. "What's in Boston?"

"Good schools. We're going to live there for a while and see if we like it," Vida said. She pressed on the gas, and Roya fell back in her seat. Vida stopped the car.

"Put on your seat belts, both of you," she said, looking at Kasra and then at Roya in the rear-view mirror.

"But Mom..." whined Roya.

"Do it now," Vida said with a slow but firm tone.

"What about Iran?" Roya asked.

"We'll go back... It might take a little bit of time."

"How long is a little bit of time?"

"What did I say about asking too many questions?" Vida said.

"Mommy..."

"I don't know. Let's see what happens," she said. "There's the sign for the highway," said Vida, pointing. She sagged in the driver's seat and rolled her neck. She turned on the radio and began humming as she drove away from Rosemary's house.

CHAPTER 27
November 1979, Thanksgiving, Boston

———

The skin on the fifteen-pound turkey was sizzling when she took the bird out of the oven. Their friends stood around the dining room table and hovered over the stuffing, corn, and green bean casserole covered with mushroom soup. Steam rose above each dish.

"What are you doing to that poor bird?" complained one of the Iranian neighbors. "What's taking so long?" They had not had a traditional Thanksgiving dinner before.

"Start serving yourselves. I'll be right there," yelled Vida.

It was a dinner party for the other Iranians in the building. Vida had rented a small apartment in a building in a nice Jewish neighborhood with good public schools in a Boston suburb. Cyrus moved into an apartment in the same building. Some called the building the Tel Aviv Towers, but in the last few months several Iranian families had moved in.

Now those people called it the Tehran Towers. The Iranian families were not familiar with the American Thanksgiving tradition, and they made loud cheering sounds when Vida carried the big bird to the dining room table. She carved the turkey the way Linda had shown her all those years they celebrated Thanksgiving in Tehran.

Earlier in the fall, school had started for the kids. After searching for a month for a library job, Vida eventually got a job as a bank teller at the same bank where she opened her accounts. Within a month she was promoted.

It was November 22, and eighteen days earlier crowds of Iranian students ransacked US property in Tehran and took fifty-two American citizens hostage at the US Embassy in Tehran, the same Embassy where Vida had visited many times because of her job. When the nightly news initially showed the blindfolded men, Vida recognized the one right in the front. He had attended the bicentennial celebration at the library.

When she had landed in New York six months earlier to get her children from Rose's home, Vida had hoped her stay in America would be short, and she would go back to her home and job quickly. She and Cyrus had agreed they would move to Boston, for a year, at most.

Now, in the Tehran Towers, the Iranian families in the building became friends and had dinner parties on the weekends. At the gatherings they discussed the political situation and debated the cause of the revolution over drinks. They all agreed the Shah would return but had no consensus on the timing.

It was late when they finished eating on Thanksgiving night.

The music was blasting in the living room, and the guests were disco dancing. Cyrus grabbed Vida's hand and whispered in her ear, "Marry me?"

For an instant she thought her heart stopped beating. She looked into his eyes.

"I mean it. I want to share my life with you. You have changed me. I can't imagine living one more day without you," he said. "What do you think?"

She wanted to throw her arms in the air, scream, and say yes, but she couldn't, not here, not now. Not in front of all these people who had been strangers a few months before.

"I love you," he said.

"I love you more," she responded. She turned around and went back into the kitchen to finish the dishes. Vida suddenly heard the phone ring.

"Roya, can you get it?" Vida called out. With all the noise, she couldn't tell if Roya heard her.

"Rooooyaaa?" she repeated.

A few minutes later Roya ran up to her. "It's Maman," she announced.

"Ohhh… Maman." Vida tugged roughly at the dishwashing gloves to free her hands. She hadn't talked to her mother in several weeks and felt a smile beaming across her face.

"Tell her I'll be right there," she said. "It's my mother calling from Iran," she announced to the others in the kitchen. *It must be four in the morning for her. This is an odd time for her to be calling.*

Vida rushed past the guests and into the bedroom.

"Maman *joon*… How are you?"

"Fine. Are you having a party?" asked her mother.

"We have a few families over. Is everything okay?"

"Yes, sure. I need to tell you something. Quickly. You might want to know," Maman said.

Vida sat down on the bed and pushed her forehead into her palm. "What's that? Is everyone okay?" she asked.

"Yes. Um… Listen to me. I need you to give your friend a message," said Maman.

"My friend?" Vida bunched her eyebrows. *What friend?*

"Remember that friend of yours?"

What friend? thought Vida.

"The one who is a widow?"

My friend who is a widow? What is she talking about?

A loaded silence lingered on the line. Maman did not respond for a moment.

"You know… the one with the two kids. She used to work for the Abraham Lincoln Library?"

In an instant Vida knew what her mother was telling her. "Yes," Vida said softly. She felt a muscle twitch in her leg. She took a deep breath and stuck her finger inside the coil of the telephone cord. They were listening. "Yes, I know her."

"If you happen to speak with her… tell her to stay away. Tell her to stay put wherever she is, and to not return to Tehran. She can't come back to Iran," Maman said.

"What?" Vida's mouth fell open.

"*Azeez*… It's not safe anymore. They came looking for her. They took her house and everything in it. They want her to come back to Iran so they can arrest her. You see what they've done with the American Embassy. They want anyone who had anything to do with that embassy. Who knows what they'll do to her if she returns. It's not safe for her. *Azeez*… It's not safe."

A sudden coldness hit at Vida's core. She felt disoriented.

"Have fun at your party. We'll talk more next time," Maman said.

Vida gently hung up the phone. She sat on the bed, her hand to her chest. *It's gone. Iran. My home. My family. I'll never see any of it again.* She took a deep breath and stood up.

Outside in the living room music was playing—the Bee Gees record Cyrus had bought the day before. In a daze, Vida watched her friends dancing in the living room with Cyrus in the middle imitating John Travolta in *Saturday Night Fever.* One of the women was standing by the kitchen door watching the group, a towel in her hand, drying one of the pots.

Vida wanted to run out of the apartment and out of the building onto Route 9. She worried and thought, *What if they go after Maman? Is Homa in danger now? At least I have the children with me.*

Then she saw Cyrus grab Roya's hand and twirl her around.

Vida smiled, and tears welled up behind her eyes. At first her hands were trembling, but then she let out a huge breath with her palm pressed to her heart.

THE END

Acknowledgments

——

By the time this book gets printed, it will have been a nearly fifteen-year journey. A huge thank you to so many people who made this happen.

I especially want to thank the incredibly strong women in my life: my mother, Maheen (Babe is her nickname), for her love, support, and for being the best role model ever. I called her so many times during the first year to try and get all the details about this story. My late grandmother, Maman, was always the symbol of a strong, smart, witty, independent woman, and my late stepgrandmother, my other Maman, for being a lesson in kindness, love, and light in all of our lives.

Thank you to my amazing brother, Kaveh (Karl), for all of his encouragement and for being my sounding board and rock, not only on this journey but always, and for making me laugh along the way.

My late stepfather, Mohsen (Michael) Moheet, was my consistent champion, voice of reason, trusted advisor, and an inspiration. "Uncle Mohsen," as I called him, taught me so much about Iran, Iranian history, politics, and culture—the good, the bad, and the ugly. Every fatherless girl should be so lucky to have an "Uncle Mohsen" in their life.

Thank you to my "little" Uncle Hassan and his wife Carmen for always being there and showing up for Kaveh, Babe, and me.

To my niece, Morgan, my nephews Alex and Andrew, and my cousins, Martin and Michael (Miko). I secretly observed so many of your actions and mannerisms when you were little, many of which ultimately got incorporated into this book to bring our childhood to life.

To my dear friend Roya, who is not only like a sister but let me use her name in the book as my character. Thank you to her incredibly accomplished and kind dad for letting me use his real name in the book. He was one of my biological father's closest friends, pediatrician for my brother and me in Iran, and a massive backbone for my mother during the years mentioned in this manuscript in Iran.

This book started as a short story I wrote in Ellen Sussman's writing class around 2001. A huge thank you to Ellen for teaching me what I know about writing, for being supportive and introducing me to so many smart and kind authors, like Heather Haven and Patty Paige, and many others with whom I ultimately connected in a writing group. My writing group read each chapter and provided comments, giving guidance and support. I could not have done this without them. I am humbled and honored to have had their time. A special thank you to authors: Ann Gelder, Beth Sears, Cheyenne Richards, Eileen Bordy, Gordon Jack, Mary Taugher, and Shelly Schuur.

Libby Roth read the rough first drafts of each chapter and was my guide throughout the early writing process. Thank you so, so much, Libby.

Back in the 2009-time frame, when I first embarked on this writing journey, my mother's close friend, Azar Ashraf, connected me with my mother's lawyer, Dr. Matine-Daftari, who was so instrumental in helping my mother during the legal battles described in this book. I ultimately spent a long day with Dr. Matine-Daftari at his Paris apartment and learned so much about the prerevolution Iranian legal system. I am so grateful for his guidance and wisdom.

Thank you to the early (and recent) readers of the entire manuscript: my amazing Babe, my brother Kaveh (Karl) Motey, Zahra Partoazam, Diane Hendrickson, Karen Faripour, Sallie Kim, Lonnie Goldman, Christina Chua, Shira Kaplan, Haleh Bakhash, Michelle Morcos Smith, my sister-in-law Laurie Cavender Motey, Ann Gelder, Roya Ansari, and Cathleen Edidin, who most recently pushed me to give birth to this book.

Over the years I had this book reviewed by two professional editors. A huge thank you to Lynn Stegner and Vicky Mlyniec for their professional comments.

In the later stage of the writing process, David Berkey got me access to archives at Stanford University and many of those news articles and image-inspired descriptions in this book. Thank you, Eleanor, for introducing me to your husband and for his help and guidance.

To Eric Koester of Manuscripts, LLC, who convinced me "to not sit on this book for another fourteen years." Eric, thank you for giving me the platform to bring this story to life. To my revisions editor Carol McKibben, whose eye to detail, patience, kindness, and wisdom were instrumental in getting my manuscript through the revisions process. Thank you, Carol, for taking such great interest in this story. A big thank you to the entire team at Manuscripts, LLC: Matteo Prayer for his first draft feedback; Laura Vaisman-Rivera; Sherman Morrison; Kristy Elam; Clayton Bohle; Gjorgji Pejkovski; and Bojana Gigovska, for keeping me on track and accountable while helping me finalize this book.

Robert, thank you for reminding me of our amazing childhood community in Tehran. Thank you for being so positive and for your patience the last six months of this writing journey.

Finally, to some of my father's relatives, I am sorry if this book comes across as harsh. I would not be who I am without the events that took place in my childhood, and I am grateful for who I am today. If it wasn't for this series of events, I would not have gone to law school. And no matter what happens, you know this book is a work of fiction, and I did take liberties to depart from the truth, more than a few times.

For any person I may have missed, my apologies for not listing your name. It has been fifteen years in the making.

This book was also made possible by a community of people who believed in me so passionately that they preordered and paid for their copies, helping promote the book before it even went to print. Thanks to all of you, many of whom are mentioned above, who read my early drafts and, most recently, gave input on the book cover. You are all amazing, and as promised, you are in the book (listed in alphabetical order by first name):

Ahmad Houshmand	Alex Motey
Ali Diba	Alina Caceres
Allison and Hossein Banisadr	F. Amanda DeBusk
Amy Aylward	Andrea Borbely
Andrea Hong	Andrew Motey
Andrew Thomases	Barbara Krebs
Barbara White	Beth Sears
Beth Siegelman	Betsy Rosenthal
Caitlin Haberberger	Carolyn Moore
Cathleen Edidin	Chris Robinson
Chris Wendel	Christi Nicolacopoulos
Cindy Joffrion	Cyrus Shargh
Darya Nasr	David Pelzner
David Spence	Dean Motazedi
Denise Altman	Denise Doyle
Diana Adle	Diane Hendrickson
E.J. Hong	Edna D'Souza
Eleanor Lacey	Elizabeth Hoffman
Ellen Miller	Ellen Sussman
Eric Davalo	Eric Koester
Eric Volkman	Farzad Tari
Fati Farmanfarmaian	Fati Sadeghi-Nejad
Faye Star	Geri Crane
Gerry Hanrahan	Gitty Kashani-Najmabadi

Golnar Rastar	Grant (Meiji) and Claudia Stewart
Haleh Najmabadi Peterson	Holly Roslow
Inna Maranets	Irfaan Premji
Jan Kang	Jeanne Dumari
Jennifer Chaloemtiarana	Jennifer McFadden
Jennifer Pileggi	Jenny Douglass
Joanne Lennon	Jonathan Rubin and Angela Tarazi
Joshua Lipp	Judith Levine
Julia Pang	Julie Flaig
Julie Learmond-Criqui	Karim Kawar
Kaveh (Karl) and Laurie Motey	Keegan Sims
Kelly Gomez	Kellyn Patros
Kimberley Basnight	Kimia Zucker
Kristina Israelski	Ladan Brabo
Laing Rikkers	Laurence (Larry) Fitterer
Laurie Richter	Leila Kamel
Leslie Lundt	Lisa Bodensteiner
Loren and Art Castronovo	Lynn Fraser
Mark Slater	Mark Stamilio
Mark and Michelle Eagle	Mark Millender
Maryam Alexandrian-Adams	Maryam Borjian
Maryam Zar	Mauri Schwartz
Melody Alemansour	Mercedeh Baghai
Michael Sanie	Michael Syatt
Michelle Deutsch	Michelle and Fred Smith
Mitra Nadim	Mitra Shahid
Monika and Tyler Garratt	Nadia Kazerani
Nastaran Heidari	Neelima Mane
Nounou Taleghani	NY Wang
Patty Paige	PattyAnn Tublin

Paul Gillane

Randy Furr

Rokhand Collins

Sally Mickel

Scott McCoy

Shannon Bell-Aliotti

Shelly King Schuur

Shira Kaplan

Stanley Kovler

Sue Hickman

Susan and Doug Wheeler

Tad Freese

Taraneh Maghame

Tina Singh

Wendy Sims

Zuhre Tutuncu

Paul Morrison

Robert J. Loomis

Roya Ansari

Scott Katz

Shadi Sami

Sharon Young

Sherbi Badal

Shiwen Cai

Sue Bunnell

Susan Decker

Susanne Khalili

Tam Dell'Oro

Thomas Ivey

Vahid Tavali

Yasmin Zarabi